ANGEL'S BLADE

A JACK SANGSTER MYSTERY

ANGEL'S BLADE

A JACK SANGSTER MYSTERY

LEWIS HINTON

The Book Guild Ltd

First published in Great Britain in 2022 by
The Book Guild Ltd
Unit E2 Airfield Business Park,
Harrison Road, Market Harborough,
Leicestershire. LE16 7UL
Tel: 0116 2792299
www.bookguild.co.uk
Email: info@bookguild.co.uk
Twitter: @bookguild

Typeset in 11pt Adobe Jenson Pro

Printed and bound by CPI Group (UK) Ltd, Croydon, CR0 4YY

ISBN 978 1915122 988

British Library Cataloguing in Publication Data.
A catalogue record for this book is available from the British Library.

MIX
Paper from
responsible sources
FSC
www.fsc.org   FSC® C013604

For my parents, and their love of all things Cornish

INTRODUCTION

The year is 1970, the month May. Jack Sangster, a special investigator with the Granville Institute, a philanthropic organisation dedicated to helping troubled youngsters, is in Cornwall helping to establish a residential academy for exceptionally gifted teenagers.

A former naval commander and oil executive, Sangster has been given this assignment due to his exceptional people and organisational skills, but his true talent lies in resolving difficult, sometimes apparently insoluble problems, especially when there are missing children involved. Sangster often works closely with both the Department of Education and the police on such cases.

His home town is Chester, but he can be sent on assignment anywhere in the country. As the story opens, Sangster has been living on and off for several months in a small hotel near Truro…

WEDNESDAY, MAY THE 27TH

5:30PM

I felt in my bones we would never see Angel alive.

And that near certainty only intensified as I looked across the creek. Until a few days ago this had been a warm and tranquil wooded inlet, but now was overcast, chilled by a west wind that upset the river as it fought with the ebb tide.

"A fifteen-year-old girl has been missing almost three days, Sangster," boomed the voice of Sir John Granville, textile magnate, philanthropist, hedonistic bon viveur of the highest order, my employer, and right now perhaps the most anxious multi-millionaire in the country. "Three days, man, so odds are our school'll be closed down. Here she is, look."

He thrust a black and white portrait into my hand, a head and shoulders shot of a blonde-haired young woman.

"Yes, I know who she is."

"She's all over the news, Sangster, that's who she is. Beautiful face like that and everyone's looking." He puffed his enormous chest outwards with some force. "Pah, pah, pah," he expelled his breath in a cascade. "Academy'll be finished unless the girl's found soon, I tell you, and the rozzers haven't a clue. Bloody incompetent, bumbling yokel force down here, I mean—"

"Excuse me, Detective Chief Superintendent Pentreath would like to speak with you both." I looked round to see a uniformed officer standing behind us. "He's in the principal's study, if you'd like to follow me."

"Hmph, very well, lead on, constable," muttered Sir John, who winked at me and mouthed the word 'yokel'. We then turned to follow the officer as he strode across the level lawn that stretched from a seawall at the creekside all the way up to the main school building, a fine yellow rendered Cornish manor house. This was the principal facility of the rather grandly titled (at least I always thought so when I saw it written or heard it said out loud), 'Granville Institute Everyman Academy for Gifted Children', a residential school for excessively gifted teenagers from all walks of life and known to us all as simply 'the Academy'.

"I'll leave you both here," said the officer, stopping by the entrance. "As I say, the chief super is in the principal's study." We walked through into the Academy's oak-lined hallway and towards an open door on the left, from which heated voices could be heard, amplified somehow by the wood panelling.

"Ahem…" said Sir John, knocking and entering, I following in his wake. "Officer said you wanted to talk to us, I—"

"Is it you?" screamed a woman, in what sounded like a strong West Country accent (which I found out later was actually from Brightlingsea, in rural east Essex). She was of early middle age, with short blonde hair and what would have been a handsome face, had her cheeks not been streaked with tears and mascara and her eyes not been red with despair.

"You that opened this place," she screamed again. "Took our Angel away. Brought her all the way across the country then lost her, didn't you?"

"Madam, I—"

"You bastard," she shouted, lunging at Sir John, who jumped back, surprisingly nimbly I thought, given his enormous bulk (he was about

2

six foot four and I guessed weighed in at well over twenty stone). "You lost my Angel, I'll—"

"Now, Mrs Blackwood," said a uniformed policewoman, intercepting the lunge. "I understand this is difficult for you but please, try to remain calm. We're certainly doing everything we can, and Sir John has come here from London today to help personally. Isn't that right, Sir John?"

"Of course, madam. I take it you are the mother of the unfortunate, I mean the missing, well, what I wanted to say was..."

"Angel," glared the woman, now sitting down, the man next to her (Mr Blackwood I assumed), placing his arm over her shoulders. "Her name's Angel."

"Now then," came the soothingly even voice of principal Cyrus Flimwell. "We're here to make sure Angel is found as soon as possible."

"That's right, Mrs Blackwood," said the woman at his side, Cyrus's wife, and joint principal Velinda (nicknamed 'Prinny' by the pupils, with her husband known to them as 'Prin', while they called each other 'Vi' and 'Cy'). "And the Devon and Cornwall police have assigned Detective Chief Superintendent Pentreath here," she added, gesturing to a thin man in a grey suit who had thus far remained silent. "And this man with Sir John is one of the Granville Institute's special investigators. He also oversaw the establishment of the academy here at St Anthony."

"Jack Sangster," I said, offering my hand.

"And what do you investigate for the Granville Institute that's so 'special', Jack Sangster?" Mrs Blackwood asked me, ignoring the offer.

"I look into problem cases, missing children, long-term truants, that sort of thing," I answered as confidently as I could, while inwardly feeling anything but confident.

"Yes, Mr Sangster is the best we have," said Mrs Flimwell. "He's helped with cases like this before, found missing children when nobody else could, and he and others from the institute will now work with the police, help anywhere they can."

Sir John nodded, as did Pentreath, although the latter with a sideways look at me that hinted resentment of outside interference in his investigation. The detective then paced to the centre of the room and spoke in a surprisingly deep register given his rather spare frame and face.

"Now, in typical cases like this, in care homes and the like—"

"We are not a care home," thundered Sir John.

"Quite so," said Pentreath. "And what I was going to say was that we typically tend to be, how shall I say, a little careful about jumping to conclusions with missing teenagers." He stopped to (rather theatrically I thought), clear his throat, presumably buying the time to choose his words carefully. "Especially repeat offenders, and especially those from certain, er… institutions like care homes. We have different protocols for that kind of child. Ahem…" He coughed again, and as he did so, the Blackwoods' faces turned almost purple. "However," Pentreath continued, "in this case I am assured Angel Blackwood is a stable girl who has never absented herself without permission before, from this school or any other."

"Yes, so how are you going to find our daughter?" said Mrs Blackwood, now close to hysterics. "Are you really doing everything you can?"

"We are—" Pentreath tried to answer but was cut short.

"It's her birthday tomorrow for heaven's sake. She'll be sixteen."

'Birthday on top of everything else?' I mouthed to Velinda who (out of Angel's mother's direct line of sight), mouthed 'Yes' back to me.

"Mr and Mrs Blackwood," said Pentreath slowly. "I can only say that last night I was specifically asked by my chief constable to take personal charge and ensure we leave no stone unturned, spare no resources until your daughter's found. Now, if you would all follow me, I'll take you to the gym."

"Gym?" Sir John muttered. "No time for that sort of thing, missing girl to find."

"Where we have set up our incident room," the DCS sighed quietly.

"Ah, lead on."

The WPC stayed with the parents, both of whom elected not to listen to a blow-by-blow account of how the police had thus far failed to find their daughter. The Flimwells, Sir John, DCS Pentreath and I, then entered the gymnasium to see a team of about twenty police officers, some uniformed some not, standing by charts and pictures on the walls, or sitting at desks which were spaced across the floor. We walked past a table with a row of telephones, where operators with headsets were busying talking and taking notes, and on to a corner with two large blackboards set up on wooden easels.

"Now then," said Pentreath, reminding me of an army officer briefing his men as he pointed to a series of chalked-up names, dates, times, and arrows that listed the chronology of events leading up to and after the disappearance of Angel Blackwood. "Here are the basics. Angel was last seen leaving a school debating club meeting at about 3pm on Sunday. The police were called when she didn't appear at dinner that evening, at 6:30pm, after which we immediately conducted a search of the school grounds and interviewed staff and pupils. At dawn yesterday, we initiated a full search of the surrounding area, with officers drafted in from all over the county and beyond, including canine units. Posters for public posting have been issued as widely as possibly, and newspapers, TV and radio informed, including nationals. As of this afternoon we have conducted detailed searches of the St Anthony area plus a sweep of the adjacent area around St Mawes. Currently, house-to-house checks are being undertaken in the Roseland, Falmouth, Penryn and Truro areas, and a forensic team is working the scene here, so we anticipate leads any time now. In fact, we…"

I lost concentration as the detective continued to repeat tried and tested methods that were general to any enquiry. Painting by numbers.

"Er, excuse me?" I eventually asked him.

"Yes Sangster?"

"Do you have any suspects? Any, as I think you say, 'leads' right now?"

"One possible suspect, a vagrant that has been seen in the area for some weeks now."

"The tramp," said Velinda Flimwell.

"The tramp?" queried Sir John.

"That's what the children nicknamed him. Dishevelled old man with a beard and overcoat, hangs around the school sometimes, had to be escorted off the premises on several occasions by Runtle. We were never quite sure how he got into the grounds, but he did. Seen loitering in some of the local villages as well. Up to no good if—"

"Hmmm…" I interrupted. "From what you say I think I may have met him at the weekend. Do you know who this 'tramp' is, Pentreath, where he lives?"

"I'm afraid not. He seems to be of no fixed abode and just pops up now and again then melts into the countryside. This area is heavily wooded you know."

"And did you identify and interview the girl's close friends?"

"All the pupils were interviewed," the DCS answered. "Forty-nine of them, nobody left out. Went through the entire register. Staff, including all the permanent teachers were interviewed as well, and we have a list of over ten part-time teachers we're working through."

"It's just that I saw Angel canoeing with one of the other pupils at the weekend. Wondered if that boy might know something."

"As I say, everyone interviewed," Pentreath continued, before explaining more about his approach, and consistently mentioning just how much effort and manpower was being allocated to the investigation. My feeling was that all this was wasted and the police were looking in the wrong place.

"Very good to search the immediate area," I finally said, "but couldn't the girl have simply left somehow, say in a car?"

"No, Sangster," said Cyrus Flimwell. "Runtle was in the gatehouse all afternoon. Other than a very few staff who live off premises, nobody came in or out that day."

"The girl could have been taken in a car boot, say, or lying in the back seat under a coat or a blanket?"

"Runtle reckons not. He said the people who came and went were either on foot from the bus stop or on bicycles. Except for my wife of course. Velinda drove out that afternoon."

"Runtle?" queried Sir John. "You keep mentioning this Runtle."

"Caretaker and gatekeeper," answered Flimwell. "Looks after the chapel as well. Old retainer here from years ago."

"What about a bicycle?" I asked.

"Same thing," said Flimwell. "The perimeter walls form a semi-circle that surrounds the academy, all around the grounds and down to the creek on both sides, and after that iron fences across the mud down to the low tide mark. You couldn't get a bike through anywhere except the main gate, and only Runtle opens that, from the gatehouse. He's a stickler for security as well, almost to the point of embarrassment with the way he can treat visitors."

Of course, I thought, recalling going over plans for the site the previous year. The academy was partly chosen for the security provided by its walls, and (much to Sir John's dismay when he saw the bill), we had installed sophisticated machinery and controls to operate the front gates from inside the gatehouse or from the main academy building.

"Isn't there a back gate by the chapel?" I asked, my memory of the layout now jogged.

"Yes," said Flimwell. "But again, only Runtle has the key. Hangs in a key cupboard in the gatehouse and he says that the back gate was padlocked at the time of Angel's disappearance. We double checked, of course, and found it locked, just as Runtle had told us."

"So, the girl either walked out in some way we don't know about, or she's still here in the school or the grounds."

"She's not here, Sangster," Pentreath stated flatly. "Rest assured of that after our searches. And our dogs picked up no scent, so if she did walk out, it was on thin air above the ground."

"How do you know the dogs didn't miss her scent completely?"

"Because they did pick up her scent on the lawn, where she was seen before lunch, but nowhere else. Especially not around the gatehouse or even the perimeter walls, where she could just possibly have climbed out, although she'd have needed a ladder."

"So, to find this missing girl, you are mainly relying on dogs' noses?" I asked, my incredulity hard to hide.

"We know our jobs, Sangster. Our tracker dogs are of bloodlines bred to catch escaped convicts on Dartmoor. The best hounds in the land, managed by the best canine unit in the force."

"But the mutts aren't foolproof, surely?"

"No, the dogs aren't foolproof, and might struggle if the quarry has a few hours start, but will still usually pick up a scent, unless it's raining heavily of course, then they can't, but Sunday was a dry day." Pentreath, seemingly desperate to justify himself (I wondered why such a senior officer would feel the need), struggled to get his words out quickly enough, causing him to pause and catch his breath. "No," he continued, after loudly exhaling. "When the alarm was raised, and we began our search, the girl's trail was still warm, and the scent would have lingered, I think."

"And the boathouse?"

"All boats, canoes and so on are accounted for. And bicycles in the sheds for that matter. Nothing missing."

"Could she have swum across the creek?"

"By no means impossible," said Flimwell. "But the Percuil River from the front lawn here at any time of the tide would be a push for most people to swim across, especially in their clothes. And," he added, "high tide was three ten on Sunday afternoon, so the river would have been at its most difficult."

"But she could have swum, maybe just out to a boat or along the river, rather than all the way to St Mawes. In theory?"

"Even if somehow, she did," said Pentreath, sounding a little exasperated, presumably at having to keep answering my questions. "We saw no footprints in the mud, and the dogs picked up no scent by the foreshore, as I said."

"Outside of the boundaries?"

"We checked the foreshore either side of the academy perimeter for well over a mile. Again, the dogs picked up no scent."

She is either still here, I thought again as he spoke, or she left some other way. I continued to wonder if someone could somehow have picked her up in a boat but said nothing. Pentreath did have a point that she would surely have been seen, or that the dogs would have found a trail somewhere along the shore.

"Thank you," I eventually said, looking pointedly at Sir John. "I think we've taken enough of your time now."

"Indeed we have, Pentreath," Sir John added. "And if you want any help from us, just say the word."

"The excellent cooperation of your staff here is more than enough help," the detective answered, gaining appreciative smiles from both Flimwells. "And if we need assistance on the detective work, we'll be sure to tell you." He then turned to a sergeant standing next to him. "Bolitho, have we interviewed Mr Sangster yet?"

"No sir."

"Sangster, if you'd be good enough to let the sergeant know your whereabouts on Sunday afternoon?"

"Of course," I said, as Sir John snorted something under his breath to the effect that Pentreath needing a good whipping. "I can tell you now. I was at St Anthony Head until around one o'clock, then drove straight to our hotel in Truro and stayed there for the rest of the afternoon."

"So, earlier on Sunday you were near here, but in Truro when the girl disappeared?" asked Pentreath, raising an eyebrow.

"Yes," I answered, as the sergeant scribbled his notes.

"Anyone corroborate that?"

"My wife, a waitress at the café by the St Anthony Head car park, the hotel guests and landlady, and oh…"

"Yes?"

"I reported a theft to the police at almost exactly three. A camera was stolen from our car boot. Was given a reference number and everything."

"On a Sunday?"

"Via a telephone switchboard."

"Got all that, Bolitho?"

"Yes sir."

"Goodbye then," I said, wanting to go before Sir John, whose face had become indignantly redder with each of Pentreath's questions, said anything we'd both regret. "Cyrus, Velinda, don't worry, we'll show ourselves out."

"Bloody sauce of the man," Sir John spluttered as we left.

"Just doing his job, Sir John."

As we arrived at the entrance hall, I felt a hand on my shoulder, and turned to see Mrs Blackwood.

"I'm sorry for the way I spoke to you, Mr Sangster, I really am sorry, but somehow I felt if anyone could find Angel, it might be you."

"I can only try to imagine what you're going through, and I'll help any way I can." I immediately felt the burden of responsibility as she said this. "But I didn't say much in the principal's study."

"I know, but somehow, call it intuition if you will, I felt that even saying almost nothing in the principals' study, you said more than that detective has since we met him."

"I'll do my best, Mrs Blackwood," I answered, my stomach knotting at the thought of someone relying on me for what I felt sure was a hopeless case. "And I'm flattered by your faith in me," I added, just managing the wateriest of smiles.

"What did you think of that rozzer Pentreath, Sangster?" Sir John asked me as we walked to the car. "The girl's mother didn't like what she heard."

"He's obviously experienced, but his methods fit Einstein's definition of insanity. That's what I think."

"What's that?"

"Keep doing the same thing over and over again and expect different results."

8PM

"So, Sangster," said Sir John, calmer than he had been but still agitated, as we navigated the green lanes of the Roseland Peninsula. "As I say, the academy may well be finished if we don't clear this up pronto. The powers that be in London are looking for any excuse to close me down, and this girl going missing will be a godsend for them." He looked at me and shouted. "You must sort it out. You must."

"Of course, I want to find Angel, but for her own safety rather than the academy. You saw her mother."

"Sorry, of course. But you know what I mean."

"I'm not a detective you know."

"Oh piffle," he said. "You've solved more than a few tricky problems for me in the last year or so. Got a first-class mind for this sort of thing."

Sir John then went quiet, seemingly lost in his own thoughts, and we drove on for about twenty minutes, mostly through country roads until we met the main Truro highway, at which point the lights of houses and streetlamps began to switch on in response to the waning daylight. A sharp left turn, just before the town, then took us along a waterside road that followed the course of the river.

After about two miles we came to the village, at the confluence of the Truro and Tresillian rivers, where I had been living on and off for the past four months, in the Watersmeet Hotel. Sir John, who had arrived by train from London that morning, would stay the night and then travel back up the following day. He took his overnight case from the car boot, along with what looked to me like a small picnic basket, walked into the hotel and announced himself loudly to Morwenna Poldhu, the landlady. She stepped back in surprise at this Dickensian looking giant with matching voice (who was, as my wife had observed, six foot four in all directions and 'because he can afford it, darling', habitually dressed like a character from some other age). Sir John then nodded to her, she signed him in and silently passed over a room key.

"I'm going to take supper in the bar, will you join me, Sir John?"

"No, Sangster, I'll just go up to my room."

"Nothing to eat, Sir John?"

"No, Sangster," Granville repeated in what he imagined was a whisper, holding up the picnic basket. "Don't trust the food down here. Doubt they wash the cutlery more than once a week either. Brought a hamper from Fortnum's. Got me own plates, knives and forks as well."

"Cheeky sod," said the landlady semi-audibly, as Sir John stumped up the stairs.

"Ah, my dear patroness?" he then asked her, looking over his shoulder and, by his friendly expression, clearly oblivious to her comment. "Could you see your way to sending me up a bottle of your doubtlessly very excellent brandy? One glass and no ice thank you. VSOP or even XO if you've got it."

"Certainly, sir, of course, sir, right away, sir," she answered with an exaggerated curtsey, the irony lost on Sir John, who turned to fix his stare on me as she walked back into the taproom and out of earshot.

"Oh, and Sangster, I know you're always saying you're not a detective but…"

"Yes?"

"Got any ideas?"

"There's a lot I'll try and cover tomorrow at the academy."

12

"Such as?"

"Well, I want to talk to that boy, Jonny."

"Who?"

"Not sure I mentioned it, but I think I saw him canoeing with Angel at the weekend. I'll see that other lad they're friendly with as well, the one they call Spider. And I want to personally search their rooms."

"But have you got any ideas, man?"

"Well… only instincts as yet, Sir John, only instincts."

9:30PM

I entered the taproom at the Watersmeet to see four locals huddled at the end of the bar, deep in conversation. Pasco, the local ferryman, Mike Jackson, owner of the boat yard opposite the hotel, David Stocker, an estate agent, and Canon Simeon Pengelly, a local vicar who also occasionally taught religious instruction at the academy. Indeed, it was almost always the same people in the bar, save for the occasional visiting tourist or residential guest (few and far between during mid-week and out of season). I nodded good evening to them, and they, each in their turn with what had become a kind of ritual, nodded back to me. For some reason I thought of Jackson, Stocker and Pasco as the three wise monkeys.

I walked up to the bar, with its long wooden counter and clutter of objects behind that barely left room for bottles, glasses and beer pumps; a battered and almost paintless lifeboat shaped money box (the letters 'RNLI' just visible along its side), various trophies (mainly for darts and boat racing), some black and white framed prints of the village in former times, a card of peanut packets that revealed more of a bikini clad model each time a packet was removed, numerous postcards from around the world, a stuffed, grinning monkey head (the origin of which I never did find out), as well as two matching paintings of a bald man in a black gown reading a book (the name on the volume was 'Nana', and in the first picture, entitled 'Attack', he sat forward, hand held up in exclamation, and in the second, entitled 'Defence', he sat thoughtfully back). In pride of place above the spirit optics hung a gilt-framed portrait of a stern-looking woman in a black dress, head shawl and broad brimmed hat. Her name, Morwenna had told me, was Mopus Jenny, ferrywoman in the village over a hundred years previous, who, amongst other things, didn't suffer fools gladly (apparently, when asked which ferry passengers caused her most trouble, Jenny answered 'Wemmin and pigs'). I always felt Jenny's eyes followed me round the room.

"Don't mind Jenny, Jack," the landlady said, as I eyed the portrait with unease. "Now how about a nice pint of Hicks?"

"Thanks, Morwenna, any pasties left?"

"Nob!" she shouted through a hatch to the kitchen. "Any of them last batch of pasties left?" An unintelligible grunt came back. "Nob says yes, Jack, but he also says you're lucky. It's the last one. Bit of salad with it, pickle, bread and butter?"

"What would I do without you, Morwenna?"

"I was thinking," she said, leaning across the bar counter and folding her arms on the surface, her mass of peroxide blonde hair (which tonight was piled high or 'locks up' as she would say), blocking out much of the light from the lamp in the ceiling behind her, and giving her head a rather curious silhouette. "That the proper question to ask me should be, 'What would I do *with* you, Morwenna?'" She leaned even further towards me, her low-cut leopard-skin blouse falling forward in an almost intimidating manner. "Or perhaps the improper question?" She winked, I reddened, and she laughed, sensing my embarrassment. "Don't you worry, I couldn't hold a candle to that wife of yours. Whole village looked at her last weekend when she came down to see you. Just like that old film star, Hedy Lamarr."

"Do you think?"

"Well." Morwenna shook her head. "Whoever your wife looks like, you're a lucky man. But Jack," she said, with another wink, "remember, any time you get lonely, I'm only..."

"Ah, Morwenna, looking younger and lovelier than ever to be sure," came a smooth and very loud Irish voice from the doorway. I turned to see its owner, a dark-haired man in his early thirties wearing a leather motorbike jacket, trousers, and boots, along with a white scarf.

"You've altogether too much blarney, Mr Slevin," the unflappable landlady replied. "And you a man of the cloth as well," she added to mine and everyone else's surprise (the group at the end of the bar had turned to stare at the figure in the doorway, Canon Pengelly seeming especially startled). "Now I've only got a ploughman's left from lunchtime if you're hungry, Mr Slevin. Last pasty's just gone."

"Ah, I dined in Truro," he said, bowing, so that a small clerical collar became visible. "Your Cornish fish and chips no less, and the best in the land I'm sure, so I'll bid you a goodnight, sweet colleen. And to you, gentlemen, a very goodnight as well." With that he made another, even more theatrical bow, then left as quickly as he came, whereupon the locals turned back to their conversation.

"Is that the chap who arrived last Friday, Morwenna? With the motorbike."

"Yes, and charming to the last, but I don't like him, Jack."

"Why not?"

"Oh, I don't know. Perhaps too charming, not a gentleman like you."

"Well thank you, but I—"

"No," she interrupted. "I'm serious, not like you, and he's a priest, so flirting doesn't sit well. Doing a study thing linked to the cathedral in Truro. Said his official title is a Monsig, a Mons, a..."

"Monsignor, Morwenna," shouted Pengelly. She shrugged, and I turned to my pasty, which was passed on its plate out of the serving hatch by the invisible Nob with his customary grunt.

"Nob says there's no pickle left," said Morwenna, shaking her beehive hair. "Sorry Jack." She thought for a moment, as I began to eat.

"That man you were with, the big one that took the room tonight, with the brandy and the hamper. Odd kind if I may say so."

"Oh, you may. Very odd. Very rich as well though."

"Ooh," she said, head on one side and hand on one hip in an affected, coquettish pose. "Exactly how rich?"

"As rich as you want, perhaps the richest man in all of England," I said, munching away. She exaggeratedly made to adjust her hair and fluttered her heavily lashed blue eyelids.

"Mmmm… interesting. Anyway, how's your pasty? What do you think of 'im?"

A few months ago, I wouldn't have known Morwenna meant the pasty, but now I'd become used to her, along with others in the village, refer to inanimate objects (including things usually called 'she', like boats), as 'him', or 'he'.

"Well, Morwenna," I said carefully. "This is a passable pasty, in fact a very good pasty."

"Glad to hear that, Jack."

"But…" She stood very still, clearly listening with anticipation, the rest of the bar silent and listening as well. "As I say, a very good pasty, Morwenna, but I'm afraid not quite up to the usual standard." I looked around, sensing unease, but continued. "I've been staying at the Watersmeet on and off since January, and this pasty, well, the beef's not as succulent as I'm used to. In fact, I'm not even sure its shredded as it should be in a proper pasty. Might be minced. And the swede—"

"Turnip," came a correcting chorus from the four locals.

"Sorry, the turnip's slightly hard, with less pepper than I've tasted before. Pastry's perhaps just a little dry as well. No, it's simply not, how shall I say it…"

"Yes Jack?"

"Er… not quite as good as usual."

There, I thought, I'd been honest, probably to the point of being asked to leave the bar for the night (after all, in the months I'd stayed at the Watersmeet, I'd seen that the fearsome landlady wasn't above throwing out regular drinkers of thirty years for quite minor misdemeanours if she felt like it). My worries were unfounded, however, as a cheer went up around the room (even in grunt form from Nob through the hatch).

"I told you boys." Morwenna leaned over her counter and planted an enormous kiss on my cheek (which I felt sure would leave a rouge lip print). "Jack's a great judge of a pasty, even for an emmet."

"A what?" I asked, having heard this word many times but never understood what it meant or why it was used.

"Ant," came a shout from Pasco at the end of the bar.

"Oh, er… thank you," I said, still none the wiser. "So, am I right in thinking it wasn't one of your pasties, Morwenna?"

"That's right, my lover, my cock," beamed Morwenna, displaying her surprisingly long front teeth. "It was made by my cousin, Angharad. She keeps a pub in St Agnes. I didn't have time to bake last weekend, so Nob drove up and got a batch from her. I use my mum's recipe and Angharad uses her mum's, and your pasty was the last of Angharad's batch."

I took a moment to make sense of her words, then breathed a sigh of relief, while noting more evidence that the invisible Nob did actually exist and sometimes even left the hotel kitchen.

"By the way, Jack," Morwenna then whispered. "Don't mind me calling you an emmet, do you?"

"An ant, Pasco just said."

"Just means someone from up-country," she laughed. "Comes from some old word for ant though, but not Cornish mind, that would be moryon. Hmmm…" She held her chin in thought.

"Ah Morwenna, I er… see."

*

"Come and join us, Sangster," called Canon Pengelly, as I passed Morwenna my empty plate. "That was brave of you with the pasty," he laughed. "And er… weren't you worried about Morwenna?" he added, while she was temporarily out of earshot, head in the serving hatch.

18

"I always think it's best to say what I think, regardless," I answered, immediately thinking this sounded a little pompous. "Well, within reason, try not to offend, you know what I mean."

"Jolly good philosophy. Now, what'll you have?"

"Oh, it's late, and been a long day, I think I'll turn in, I…"

"Nonsense. Morwenna, large Grouse for Sangster please. No ice. That's right, isn't it?"

"You remember well, Pengelly." I walked over to the group as Morwenna handed me the whisky. "Well, good health," I said, wondering if their excited discussion was because they had caught wind of Angel's disappearance, and also wondering how best I could avoid any questions.

"Now then, Sangster," the canon said, draining his own glass and indicating the need for a refill by raising it above his head. "We've been debating, and I say that…"

"Aw, rubbish," said the ever-practical Mike Jackson. "Jesus in Cornwall. Just wishful thinking by you lot in your dog collars."

"Ah," said Pasco, raising his enormous bushy eyebrows. "Maybe not such wishful thinking, we all know the stories. And what about that Henry Blake?"

"Pardon?" I said, now completely confused, as well as relieved that the subject under debate was one other than Angel.

"Jerusalem."

"That was Parry, wasn't it, Pasco?" said a surprisingly well-informed Stocker.

"That's the music, I'm talking about the words, now how's it go?" He started to sing. "And did those feet, in ancient times, walk upon England's pastures green, and did the holy lamb of God, in England's… mmm… mmm."

"Thank you, Pasco," interrupted Jackson, placing his hand over the ferryman's mouth, while Pasco continued to try and sing. "That's lovely, but Morwenna has no music license and I think it's drinking-up time." The landlady nodded, and with that the others, including Pasco but excluding Canon Pengelly, finished their drinks and stood up.

19

"Goodnight, Morwenna, Jack, Simeon."

"Goodnight, gents."

I was left in the bar with Pengelly, who then declared to Morwenna that he would take a room at the hotel.

"It's late, Simeon, but no trouble. The top floor front room is already made up – 12a, key's behind the hall desk."

"You're staying the night?" I asked the canon, who nodded. "Hadn't you better call someone? Won't Mrs Pengelly be worried?"

"I will call my housekeeper first thing in the morning, but there's no Mrs Pengelly to worry about me," he said, looking directly at my eyes to emphasise this. "Weather's coming in, and it's a long ride back to Truro. Best I stay."

I listened to the rain, driving in across the river and battering the windowpanes, and recalled hearing that Pengelly cycled everywhere, having lost his driver's license for drinking while at the wheel. And being unable to drive meant the canon now did an awful lot of cycling, as he looked after several churches in different villages spread over a wide area ('services in each, every fourth Sunday, Sangster'), including the ancient chapel that was attached to the academy building. In fact, after meeting Pengelly in this same bar when I first arrived in Cornwall and hearing him talk eloquently about the Anglican church and theology in general, I had recommended to the Flimwells they engage the canon to teach religious education at the academy. My instinct about the man had been correct, Simeon Pengelly proving a popular and effective mentor with the academy's very demanding pupils.

"Another scotch, Sangster?"

"No, it's my shout. Let me get you one, Pengelly."

"Very well, but I insist, insist mark you, that you join me."

"Alright, last one," I sighed. We toasted one another, while Morwenna leaned patiently on the bar filing her nails, which were improbably long and curved and painted with a dark gold varnish.

"Did you go to the academy today, Sangster?"

"Yes, Pengelly, I do most days," I answered, wondering where this was leading.

"Was in Truro all today and yesterday myself," he said, perhaps slightly uncomfortably, I couldn't be sure. "And was that Sir John Granville you arrived with just now?" I nodded. "Any reason for the great man being here in person?"

"He visits the academy occasionally." I said this as casually as I could. "Now then, Pengelly," I added in an attempt to change the subject. "What was that all about?"

"What, with Pasco singing Jerusalem?"

"Yes," I laughed.

"You really want to know?"

"I think so."

"It takes a bit of explaining, so we'll need a few minutes."

"Okay."

"Then let me tell you the story of our Lord visiting Cornwall." With that he drank his whisky and ordered two more large measures before I could say no. "First off, have you heard of Joseph of Arimathea?"

"Er… no, I'm a complete heathen, Pengelly. My wife would probably have heard of this man, but not me. Sorry."

"Well, not to be confused with Jesus' father Joseph of Nazareth, this Joseph was a secret disciple of Jesus, and some say a close relative, perhaps an uncle, even a great uncle. Bible's not too clear, but either way, Joseph had been a friend since Jesus was very young and is at the heart of the Cornish connection. So, Sangster, the legend goes like this, and interrupt me if I'm telling you things you already know."

Canon Pengelly then, occasionally having to raise his voice above the sound of the now torrential rain, related a curious and (to me) entirely unknown folk tale, interspersed with his own views and supporting 'facts'.

Jesus' tomb in Jerusalem was apparently owned by this Joseph, who was granted the right by the ruling Roman administration to retrieve the body from the cross and inter the corpse. On the third day after the crucifixion ('so Easter Sunday, Sangster'), the tomb was found empty, and thus the miracle of the resurrection was born. But the legend that Pengelly wished to relate began in an earlier time, during the so-called 'lost years'. Jesus, he said, is documented in the scriptures up until the age of twelve, but not afterwards, at least not until he is over thirty. During that time, scholars can only suppose what happened to him, but most surmise that he travelled. The life experience and understanding of esoteric doctrines exhibited in his later teachings, Pengelly asserted, proved Jesus hadn't remained in the small town of Nazareth, or even Palestine itself for long. Rather, such arcane knowledge would have been gleaned from diverse cultures in far off lands, like India, Ethiopia, and most importantly for the Cornish legend, perhaps Britain with its druidic culture.

Listening to the canon passionately relating what he felt to be (almost literally) 'gospel truth', I couldn't help thinking that blind faith led the man to ignore the obvious questions.

"But, Pengelly," I eventually interrupted, "if Jesus was as talented as the Bible implies, then he could easily have devised the Christian doctrine without outside help."

"Well, er..."

"Look, think about Shakespeare. I'm no scholar, but to my uneducated mind he was simply talented beyond any other in his field and, as a consequence of that supreme talent, numerous 'learned' people through the centuries decided he couldn't have written his own plays."

"Don't see the point, Sangster."

"Plus," I went on, feeling I'd already explained 'the point', and that anyway, my Shakespeare analogy sounded somewhat pretentious when I'd said it out loud. "If Jesus was the 'Son of God', then he would be divinely inspired, so no need for all that travel anyway."

"Colossians, chapter 3 verse 23."

"I'm sorry?"

"Bible quote, basically saying God helps those who help themselves. Jesus was put on Earth in the form of man, so he would surely have sought inspiration as a man, and not relied on God."

It was this kind of circular thinking that usually told me a religious debate had likely run its course, so I said nothing more. I did find myself wondering though, as Pengelly began to talk again, whether Jesus, if he had lived at all, really believed he was the Son of God, or whether, like all of us, he had doubts. Perhaps Jesus even knew deep down he was just a man.

Joseph of Arimathea, according to Pengelly, was a wealthy merchant, and crucially for the Cornish legend, involved in the tin trade. Tin was an essential component of bronze, a metal widely used at the time of Christ. The principal source of that tin was Cornwall, and ships from the Mediterranean had already been sailing to the Cassiterides ('the Tin Islands, Sangster, as Britain was known to certain mariners in those days'), to trade for this most precious of commodities for many centuries. Jesus, following in his father's footsteps and apprenticed as a carpenter, might logically have accompanied Joseph on voyages to Britain. On one such trip, Pengelly further asserted, Joseph's ship was damaged in a storm off St Anthony Head, colliding with rocks by a cove called Carricknath, before eventually making landfall in a sheltered creek on the Percuil River (by coincidence the wooded arm of the Fal estuary that led to the inlet by the academy). When I questioned Pengelly as to evidence, he mentioned written sources describing this and other voyages to Cornwall. These included one made after the crucifixion, where Joseph of Arimathea brought the crown of thorns worn by Jesus on the cross to Britain, although the canon offered no details of his sources.

My ears had especially pricked up when he mentioned the Percuil River, and despite the whisky and his long explanation already testing my attention span, I listened intently to the canon's next words.

A stone arch in the academy chapel, he said, was carved with odd symbols that seemed to indicate Jesus did indeed visit Cornwall. The carvings were certainly ancient ('we don't know how old, Sangster'), and on a guided tour Pengelly was conducting some years before, one guest, an archaeologist, became very excited when seeing the symbols. This person claimed, according to Pengelly, that the carvings were of a type that he had only seen once before, long ago in Egypt. He could interpret the glyphs and explained that they told of Jesus coming to the place with his uncle at a particular time of year.

"And there was a recurring symbol related to Jesus, this man pointed out. You can see it yourself in the chapel."

"What's that?"

"The Ichthys."

"Sorry?"

"The fish, Sangster. Always associated with anything to do with Jesus Christ. It all leads to our Lord coming to Cornwall, and I've spent much of my adult life trying to prove it."

"I'm sure," I murmured, assuming that was the end of the conversation.

Pengelly, on the other hand, assumed nothing of the sort, and was now in full flow, going on to say he felt the whole story added up, as the Fal would be one of the first natural harbours encountered by anyone sailing to Cornwall from the Atlantic. To support the story further, the canon alleged that about a hundred and fifty years ago, an ingot of tin had been dredged up from the mud of the Percuil, and supposedly provenanced to be of Phoenician origin ('modern day Lebanon, Sangster, they were great mariners around the time of Christ, and you can see that bar of tin in the Truro town museum').

"So, Pengelly," I said, feeling the whisky begin to slow my mind. "That really is fascinating, but now I must go to bed. I have a missing girl to investigate tomorrow."

Oh no, Sangster, I mentally cursed myself, now I'm going to have to talk about Angel.

"So, I hear," he said, his eyes drooping into a frown. "Photo's been posted up all over the place and I guessed that was why Sir John was here but didn't like to pry. I knew her of course."

"Did you personally teach Angel?"

"Oh yes. Even took the girl up to London last month. Got her a day pass to the British Museum."

"Of course, you did, I remember now."

"In fact, Sangster, it was on that trip that she started taking a great interest in the legend of Jesus in Cornwall. Asked if she could come to Truro to study, in the cathedral library and the town museum. Devoured everything she could on the subject, picked my brains clean as well. Remarkable girl." He paused, a faraway look in his eyes. "You know, Sangster," he finally said. "They're a bright bunch at your Granville Academy, but Angel is the brightest star in your firmament."

"How so?" I asked, his gushing about this soon to be sixteen-year-old schoolgirl beginning to sound alarm bells in my mind.

"Well, just cleverer than the rest. But if you asked me why, I would struggle to answer."

"Well, try for me."

"Alright. I know its unfashionable to judge her in this way, but Angel's attractive, stunning you might even say, so she had none of the esteem troubles that a teenage girl might have."

"Yes, of course I've seen her, and she is beautiful. Some girls do struggle with the pressures of good looks as well though, Pengelly." He nodded, then continued.

"And she had a photographic memory, plus the drive to consume books at a staggering rate. And that drive was matched by a generous dose of common sense that made Angel a practical but spectacular scholar. And unlike most of the kids at the academy, a happy scholar as well."

"Well, it seems clear she's clever, so why would you struggle to answer?"

"Because er… I… can't answer." The canon's hesitation, he then explained, was not because he didn't want to tell me, but because he couldn't find the words. Angel, he felt, was perhaps cleverer than he knew how to be. "She had insight," Pengelly eventually said. "Could look at all the facts, use her intuition, take everything she had ever learned and put it all together, instantly and without hesitation. She was just quicker. And she said she didn't sleep more than three or four hours a night, so could devote all that extra time to the pursuit of knowledge. As I say, a quite remarkable girl."

"You use the past tense?"

"No, I do not, at least not on purpose. The thought that a mind like Angel's has been taken from us is a terrible thought. In fact, were I to have a child, Sangster, and if that child possessed even one tenth the mind of Angel, I would be the very proudest of fathers. Of course," he added softly, eyes watering slightly. "The Lord has seen fit to make sure that won't happen."

"Hmmm…" I said. "It's difficult and, if I may say so, I think I understand. My wife and I have also had to accept we will always be childless."

"No Sangster, you don't understand. It's not medical. There'll be no children for me because I do not… I do not love women, if you take my meaning."

"Ah yes," I responded after a few moments' reflection, wondering whether that did or did not exclude him as a suspect in Angel's disappearance. "I can see the problem with your not having children, but otherwise, does this er, way of being bother you unduly?"

"I think 'bother' doesn't quite cut it, Sangster. First off, to be like me was illegal until…"

"I know, Pengelly, illegal until three years ago. They used to call it 'The Blackmailer's Law.'"

"I know that only too well," he said, eyes cast downwards with sad resignation.

"But," I said as brightly as I could, in an attempt to lift him from his mood, "it's not illegal anymore, and views change. I was in the navy for eighteen years, and there most of us simply accepted men with those proclivities as normal."

"Perhaps, but you don't know what it was like for me before 1967. Is still like for me today. People's attitudes. The church's attitude."

"Perhaps I don't."

"Trust me, you don't, and second off, I have my faith. The Bible is quite clear."

"What does it say?"

"'Thou shalt not lie with mankind, as with womankind: it is an abomination.' Leviticus, chapter 18, verse 22."

26

"And you believe this must be taken literally?"

"It is the word of God, Sangster. Mind you…" he began muttering something about lobsters also being a similar abomination in the eyes of the Almighty.

"Lobsters?" I laughed.

"Oh, nothing, shouldn't have mentioned the lobsters, but do you see what I mean?"

"Hmmm… yes." I considered his conundrum. "Do you, er… have any immediate temptation, you know, anyone right now you perhaps would like to…?"

"I may, Sangster, I may, but the Bible, how do I reconcile that with my nature?"

"Do the right thing, Pengelly, regardless of what anyone else thinks." I realised I'd said this with a slight slur, while finishing the last of the whisky, but carried on talking anyway. "And if you do, I am sure your God, whoever or whatever he is, will look down upon you with affection."

"Jack," said Morwenna as she continued her manicure behind the bar. "You're pissed."

10:30PM

I lay on my bed, back against a propped-up pillow. My mind was spinning too fast for sleep, and somehow, the story of Jesus' link to St Anthony, plus other things during recent days that I couldn't put my finger on, were all coming together to tell me that the solution to Angel's disappearance could be found if I dug deep enough. And despite having spent the evening in company, first Sir John's, then the locals in the bar, the flirting of Morwenna and the alternative history lesson and outpourings of heart-felt unfulfillment from Canon Pengelly, I felt lonely.

I looked to the bedside table and saw that the hands of my alarm clock said ten forty. Sarah might still be up, so I pulled on my dressing gown, grabbed some coins, and after passing the bedroom mirror and hastily rubbing off Morwenna's lipstick print from my cheek, crept down the stairs to the lobby.

"Sarah, yes, glad you're up... yes, all fine... no, I'm just calling to see if you're okay... why am I asking you?" There was a silence. "Because I miss you." Another silence. "Oh, and I was talking to a chap in the bar this evening, and I thought what he said might be up your street... yes, very much Levantine studies."

I proceeded to relate a short version of the canon's story about Jesus and Joseph visiting Cornwall. Sarah, unsurprisingly, was fully aware of the legends (although not the details about this part of Cornwall).

"Yes darling, it's actually a well-known theory. There are also plenty of people who think Joseph came back to England after the crucifixion and founded an abbey in, er… Glastonbury, that's it. All hearsay of course…" She paused for a moment. "Jack, it's lovely you called late, but you sound worried. There's something on your mind, isn't there?"

"The academy's got a young girl missing, and Granville's asked me to help sort it out. She's been gone more than two days and I keep thinking she's probably dead, and if she is dead, who knows what happened to her beforehand. Sir John says he's relying on me!"

"Why?"

"Because the police have got nowhere so far and so Granville, the old rascal, has lost faith in them and put the whole problem on my back. He's worried the authorities will use this girl's disappearance as a reason to close the academy down."

"That's awful, darling?"

"Yes, and it gets worse. The parents, well actually the mother, latched onto me as the only one who can find her daughter, I mean, I've dealt with problem kids, serial truant cases and worse, but this one's police work."

"What about those cases you solved last year, the one with the missing boy who blew up that mine?"

"Quarry, it was a quarry he blew up."

"Alright, quarry then, and that time you ended up owning a greyhound?"

"Well…"

"And that awful business in Wales at Easter."

"Not the same somehow, it's—"

"You know what, Jack?" Sarah interrupted. "The girl's mother was right. People somehow place trust in you. And you'll see things the police may miss. Now, I hope that landlady, what's her name?"

"Morwenna."

"I hope she's not, er... putting her trust in you too much. She fancies you, you know that."

"She was also impressed with you, Sarah," I replied quickly. "Very impressed from what she said." We were both silent for a moment. "Anyway, it's late and I'm just calling to say I miss you. Now tell me what you're wearing."

"What, at this time of night? It's very boring."

"Well, lie if you want."

"Alright, I'm wearing a black negligée, matching fully fashioned stockings of course, spiked-heel court shoes, that black velvet choker you like, and..."

"Sarah, what are you actually wearing?"

"Don't want to say."

"Tell me, Sarah."

"Just one of your shirts, Jack."

"Not that dirty shirt you took back home by mistake last weekend?"

"Yes, and it wasn't by mistake."

"Did you wash it yet?"

"No, and when I'm not wearing the shirt, I stuff it in my pillowcase."

*

As I crept back up the stairs I heard footsteps and, looking along the landing, saw the figure of Monsignor Kelly, motorcycle leathers now replaced by a silk dressing gown. He turned up a side stair with a sign by the bannister. 'Room 12a'. I smiled, remembering Pengelly's startled expression when the Monsignor had stood in the doorway of the bar. Perhaps the canon was 'doing the right thing, regardless' after all.

Back in my room, despite talking with Sarah, I still couldn't sleep, recent events racing through my mind. I was sure there must be something that hinted at Angel's whereabouts, but what? I cast my mind back to the previous Friday. I'd taken an early train up to London to run over the academy's funding with Ernest Prendergast, the institute's chief accountant. Sarah travelled down to London from

Chester to take the evening train with me to Cornwall, where she would stay the weekend and return to Chester on the Monday, in time for lectures in Manchester the following day.

Everything had seemed so hopeful that weekend, but now, just a few days later, Angel had disappeared. And despite telling Sir John I had instincts, all I could see in front of me was a brick wall, although for no reason I could have explained I felt more hopeful than I had earlier, as if the answer lay just behind that wall. Perhaps something I saw or heard during Sarah's visit might lead me to Angel.

Sarah and I had arranged to meet under the Paddington Station clock at five, and we nearly missed the train…

FRIDAY,
MAY THE 22ND
(THE PREVIOUS WEEKEND)

17:34PM

"There are two bloody clocks," I shouted to Sarah, who was standing clutching her weekend bag and wildly looking around the station. "Come on, less than a minute before the train leaves, now run. Platform Two."

And so we ran, jumping breathlessly through the door of the end carriage as the guard leaned out of his van and blew his whistle. Slamming the door behind us, I felt the train groan as it began to pull away from the station.

"Oh Jack," sighed Sarah, dropping her bag and throwing her arms around me. "That was close. You waited under the wrong clock."

"Yes, a bit too close," I said, panting. "This is the last service that gets us to Truro tonight." I panted again, feeling the floor rock from side to side as we gathered speed. "Anyway, we made it, but I think our seats are at the other end, let's walk up."

We stumbled down open aisles between pairs of seats and through corridors with doors to compartments. After wobbling along like this for a few minutes we came to a restaurant car with linen-covered tables, polished bone china that carried the logo 'GWR' (leftovers from the old Great Western Railway), sparkling glasses, gleaming cutlery, freshly filled flower vases and printed menus with gilt edging. ('Just look at the way they've laid those lovely tables, darling.') Our seats were in the next carriage and, as I pulled open our compartment door, I breathlessly realised we had walked almost the full length of the train.

"Never mind the walk, we've got the compartment to ourselves, Jack. Look, little curtains, and old-fashioned lamp shades. How sweet."

"First class is one of very few perks I get from the institute, so let's make the most of it Sarah, I—"

"Ladies and Gentlemen," the voice of the guard from the tannoy interrupted me. "This is your five thirty-five express service from London Paddington to Penzance, calling at Exeter St David's, Taunton…" He droned on, listing innumerable stations, including Truro. "St Erth and Penzance," he finally said.

"How long does it take?" asked Sarah. "All those stations."

"About five hours to Truro," I answered, as the compartment door opened, and a steward appeared.

"Tickets please." Our tickets were duly clipped. "Thank you, sir. Now then, the Pullman car opens at seven. Will you and madam be dining with us tonight, sir?"

"Of course," I answered, looking at Sarah, who was nodding vigorously.

"We're both looking forward to sampling the railway's hospitality," she added, the steward nodding back. "You look as if you've been looking after passengers for a while."

"Mervyn Davies, madam, been working these trains for nigh on thirty-five years now, 'cept for a stint during the war."

"Well, it's my first time, dining with you and, as I say, I'm very much looking forward to it."

"Good, madam, then we'll look forward to seeing you later. Any time after seven, and up until about eight thirty. Kitchen closes at Plymouth." He went into the corridor then poked his head back through the door. "Oh, and most tables are for four, but I'll do my best to reserve you a two-seater. More private, like."

"This is rather romantic, darling," said Sarah, as we found ourselves alone in the compartment once again. "What a shame it isn't one of those trains with cabins and beds."

"Yes, what a shame," I said, assuming Sarah was having visions of Orient-Express-like opulence. I shuddered, her words actually bringing to mind the inaccurately named British Rail overnight 'sleeper' service, a guaranteed recipe for insomnia I'd used several times since being sent to Cornwall.

"Now then, I need to freshen up, Jack. Where's the, er…"

"End of the corridor, on the right. Go the other way and you'll end up walking through the dining car and on to the second-class loo."

"Ooh, second-class loo, that would never do," she laughed.

9:30PM

"Amazing, darling," said Sarah, as the steward cleared the last of our plates. "I mean, British Rail's food is legendary." She laughed. "For all the wrong reasons, but that." She pointed at the table. "That was a meal, well... that I would actually have paid for."

And it was amazing, with three immaculately presented courses and accompanying wine, all managed with consummate ease, despite the confines of the dining car, by our friendly steward, Mervyn (how he managed to safely serve soup as the train pitched and rolled its way westwards was a particular mystery).

"Coffee sir, madam?"

"Yes please." Once again, Mervyn showed uncanny balance, pouring the hot brown liquid into our tiny china cups without spilling a drop. As he did so, Sarah's eyes suddenly sparkled with streetlight reflections shining through the carriage window as we hurtled past an isolated village, and I found myself wondering if a sleeper train, regardless of its comfort, wouldn't have been such a bad idea after all.

*

"So, tell me," said Sarah, finishing the last of her coffee. "I know you don't like to talk shop, but how is everything going with the academy? I haven't seen you for over a month, and you don't mention it much on the phone."

"Almost six weeks actually."

"Seems like it as well, Jack," she said with a sigh. "Anyway, is the school working, and did you get the extra funding today?"

"The school's working, I suppose, although I still think we should have waited until the autumn term to admit pupils. And yes, the new funding's secure."

I had been against opening too early, my original plans for the academy, including a period of settling in for teaching, administration, and maintenance staff, plus ensuring classrooms, a gym, dormitories, the infirmary and so on were properly equipped and operational. Sir John, impatient as always, overrode me, and decided the academy would open first for modern and classical languages, art, and music, and later for sciences (thus allowing time to build laboratories and other more complex facilities). By February, his team had already identified fifty children gifted in these disciplines from schools around the country and, more importantly, offered them places at the academy starting after Easter. Sir John's solution to finding appropriate teachers (many of whom had been university lecturers), part way through the school year and at short notice had been to simply double their salaries and pay all of their lodging and other expenses. This recruitment policy, of course, had the effect of alienating an already hostile Department of Education even further ('Stuffed shirts in London think we're elitist, Sangster, close us down if they could').

I also explained to Sarah that the children themselves presented a challenge. This initial intake was aged between fourteen and seventeen years old, and besides all the usual problems associated with the pastoral care of teenagers, especially in a coeducational boarding school, the pupils' exceptional intellects brought many more complications. Restless young minds, questioning everything, easily bored, needing constant stimulation. Principal Velinda Flimwell had prior experience teaching exceptionally gifted pupils, and I recalled her description of such children during the interview at the institute's office in London.

"They have the same special needs as those with severely impaired mental faculties," she had said, quite shocking me. "A child with an IQ off the scale can often be considered a handicapped child as well. So, if your academy is to thrive, you must cater for those special needs, and it won't be easy."

But despite a few teething problems, and in a large part due to Velinda and her husband Cyrus proving to be the superb head teaching team we had hoped for, the academy was able to open after Easter. Cyrus, a qualified chartered accountant, was the administrative brains of the pair, whilst the more flamboyant Velinda was the natural head teacher, empathetic towards, if not fully able to comprehend, the particular needs of the academy's exceptional young charges.

And with the first tranche of pupils admitted successfully, the embryonic academy was thus far going very well. In fact, surprisingly well, to the point that Sir John had agreed, subject to Prendergast reviewing my numbers, to release additional funding for what had become known as 'phase two', which would involve staff and facilities for a further two hundred pupil intake in September.

"Well that all sounds marvellous, darling. Shall we go back to our seats?"

"Ah," I yawned. "Yes let's." I yawned again.

"You look as if you've got an after-dinner nap coming on," grinned Sarah, as we stood up and walked back through the Pullman car, which was still full of diners. Some were couples like us, some sat at four-seater tables, where strangers had become friends in the few hours since we left London.

"Look," whispered Sarah as we passed one such table, "he's got leather trousers on."

"Who?"

"That priest, with the long black hair and the dog collar." She jerked her head backwards. "Handsome man, youngish, big gold cross round his neck, in the window seat facing backwards, on the table with those three old ladies. I've been watching him all evening." I turned to look, briefly catching sight of the passenger in question, before being pushed forward by Sarah. "Don't stare, darling."

10:30PM

'Next stop is Truro, ladies and gentlemen, Truro next stop,' said the voice from the tannoy.

"Come on, Jack," said Sarah, slamming shut a book she had been reading. "Open your eyes, we're almost here." I started at her voice, blinked, then stood up and lifted our bags down from the overhead luggage rack, feeling the train slow, then hiss as the brakes were applied more heavily and the station buildings came into view. As we pulled to a stop I lurched forward against Sarah, forgetting, as always, to brace myself.

"Steady, Jack."

"Sorry, it's your animal magnetism, Sarah. Irresistible."

"Come on," she said, giving me a peck on the cheek as we left our compartment and stepped onto the platform where Mervyn stood smiling and holding the door open.

"Thank you for the wonderful service, and the lovely smooth journey," said Sarah.

"You're very welcome, madam," he beamed. "These two old warships do a great job, very dependable," he added, before climbing aboard again, closing the door, and peering out of the window towards the rear of the train. "Just checking that bike's off safely. Ah yes, there it goes."

I looked around to see the motorcycle in question being wheeled down a wooden ramp from the guard's van at the end of the train. The ramp was then drawn up and the whistle blown, after which the train hissed once more and slowly pulled away from the platform. Our steward waved to us as it went.

"I think the bike belongs to that priest, darling, you know, in the dining car."

"Yes," I said, recognising the priest's silhouette by the hair. "I believe that's him."

"What a very odd priest," Sarah said to me as we walked along the platform. "And why bring a motorbike on a train?"

"He's youngish so it's as good a way as any to get about in Cornwall I suppose, and the train's a lot easier than riding all the way from London." I looked back as the owner of the bike, who had been met on the platform (by someone whose silhouette also seemed familiar), wheeled his machine towards a side gate at the far end of the platform.

"And what do you think that steward meant by 'old warships'?"

"Warship class diesel locomotives," I laughed, recognising Sarah's habit of asking more and more questions when she was excited. "They use two of them, joined together, to pull the train."

"Oh."

*

"Isn't this quiet, Jack?" said Sarah, as we stepped out of the car next to the Watersmeet, which was all in darkness except for a pale lamp which illuminated a sign over the front door:

'St Austell Ales. Morwenna Poldhu, licensed to sell wine, beer, spirits and tobacco for consumption on these premises.'

"And the sky, look at the sky," she cried, pointing upwards. I looked up as well, to the vague grey snake of the Milky Way, straddling countless individual stars that shone through the Cornish night, and visible to a much greater extent than it ever would be near the glow of a city.

"Shh, Sarah," I said quietly, putting my finger on her lips. "Everyone's in bed here by about eleven."

"But it is beautiful, isn't it?" she whispered as we walked up the steps to the hotel.

"Yes, it is, and wait until you see the village in the morning. A clear night sky like this usually means we'll have nice weather tomorrow."

"Jack, isn't that the motorbike we saw at the station?" I looked down to see a large black Triumph machine parked behind our car, looking very like the one that had been wheeled down the ramp from the guard's van.

"Similar size and shape yes, but I couldn't be sure it's exactly the same bike. Now then, where's that key?" I fumbled in my pocket for a moment then found the hotel night key, given to me by Morwenna for use after hours. "Come on, Sarah," I said as the door unlocked. "And quietly up the stairs."

SATURDAY,
MAY THE 23RD
8:30AM

"Oh Jack, the river," cried Sarah, throwing the French windows of our bedroom wide open and stepping onto the small balcony beyond. "It's just... it's wonderful. Looks like the Orinoco or something with all those trees coming down to the water's edge."

And the view was spectacular, the hotel looking out over the tidal tree-lined t-shaped confluence of the Truro and Tresillian Rivers, which formed a larger channel that curved out of sight to the south. This morning the tide was at half ebb, so that the water was well below the lowest tree branches, which were cut off in an unnatural looking straight line (the salt-water killed the growth where it touched the trees, locals had explained to me). Mewing seagulls vied with the buzzing of numerous small boats ferrying people out to larger yachts that were moored up and down the creek, their owners preparing to leave for the day. I had watched this scene change with the passing of winter and the greening of spring, and rain, wind or shine, there was always something different to see.

"Have you got your Polaroid in the bag?"

"Yes, next to the big camera case, why?"

"I want to catch this moment, with you standing by the window."

"Alright," she said, instinctively adjusting her hair and night dress as I picked up the camera, removed the case, pointed, and clicked.

"What do I do now, Sarah?"

"Wait, darling."

And so, we waited, several minutes passing before a tiny oblong plastic sheet slowly edged out from the back of the camera. "Right, now take that and carefully peel off the front covering." I peeled as instructed, watching as the chemicals met the air of the room and a black and white image of Sarah's head and neck, framed by the window, gradually appeared.

"I'd like to keep this in my pocket, Sarah, but it's a bit sticky."

"Give it to me," she said, reaching into the bag and pulling out a packet of plastic sleeves. "You put the instant picture into one of these, then press all over and it's preserved forever." She thumbed the sleeve until all the air had gone and then passed me the photo. "There you are, Jack, for your wallet. I'll be watching you everywhere you go now."

"You don't need to watch me, Sarah."

"Don't I?"

"Don't be silly, now look…" I pointed out of the window and to the right. "If we went far enough down that river we'd end up at the academy."

"Oh, it's beautiful," she shouted, any worries about keeping an eye on me now seemingly gone. "Is that the boat you mentioned that goes to Falmouth?" she then asked, as a sky-blue painted pleasure steamer with white deck housing, a scarlet funnel, and dressed overall with coloured pennants, rounded the point opposite.

"Yes, that's the *Kernow Belle*," I answered, looking at my alarm clock as the boat slowed to moor by the village jetty. "Eight thirty now, so she'll sail on to Truro after this, pick up passengers and then come back here, for about ten o'clock, I think."

"Ten o'clock?"

"Yes," I said, pulling off my pyjama top. "So, if we want to catch that boat, we'd better get down to breakfast."

"Alright, Jack, as long as you don't have kippers. I won't kiss you after you've eaten kippers."

"Well, perhaps, if you kissed me before breakfast..."

We managed to wait another twenty minutes then go down to breakfast, where I did eat kippers after all.

10 AM

"Motorbike's gone," I said to Sarah as we stepped into the morning sunshine, our car now the only vehicle parked by the hotel.

"Yes, I heard it leave this morning, quite early. Come on, darling, show me the place where we get the boat." We turned left and walked along the road, which dipped down to a public slipway next to the boatyard and a floating jetty for the steamer. People were already waiting in a queue for the ten o'clock boat.

"Morning," I called to Mike Jackson, who was busy painting the underside of a sailing yacht laid up on a cradle beside the jetty.

"Hello Sangster," he called back. "And this must be, er…"

"Sarah," I shouted, as Sarah waved.

"Pleasure to meet you, Sarah," said Jackson. "Perhaps I'll see you both tonight in the hotel bar but got to get on now. Antifouling." He pointed to the red paint on the boat's keel. "Needs to dry between tides," he added, turning back to his paintbrush.

Clang! Clang! Clang!

Most of the waiting passengers turned to the left, as the raucous sound of a bell shattered the morning.

"What's that, Jack? I nearly jumped out of my skin."

"You ring that to call the ferryman," I explained, looking down at a grey bell mounted on the wall by the slipway, next to where a group of hikers stood. "His name's Pasco. Regular at the hotel, and when he's not in the bar he lives over there." I pointed over to a pair of cottages on the other side of the creek. "His is the far house by the point, and that little stone shelter thing by the water's edge is called the Waiting Room. He's supposed to sit in it and wait for the bell, but I'm not sure he ever does." I squinted across the water. "No, maybe Pasco does at that, he's already on his way with a passenger. See that rowing boat?"

"Oh yes, looks like he's ferrying a cyclist. I can see a bike lying across the front of the boat."

"That will be Canon Pengelly. He's another regular at the hotel bar, and he rides everywhere."

"Why?"

"Doesn't drive and looks after several local churches, including the one by the academy. I guess this ferry's the quickest way back to Truro from Roseland."

"The peninsula on the east side of the river?"

"You've been reading up, haven't you, Sarah?" She nodded. "Well, the academy's at the bottom of it, near a place called St Anthony."

"Can't wait to see the academy, and look," she said as the sky-blue steamer announced its presence upriver with a whoop. "Here comes our boat again."

*

"Only last week we saw a seal, ladies and gentlemen," came the indistinct voice of the guide through a loudspeaker on the mast of the *Kernow Belle*. "They very occasionally swim this far up the river."

"I never seen one in sixty years going on these boats," said a very old man with a long, flowing, dishevelled beard, holding a head-height walking stick made of highly polished gnarled wood, and incongruously dressed in a threadbare overcoat (worn buttoned up despite the sunshine). He stood next to us as we leaned against the rail on the top deck. "Reckon it's always last week they've seen a seal," the old man wheezed, bending double with laughter, and coughing as he did so. I laughed with him, then continued to admire the view, as tree-lined shores passed by, occasionally revealing a building, such as a church spire or stone boathouse and, at one point, just for a moment, a grand, turreted house with lawns sloping down to the water.

"That's a calendar house, Jack. I caught a glimpse, then it was gone."

"A what Sarah?"

"It has three hundred and sixty-five windows. One for each day of the year."

"How did you know that?"

"That book I was looking at on the train."

The *Kernow Belle* continued its journey, while the river widened as more side-creeks joined with it, including the confluence with the Fal proper, at which point a row of massive concrete hulls chained together along the centre of the channel came into view. "These are old barges, ladies and gentlemen, used to carry fresh water during the D-Day landings," crackled our ever-informative guide. The steamer travelled on, close by the towering hulls of two impossibly large cargo ships ('these ships are laid up in the river until work can be found for them'), and after those, past a chain ferry for cars ('King Harry Ferry, ladies and gentlemen, nobody knows which Harry though'). The ferry named for the unknown Harry travelled slowly sideways across the channel, the captain of the *Belle* carefully navigating to one side. As he did so, the passengers on our deck, including the old man, waved, and the car ferry passengers waved back. Sarah and I followed suit.

The river eventually led to an expanse of water ('Carrick Roads, ladies and gentlemen, over a mile wide and three miles long, the third largest natural harbour in the world'), where I felt the boat increase speed, the engines making more noise and the wake behind us now whiter and wider. From there we steamed through various yacht moorings and passed vessels underway, including a fleet of old-fashioned looking, many-sailed wooden yachts ('Working boats, ladies and gentlemen, used to dredge oysters'), until the docks of Falmouth came into view.

11:00AM

"Thank you, sir, thank you, madam." The *Kernow Belle* boatman helped us disembark onto the pier with a grin. "Last boat back's at four-thirty."

"Now then," I said looking round. "We need the St Mawes Ferry."

"Another boat, darling?"

"Second of three I'm afraid, Sarah. We get the last ferry from St Mawes to St Anthony."

"Don't be afraid, darling, I love these boats, now is that ours?" She pointed to a small wooden ferry boat docked at the end of the pier next to a placard saying simply 'St Mawes'.

"Almost an hour's wait," I said, looking at a sign showing twelve noon as the next crossing. "Shall we go for a wander?"

"Lead on, Jack."

We walked along the pier and then left up a hill and along Falmouth's narrow high street, coming before long to a sign on the wall and an arrow next to it pointing down a steep alley.

'Fo'c'sle Locker, Chandlery'

"D'you mind if we have a look in there," I said to Sarah. "I know it's been fine since you arrived, but it rains an awful lot here. Could do with something waterproof."

"Okay, interesting name for a shop." We turned into the alley and stepped gingerly down the slope, which led, it seemed, directly into the water below. "Interesting little ope."

"Sorry?"

"This alley, you call it an ope."

"How did you know that?"

"And look at her." Sarah ignored my question as we arrived at the entrance to the Fo'c'sle Locker, a low doorway on the right (invisible from the top of the alley), which was guarded by an enormous painted ship's figurehead that looked at us with baleful eyes. I started when the figurehead seemed to speak.

"No need to worry about Sally, love, she's not going anywhere."

"Pardon?"

A young blonde woman in a striped Breton sweater, calf-length jeans, canvas deck shoes and a red and white kerchief around her neck, appeared from behind the statue.

"Sally, our figurehead, love," she said, hair blowing sideways in the breeze.

"She's a big girl." I jerked my head towards Sally's larger than life form.

"Oh yes, came from a ship called HMS *Amazon*."

"I can imagine."

"What can I do for you, love?"

"My husband's looking for an oilskin," Sarah said, stepping between me and the woman.

"Then you're at the right place. Come inside."

And in we went, me ducking through the low doorway, which was guarded by another, smaller figurehead above the threshold (clinging on to what looked like an old sailing ship's bowsprit). Once inside, and blinking in the dimness, I looked around to see an Aladdin's cave for yachtsmen, a long, low ceilinged room stacked with every conceivable nautical accessory; brass ships' clocks, compasses, bells and barometers, reels of rope and yarn, coloured lamps hanging off the ceiling, lifebelts, charts, tins of marine varnish and paint, fishing equipment (including a pile of lobster pots), flags of every kind, an enormous foghorn standing upright on the floor, and in a wooden crate next to it, live bait (I watched Sarah grimace as she sniffed the air and watched the maggots wriggle). There seemed no rhyme or reason as to how the goods were arranged, and I looked in vain for waterproof clothing until our hostess gestured to an area at the far end of the shop where a hanging rail held oilskins of all shapes and sizes.

"You looking for a jacket or full-length, love?" she asked me, running her hand along the garments.

"He'd just like a jacket I think, wouldn't you, darling?"

"Er… yes, jacket should be okay. I'm a fifty chest but it needs to be big enough to go over a coat."

"Try this, it's a size up."

I slipped the proffered oilskin over my sports jacket, then carefully did up the newly stiff buttons.

"Yes, that seems fine."

"Matching sou-wester, love, keep all that lovely salt and pepper hair dry?"

"Um… no thanks. Jacket's already got a hood, hasn't it?"

"Yes, nice big hood. Will that be all?"

"That'll be all," said Sarah. "Sorry, we're in a hurry, can we pay?"

"Matching sou-wester indeed," snapped Sarah as we emerged into the light of the 'ope'. "Keep all that salt and pepper hair dry."

"Just sales patter, now come on," I said, taking her arm as we stepped back up to the high street. "We've actually still got half an hour to look around."

"D'you know what, Jack," said Sarah, pointing to a men's clothing store across the road. "I think you could do worse than buy a new jacket."

"I just did."

"Not an oilskin, silly, a modern one. I mean, that tweed sports coat hasn't been fashionable since about 1955."

"I like it, it's comfortable."

"It's old, now come on, they've got some lovely casual jackets in the window."

We entered the shop, which, to my relief, was run by two men, with whom Sarah spent some time discussing my sartorial needs. Almost half an hour later we were back in the high street, me now wearing a navy blue 'Harrington' zip-up jacket with tartan lining and elasticated waist and cuffs ('I think he'd like to wear it out of the shop, wouldn't you, Jack?'). My trusty tweed was then consigned to a carrier bag, along with the oilskin.

"You look a treat, darling. Takes years off you."

"Never mind that, have you seen the time?" A clock above our heads showed two minutes to twelve. "We need to get moving."

"Looks like they're about to go," I shouted as we arrived at the pier to see the St Mawes boat preparing to leave. We ran to it, clambering down a ladder, throwing the carrier bag in first then jumping on board just as the boatman cast off the mooring ropes. Sitting down, I noticed the old man in the overcoat from the *Kernow Belle* standing in the bows. His eye caught mine and he nodded, then turned his gaze towards the far shore, hair and beard flowing in the breeze as the little ferry pressed through the waves to its destination, about a mile across the harbour from Falmouth. Sarah, excited as ever by new experiences and with shopping now seemingly forgotten, began pointing out more landmarks.

"That's St Mawes Castle, I could tell you some history about that."

"I'm sure."

"And there," she said, waving her hand at a white tower that seemed to sit impossibly on the rocks at the mouth of the harbour. "That's St Anthony Lighthouse."

"We could drive there tomorrow if you like."

"Yes let's."

Arriving in St Mawes, we found we had just missed the St Anthony crossing, a sign by the empty berth stated in chalk writing that there was an hour's wait for the next boat. I looked across the water to see the ferry itself not far from shore, weaving away from us between the boats moored in the river.

"The ferry gods are against us today."

"Not necessarily," said Sarah, pointing to a café. "Now we've time for a cream tea."

"It's not even half twelve."

"It can count as lunch." She took me by the hand and pulled me into the café, where a waitress led us to a window table and took our order. "And look." Sarah pointed out of the window as we waited. "That motorbike again, the one from the station and the hotel. See." I duly looked, to see a black Triumph parked just along the road.

"Certainly looks like the same one. I mean, there can't be too many black Bonnevilles around here. I'll try and remember that number plate, I—"

"Two cream teas?" interrupted the waitress, placing a tray in front of us.

"Yes, thank you," said Sarah. "I'm so looking forward to this, Jack," she added, the mysterious Triumph now clearly forgotten. "Now then, you must put the jam on the scones first. Then the cream."

"Isn't it the other way round?"

"No, that's Devon, darling."

*

Cream teas consumed, we boarded the St Anthony ferry (actually no more than a small open boat with an outboard engine), to find the bearded man we had met earlier sitting on a seat in the bows.

"Been shopping?" he said, looking at the carrier bag.

"Oilskins. Never know when I'll need them."

"Next week, Friday, late afternoon I'd reckon. See you've a different jacket on and all."

I smiled and nodded, as the boatman pulled his starter cord in a series of short revs before the outboard spluttered into life.

"Going over to that new school in St Anthony?" the old man then asked, as the ferry carried the three of us across the river.

"We are," I shouted over the noise of the engine.

"Heard they call it The Academy."

"That's right, you know it?"

"Oh yes. Met a few of the kids there. Bright lot, eh?"

"Indeed. Set up specially for gifted children. And that's it to the right, Sarah," I said, as the main school building and its lawns sweeping down to the water's edge came into view.

"Gifted," the old man said with a faraway look in his eyes. "Ah yes, I do hope they are, at least the one I need."

"And you," Sarah asked him. "You live over there in St Anthony?"

"Oh no, but I come here from time to time."

"Truro then?"

"Around and about, here in the Old World, and in America." He stood up as he said this and stared westwards, causing the little boat to pitch from side to side, then steadied himself and sat down again but continued his faraway gaze, now appearing to speak more to the wind than to us. "Wherever I'm needed to protect the righteous."

Sarah giggled and nudged me.

"America and the righteous," she sniggered, pointing to the top of what looked like a whisky bottle protruding from one of the old man's many coat pockets. "More like the self-righteous, he'll be lucky if he gets to the other side of here without falling in."

"Shh." I put my finger to Sarah's lips, worried the old man might see her laughing, but he continued to look ahead, seemingly oblivious of our presence.

As the ferry continued to chug forwards, I looked upstream to see two kayaks in the distance, one red and the other yellow, paddled by a girl and a boy that I thought I might have seen before at the academy. I watched as the canoes followed the course of the river, turning into a clump of overhanging trees, before suddenly disappearing from view. A few moments later our ferry pulled up against a small wooden jetty at the end of a narrow lane that wound away into the thick woodland that covered the banks of the creek as far as the eye could see. Three boys I also recognised from the academy were waiting, and impatiently went to jump into the ferry until the boatman shouted at them to stop while the passengers got onto dry land. The old man disembarked first, followed by Sarah and me.

"I'll be here every hour, on the half hour, until six this evening," said the boatman, as he let us off. "Busy day today, both ways," he added, as the three boys climbed into the boat.

"Thank you," I replied. "And goodbye to you as well," I added, addressing the old man.

"There's nobody here, darling," said Sarah, looking down the empty lane. "He's vanished."

1 PM

"That's strange," said Sarah as we walked up the lane towards the main gates to the academy.

"What's strange?"

"That man in the boat was wearing a battered old Hamsa."

"Hamsa?"

"Jewish amulet. It's in the shape of a hand, usually with an eye in the middle. I remember people wearing them when I was a kid. His was hanging from a dull looking silver chain bracelet."

"Then our old man is Jewish. Nothing strange in that."

"Not in itself, Jack, but it somehow seems odd, an old man dressed like that wearing such an elaborate thing."

We walked on, arriving at the academy gatehouse, and forgetting the old man as the rotund figure of Runtle appeared out of a small door (the 'postern' as he liked to call it), to the side of the main gates.

"Ah, Mr Sangster, come through."

"Sarah, this is Runtle, our caretaker," I said, watching her appraise the diminutive old caretaker's ruddy face, his mop of grey curly hair and (as I imagined Sarah would have said out of his earshot), 'five by five' figure.

"Pleased to meet you, Mr. Runtle."

"Ma'am," said Runtle, deferentially. "The Flimwells are outside on the front lawn, if you'd like to walk on up." We proceeded along the main driveway, flanked on either side by lush rhododendrons, Sarah commenting on the massive gates and high perimeter walls ('a bit like a prison, darling'). We passed several small groups of pupils walking in the grounds, always apparently in deep discussion and, as we approached the school building, the sound of violins could be heard echoing through the bushes. Turning a corner, we saw a string quartet seated on chairs laid out across the lawn, with the two principals, along with several other staff members and pupils, standing watching as the children played.

*

"Mrs Sangster," beamed Velinda Flimwell, clapping as the music finished. "How lovely you could come down and visit us from, er…"

"Chester, and call me Sarah, please." She gestured across the lawn and towards the building. "I couldn't wait to see the academy. Jack's told me so much about the place, and about you and your husband."

"Nothing good I hope," joked Cyrus.

"All good," said Sarah. "Jack and I saw a couple of youngsters kayaking just now. From the school?"

"I think that would have been Angel Blackwood you saw, and one of her friends. We're encouraging the kids to take an interest in the water, and they're gradually doing up the boats we inherited. Some of them have been working every night, and they need to. Boats were left to rot by the previous owners."

"And what was that beautiful music?"

"*Musica notturna delle strade di Madrid*, by Boccherini."

"Night music of the streets of Madrid," translated Sarah. "The kids must have practised for weeks. That sounded almost perfect." She paused for a moment. "No, not almost. It was perfect."

"Practised for weeks you say?" questioned Cyrus, his eyes (I felt), lingering for just a moment too long on Sarah's mini-skirted legs (she seemed not to notice).

"Hours more like," laughed Velinda. "They were literally given the sheet music after breakfast this morning. Today's the first time they have played that piece together."

"Unbelievable," said Sarah shaking her head.

"Many things these children can do defy belief," Velinda went on to say. "But our academy's young people are nevertheless just children at the end of the day, with everything that means, good and bad. Now then, Sarah, I believe my husband needs to borrow your husband for a while, so may I show you round the academy in the meantime?"

Sarah nodded and we went our separate ways, she on her tour and I to the school office, where I explained Prendergast's plans for the funding of phase two. An hour later we were all back standing on the front lawn, at which point I saw that two buses now stood parked in the driveway.

"Trip to the cinema this evening, Sangster," said Cyrus, noticing my gaze. "The new Beatles film, *Let it Be*, showing at the Regal in Redruth." He shook his head and looked at the ground. "It'll be like herding cats, getting this lot there and back safely."

"Well, they're in capable hands and I'm sure the kids and the staff will love the film," I said. "Anyway, we'd better be getting along. Ferry back to St Mawes is in ten minutes."

We said our goodbyes and walked back to the gatehouse, where Runtle once again let us through the postern, the main gates staying firmly shut ('don't like opening them big gates for nobody, not even them buses'). The academy's security, I thought to myself as the postern door slammed shut, was in safe if somewhat eccentric hands.

*

"Good people the Flimwells," I said to Sarah as we walked down the lane towards the landing stage. "Couldn't have done this without them."

"Er… yes."

"Mmmm?"

"Well, he's a bit too touchy feely, that Cyrus," Sarah replied, looking away from me.

"What do you mean?"

"Oh, he kept placing his hand on my back as we walked. Once a bit lower down."

"Not too low I hope?"

"Oh no, just lower."

"Normal enough."

"Seemed unnecessary, happened too many times. And I saw him looking at me out of the corner of his eye, in that way men do."

"Normal enough again."

"A woman knows the signals."

"Well," I said, remembering Flimwell's overlong glances at Sarah. "A lot of men can't help themselves."

"Thank you, I'd never have known that." I placed my arm around her shoulders.

"There's nothing he did I should be worried about is there?"

"No Jack, nothing like that."

3 PM

Sarah was uncharacteristically quiet as we took the succession of boats back to the hotel. I'd assumed she was taking in the scenery, but nevertheless felt some unease when her mood didn't change. Usually, in a new situation like this, I would have been bombarded with questions and observations. Right now, it was all silence.

"Penny for your thoughts?" I eventually asked, as the *Kernow Belle* left the wide expanse of the Carrick Roads and entered the narrow inlet of the River Fal on the final leg of our journey. The reduced sound of its slowing engine making conversation all the easier. "It isn't Cyrus Flimwell, is it?"

"Oh God no, Jack," she whispered, still looking into the distance. "It's the children, I've never... I..." Her voice trailed off completely, words apparently failing her.

"Never what. Sarah?"

"They frighten me. Where did you find all these children?"

"The Granville Institute has scouts that check with as many schools as possible, all around the country. Exceptionally bright kids are identified and invited to the academy. Families from any walk of life, all expenses paid. But," I then asked, looking at her troubled expression, "why would they frighten you?"

"I can't put my finger on it, they just do," Sarah answered ('they just do' being the phrase she often used when unable to explain her intuition). "I mean, we came across a group sitting around a table in the library practicing some sort of telepathy."

"Practicing telepathy, how?"

"With playing cards, guessing what card had been drawn from a deck when it was placed face down. And they seemed to be getting it right most of the time. Made the hairs on my arms stand right up."

"Kids' card games, Sarah," I said. "That's all, and these kids just play them a bit differently. What else about the children bothered you?"

"They seemed old beyond their years. I spoke to one boy who knew far more than I do about pre-Christian Levantine cultures, and I have a doctorate."

"I know that, Sarah."

"Of course you do, darling, but this boy not only knew much more than me but had also memorised books that I normally only recommend as reading for the post-graduate course." I raised an eyebrow. "No, there was no question that he knew the books by heart, and according to Velinda Flimwell, he'd even memorised the Bible. Both testaments, word perfect for heaven's sake, and he was just seventeen."

"What was his name?"

"One of the other kids referred to him as 'Spider.'"

"Ah yes, I know the lad you mean. Tall and very skinny? Black hair, longish?"

"Yes, that's him, Jack."

"His real name's Simon Founds I think."

"Why Spider then?"

"Not sure, but nobody ever calls him Simon, not even the teachers. Bit of a natural leader to the others kids he is. In fact, if the academy was the type of school to appoint a head boy, it might have been Spider."

"I'm sure, but he also correctly guessed my name, Sarah Sangster.

Told me he would guess it and then did. I mean, how could he know that?"

"Might have seen you arriving with me, noticed you wear a wedding ring and, as he knows who I am, guessed the name Sangster. And Velinda must have called you Sarah within his earshot."

"No, I'm quite sure she didn't. Oh, I wonder?" She pulled back her sleeve and touched a metal band around her wrist. "This bracelet has Sarah etched onto it."

"Yes, but in Hebrew script."

"The boy must have read it."

"And instantly translated it," I said, half laughing before stopping myself in the face of Sarah's unease. "Very observant of young Spider and, as you say, a little bit frightening."

"But some of the other kids, Jack, they look through you. It's almost as if they are seeing things that we can't."

"The kids at the academy are odd in many ways, Sarah," I said, putting my arm around her shoulders. "And as a result of their intellect they often suffer, just like children with other aberrations. That's one reason the institute wanted to open the academy. To give these children a safe place, somewhere they can grow up in peace."

"I do hope they are safe," said Sarah, shivering despite the late afternoon sunshine.

"Let's forget about the institute and the academy for now," I said, as the boat rounded the point opposite the Watersmeet. "You don't leave for Chester until Monday morning, so we've got tonight and the whole of tomorrow to ourselves."

I leaned over and kissed her.

"Phew," she said pulling back. "It's the afternoon and I can still smell those kippers. Not sure I can spend an evening all alone with you as well, Jack Sangster. Not without a gas mask."

8 PM

And kippers or no kippers, we didn't have the Saturday night
to ourselves at all. This was partly thanks to the Trelawny
Male Voice Choir, who, along with wives and girlfriends, were
celebrating in the Watersmeet (quite what they were celebrating I
never found out).

Sarah and I dined in a relatively insulated alcove ("Quietest seats
in the house tonight Jack," said Morwenna as she showed us to the
table), while the main party took up most of the rest of the taproom.
The group (men all looking over forty and wearing blazers and ties,
women commensurately aged and attired in semi-formal dresses),
were loud enough, but polite, and despite Sarah and I having to shout
to each other every now and again over their conversation, added to
the atmosphere. As the evening wore on, I realised I had missed Sarah
so much that it would take a lot more than this jolly if somewhat over
exuberant group to spoil my evening.

Our meal over, I felt happy and relaxed and, coffee finished, was
about to suggest to Sarah we retired when the outside door opened.
Pasco, Stocker and Jackson then entered, waving to me as they walked
through the room, unsteady steps up to the bar showing that this

clearly wasn't going to be their first drink of the evening. The three looked at the gathered choir men, then turned away again, Pasco loudly (and slurringly), ordering three pints of beer.

"And we'll buy a couple of drinks for our friends in the corner," shouted Pasco, as the men of the choir slowed their conversation. Then, without any cue I could see, almost, I felt, like birds assembling on telegraph poles in the autumn, the whole group began to sing as one.

> And shall Trelawney live?
> Or shall Trelawney die?
> Here's twenty thousand Cornish men,
> Shall know the reason why!

"Ah, bollocks," shouted Pasco, slamming down his glass. "Whole song's rubbish." The singing tailed off, and a large (in all ways) man sitting at the front table stood up.

"Who says that?"

"I do," said Pasco. "That Trelawny story's made up. 'Twas taken from some other thing, a hundred years before. There never were twenty thousand Cornishmen went up there to rescue him."

"It's our Cornish anthem," said the big man, pacing forwards. "Wanna make something of that?"

"Ah, do what you like," said Pasco. "Because I'm having my best evening for a while, and I don't need nobody spoiling it. Isn't that right?" He looked over his shoulder at Stocker and Jackson, who were staring down at their drinks.

"He's questioning what we do, lads, questioning Cornwall," said the big man, and at that, several of the choir men stood up behind their leader.

"No, I'm not, I'm just questioning you," Pasco replied, also standing up. "O's ta clappya Kernowek?" he then shouted (in an incomprehensible tongue, the lilt of which nevertheless seemed somehow familiar to me), pointing his finger at the now clearly bemused choristers. "Na?" He continued pointing, then shrugged his shoulders and turned away. "Ke dhe ves."

"Don't you turn your back on me," the big man shouted. "Now like I said, wanna make something of it?"

"Bother hitting an emmet like you, never," said Pasco, turning round again to face his adversary.

"Calling me an emmet?" the big man yelled back, then stepped closer to Pasco. Stocker and Jackson stayed back, continuing to stare into their drinks. I watched Pasco's bravado shrink as he saw his companions' demeanours, and also saw Morwenna shake her head at me (presumably to say that potential trouble needed dissipating).

"Jack," Sarah whispered in my ear. "Do something."

"Not our fight," I whispered back.

"But the landlady's looking at us, see?" Morwenna was now mouthing 'please' at me while making stop signs with her palm against the fingertips of her other hand.

"I'll try," I sighed, then stood up, took a deep breath, and walked to the bar, by which time the big chorister was almost toe to toe with the much smaller Pasco.

"That's enough, friend," I said to the choir man, pushing in between them. "Come on, we're all here for a good time. Why not sing another song?"

"You what?" he said, looking at me with complete surprise but nevertheless standing back a pace.

"No trouble tonight, friend. It won't work out well for you." I looked him directly in the eye, and he said nothing, while one of the other choristers leaned forward and whispered something in his ear.

"Let's just relax." I turned and spoke to Morwenna. "Can you manage a round of drinks for this lot?" She nodded. "So, friend," I said loudly. "Drinks for you, your fellow choristers and your ladies. Compliments of the house. Just come and order at the bar. That okay?"

"Er… yes mate," he stammered, "I reckon it is. Thank you."

"Jack," said Morwenna, as the big man went and explained to his friends that they could order free drinks. "You make me quite weak at the knees."

"Well, I just…"

"And me," said Pasco, slapping his arm around my shoulders. "Sorry, Pasco?"

"You saved me, and I was, hic," he hiccupped, "bang out of order. But, Sangster, tonight I do have reason to celebrate."

"How's that?"

"Plumb line."

"What?"

"His plumb line," said Stocker, while Jackson, too drunk to speak I suspected, mouthed the words, and grinned. Both men held their heads high now that the trouble had dissipated.

"This," said Pasco, reaching into a canvas bag and pulling out a multi-coloured rope with a ring-shaped lead fishing weight tied to the end. "Now let me explain, it'll just take a minute, I…"

"Hold on," I said, realising this was going to need longer than a minute's explanation. "Morwenna," I said, while gesturing to Sarah that Pasco wanted to talk. "Could you take my wife another coffee please?"

"Course, Jack, and this coffee's on the house as well. Now, my lover, something for you? You've only been drinking water all evening."

"That's nice of you, but no thanks, Morwenna, I'm trying to do the healthy thing tonight. Planning a day's rambling tomorrow, on Bodmin Moor."

"Good way to be," she said, walking over to Sarah with the coffee and whispering something as she set the cup down on the table that made them both laugh out loud.

"Now then, Pasco," I said, pointing to the rope with the lead weight. "What's that when it's at home?"

"Me plumb line. I use it to douse."

"What, douse for water, like a diviner does?" He nodded. "I thought you needed a forked hazel twig for that." A scene from a western where the hero found water in the desert using such a stick came into my mind.

66

"I don't douse for water, I do it for roads."

"Roads?"

"Yes, I started when I was a boy."

"Here?"

"No, Camborne born and bred. Only started dousing round here when I got the ferryman's job. That was twenty years ago now, mind."

"But roads you say?"

"Yes, have you ever heard of The Old Straight Track, Jack?"

"No."

"Ley lines?"

"No."

"Haven't heard of much, have you?" Pasco snorted, taking a long drink then staggering so that I had to steady him with my arm.

"Clearly not, but somehow I feel you're going to enlighten me."

"Well, what I do is swing my plumb line to pick up the paths of the ancient roadways of Cornwall. Sometimes in England as well." I smiled inwardly, as I always did when hearing the locals distinguish Cornwall from England. "Those 'Old Straight Tracks', as some people call them," continued Pasco, his voice shrill with enthusiasm. "Had all those feet on them, marching and so on over the years, from Roman times, perhaps before that even. And then there's the Earth's natural lines of energy. Leys as they call them. All these leave their mark, Sangster."

"Mark?"

"Memory if you like. In the ground. And I can pick that memory up by using this plumb line, like so." He held the rope up and let the weight dangle free. "Then walk and wait for it to start swinging." He pushed the weight, which began to move in circles. "Once it swings, I know I'm on a track. After that I just keep walking until the swinging stops. Usually only stops when I get to the sea, sometimes not even then. I even found a track from Land's End to the Scillies. Those islands must have been joined to the mainland once upon a time. I've mapped hundreds of miles of ancient trackway in south-west Cornwall alone."

"And you really think this works? Can't it be affected by wind, or if you somehow miss your footing?"

67

"Oh, it works alright," said Stocker. "It's been proven time and time again, against old records, and today's probably Pasco's finest hour. Tell him Pasco."

"That's what I was trying to do, Stocker," said Pasco, dismissing his friend with a wave. "Now, Sangster, this part of the river's had a crossing since the time of the Romans at least. Well documented, going from the slipway down there, by my bell, over to my cottage."

"At least that's what everyone thought, isn't it, Pasco?" Stocker chimed in.

"Will you stop interrupting me," said Pasco, pushing his glass towards Morwenna for a refill. "Now, where was I? Yes, the crossing. You see, I always got a swing on this side of the water, but never a swing by my cottage. Couldn't find where the track came out on the other side. Made me mad it did, mapping all them trackways around the county, but not being able to map the one to me own front door."

"I can understand you might be mad," I grinned.

"That's right." He missed my grin and took a swig of beer. "But anyway, yesterday I was doing a spot of ebbing about half a mile up the river..."

"Ebbing?"

"Ebbing, Sangster," said Stocker. "You go out across the mud in your waders and stretch a net across the creek at half ebb tide. Current makes fish swim into it, mainly sea bass at this time of year."

"I see."

"Anyway, if I may continue, Stocker," snorted Pasco, "I put my hand into my bag for a line and pulled out my rogue's yarn by mistake."

"Rogue's yarn?" I queried again.

"Multi-coloured rope we mostly use to tie up our boats," said Stocker. "You make it yourself."

"Your wife Mabel makes yours, Stocker," said Jackson.

"So she does, and each one's unique. Means nobody can steal it."

"I see," I repeated, beginning to feel more and more enlightened.

"And you know what happened when I pulled it out, Sangster?" Pasco shouted.

I shook my head.

"It only began to swing, that's what. Couldn't believe it at first, but swing it did, so I walked across the mud and onto the bank, where I followed the track, up towards Tregnothnan Manor. And I can prove it."

"He can," said Stocker, while Jackson once again mouthed the word with a grin.

"How?"

"Well, I spoke to the parson."

"Canon Pengelly you mean?" I remembered the canon being ferried across the river that morning.

"The same, and he granted me access to the cathedral library, and I spent most of today there. Went through all the bishop's books and papers I did, and you know, I'd almost given up hope of finding anything when it happened. I was about to leave, and just finishing tidying up, when I dropped a book and there 'e was. Fell out on the floor, an old map of the Fal estuary, showing all the places where tracks crossed creeks. Old ferry crossings, Parson reckons. Showed our crossing going over the river at an angle from the village to the opposite bank, just where I'd picked it up with my plumb line."

"Then this route is surely known to other people?"

"Nope. Map was folded and tucked into the binding of the book. If I hadn't dropped that book, the map would still be there now, unseen and unknown. Printed on animal skin it was, almost fell apart in my hands. Parson said that meant it was old. Parson also said he'd never seen it before and reckoned nobody else had either. Said all the maps of the area he'd ever seen show the track going straight over to my cottage, even the very old ones."

"Pasco the great," said Stocker raising his glass, along with Jackson, who almost missed his mouth and continued grinning silently.

"Quiet, Stocker," said Pasco, oblivious to the accolade. "Anyway, Sangster, Parson says he's going to have my map framed and presented to the museum. With my name on it."

"Well, that's wonderful news," I said. "Quite a find. Now I must go back to my wife if you don't mind. We've an early start tomorrow." Pasco nodded, then started coiling up his plumb line, which, after several unsuccessful fumbles, he finally managed to push back into the canvas bag. "Oh, and Pasco?"

"Yes, Sangster?"

"Just whisper to me, because they're still sitting over there," I said. "But what was that you said to the choir man?"

"Cornish. Asked him if he spoke it."

"And then?"

"Told him to go away. All that singing Trelawny, and he don't even know his Cornish, does he, Morwenna?" She said nothing. "Anyway, Sangster, Morwenna speaks better Cornish than I." Morwenna shook her head and turned away. "There's more to that woman than meets the eye," Pasco went on. "Much more."

"I'm sure, but you do speak this old language yourself?"

"Yep, and perhaps not properly, but I'm one of very few now who remember it at all. Expect Cornish'll be extinct when my generation's done."

As he said this, I suddenly realised why the sound of Pasco's words had seemed familiar. It was a day at the academy several weeks ago, when I'd bumped into a very flustered Runtle leaving one of the classrooms.

"Speaking the old language, she was," he said to me, cheeks flushed as he rushed off down the corridor. "The old language I tell you, Mr Sangster, thought it was forgotten by youngsters till I heard her talking." He had pointed over his shoulder, towards the classroom door. I'd then looked into the room and seen Angel Blackwood standing by the blackboard, reciting words out loud, every now and again stopping to scrawl something in chalk before carrying on speaking. I remember being struck not just at the oddness of the words, but at the speed with which she spoke and wrote on the board. Almost superhuman.

"Well, I know a young person who can speak Cornish, Pasco."

"How d'yer know it was Cornish she was speaking?"

"Runtle, caretaker at the academy, he swore she was."

70

"Ah, Runtle."

"You know him?"

"Yes, I know that fat old tuss. Reckon it was probably French or Latin or summat else he heard. Like I said, Cornish'll be finished before too long."

"I do hope not," I said to Pasco, who sniffed and shrugged. "Well anyway, goodnight then, and once again, well done finding the track."

I went back to my table, to find Sarah quietly reading a book.

"Did you see all that?"

"Of course darling, but this book, the one I started on the train, it's fascinating." She held up the cover.

'The History and Geography of the Roseland Peninsula'

"Oh, yes, fascinating. Now, if you can tear yourself away from it, I'd like to go up."

Sarah closed the book without a word, rose from the table and we walked together to the door. As we passed the choir group, I nodded to the big man, who waved back and bid us goodnight, as did his companions.

Jack, I thought to myself. You did a good job calming that situation down. Excellent job. You've still got it.

10PM

"Tell me, Sarah," I said as we undressed for bed a few minutes later. "What were you laughing about with Morwenna?"

"Oh, nothing, darling."

"Tell me."

"Well, why did you think the big man from the choir backed down so easily when you faced up to him over the argument with that Pasco character?"

"Er... to be honest, I'm not sure."

"Apparently," she said giggling. "He thought, in fact it seems... that choir group all thought... no, I don't want to spoil it. You were so brave."

"Thought what exactly?"

"Thought you were a copper. There, I've said it."

"A policeman, why?"

"They just did, I don't know. Morwenna said she overheard them saying it. Convinced, she said they were, and a very senior copper at that." Sarah sniggered. "Must be all that grey hair and your erect military bearing. Gives you a natural authority." She sniggered again. "Gravitas even."

I grimaced, counting myself lucky and thinking for a moment about the likely outcome of being mistaken for an off-duty policeman in some of the inner city pubs I knew.

"I have an erect military bearing?" was all I finally said.

"Oh yes, Jack, makes me quite weak at the knees."

"That's the second time someone's said that to me tonight."

SUNDAY,
MAY THE 24TH
7:30AM

The following day we drove early to Camelford, then made a circular walk across Bodmin Moor. Our route took us first to the oddly shaped granite outcrop of Rough Tor before crossing the heather-clad moorlands for a further mile or so to mount a hill named Brown Willy, Cornwall's highest point, where we sat and drank a thermos of coffee provided by Morwenna. The ramble was pleasant enough, except for a meeting with a local shepherd, who was standing over the mauled carcass of a sheep.

"Dogs," he just said to us. "Blasted dogs again. Folk let them off the leash and this is what happens. And the police don't do nothing!" I gulped, looking at the dead creature, throat torn out and body ripped longways, almost in two, with most of the internal organs gone. I saw Sarah turning green (she told me later I had also turned green), then bade the shepherd a good day and we walked on, both silent other than saying the occasional hello to fellow ramblers. We arrived back at our starting point late morning and, as I climbed the stile into the car park, I felt Sarah shaking my shoulder and saw her pointing back to the moor.

"I wish we had a cine camera, Jack," she said. "Or any camera, even the little instant one. I left both of mine back at the hotel."

"Why?"

"Well look, over there. Must be our shepherd's killer dog."

I turned to see, over half a mile away but nevertheless quite distinct, a black animal, walking across the heather towards Rough Tor, its size, shape, and gait reminding me of a black panther I'd once seen in India.

"Looks a bit like the way a big cat walks to me," I said, as the creature disappeared behind some rocks. "Of course, it can't be a panther. Must be a big black dog, or perhaps just a calf or a foal?"

"Who knows, darling?" Sarah said with a shrug before walking towards the car. "Come on, we've still got time to drive down to the lighthouse if we're quick, and perhaps we could drop in to see them at the academy. It's nearby, isn't it?"

"Yes, a couple of miles."

"Oh, and I'd like to pick up my big camera on the way."

"I suppose so," I answered, anticipating the awkward detour needed to go via the hotel. The creek-side road from Truro to the village was a dead end, one way in one way out, and the turning off the main road towards the academy and the lighthouse several miles before Truro, all of which meant extra driving.

12NOON

Nevertheless, in not much more than an hour we were pulling into a car park on the top of the St Anthony headland, which, apart from a few cars and motorbikes, was largely deserted. A flat roofed café and toilet block stood close by, and next to that I could see a gated path that presumably led down to the lighthouse, which stood firmly on rocks by the water's edge, some hundred feet or more below us.

"Can we get down there?" Sarah asked, hair blowing in every direction as we stepped out of the car.

"We can try," I answered, only to be disappointed by a sign that came into view as we arrived at the gate.

'Property of Trinity House. No entrance. No public right of way.'

"Ah well, at least the view's good, Sarah." I gestured past the café, towards the broad inlet of the Percuil River, dotted with yacht moorings that led up to the harbour walls and terraces of St Mawes village.

"I read about that last night," said Sarah, staring ahead.

"Read about what?"

"St Mawes Castle, the one we saw from the boat yesterday." She pointed to a squat, round towered building on the headland opposite, its stonework spotless, its grounds perfectly manicured. "Built by Henry the Eighth to defend the harbour."

"All those wives, surprised he had time for bricklaying as well."

"Don't be silly. And there's an identical one on the other side, so they could both send a cannon ball into the middle of the channel. Had it completely covered from marauding pirates and so on. Museums now, I think. Be nice to have a closer look."

"If we walk up that way we'll eventually just end up at the academy, and that castle will still be the other side of the river."

"Then let's go the other way."

"If you like, I think the coast path goes on round the headland."

And so we went the other way, past a signpost that said simply and enigmatically 'Battery'. The rocky path wound through low thorny shrubs and flowers of different colours, and was never sheltered from the wind, which in places gusted strongly enough to push us back in our tracks.

"Oh…" Sarah would say, breath seemingly taken away each time we rounded a bend to a new view of the Atlantic Ocean. Stopping when she said this, and holding her camera, heavy in her hands with its extended telephoto lens, she would lean forward to steady herself against the wind. And each time she did I worried the gusts would suddenly cease and she'd fall flat on her face, so braced myself to catch her, relaxing only when I heard the series of shutter clicks that meant she had captured that particular view as she wanted.

And the scenery was certainly breath taking, the high cliffs falling down to a sea which today was chopped by the offshore wind, throwing up countless white horses that came to the end of their short and angry lives against the rocky foreshore or when they clashed with each other in the headland currents.

Looking across the mouth of the harbour to the Falmouth side, Pendennis Castle, sister to the St Mawes Castle that Sarah had been so fascinated with, could be seen a mile or so distant. I wondered if anyone had bothered to tell these neatly kept Tudor relics, standing guard against some unnamed foe, that their time had come and gone, as had the Spanish Armada, and it was now no dishonour to fade into a gentle retirement.

Looking further, the outline of the Lizard Peninsula cast a dark line on the horizon, until that too disappeared, leaving (I imagined) open ocean with no landfall until America. And then there was the coastline to our right, the white tower of the lighthouse now framed by the sea, and just beyond that a rocky point with sheer cliffs that glittered with the western sunlight.

"Hold my arm," cried Sarah above the noise of the wind, as we came to one particularly high point above the headland. "I've got to get a shot of this sea, Jack." I held her and she stepped forward to the edge of the path, camera poised to shoot. "Right, now... Oh my God, what's that, I—"

I urged her in my mind to take the picture so we could step backwards from the cliffs, but the tell-tale shutter clicks never came. Instead, there was a crunching noise as the path crumbled beneath Sarah's feet so that her body pulled forward and lurched over the edge, propelled harder by a sudden gust. Holding tight to her arm, I was dragged forward as she fell, eventually lying flat on my front, still clutching Sarah's sleeve, which I felt gradually slipping through my grip. She screamed and I hauled my left arm onto my right and began to pull.

"I've got you," I shouted. "Now come on." Gradually, Sarah's head appeared and, in a few seconds, she was scrambling up and onto the grass next to me. Heart pounding, I was about to put my arms around Sarah and ask if she was alright, when she stood up, dusted herself off, and started running along the path.

"Come on, Jack, we'll miss it. Quick."

I stood up and followed her as best I could, unable to think, as she kept running, coming at last to a square concrete and stone building that blocked our way (the Battery, I guessed). I then watched Sarah level her camera out to sea and start frantically clicking. I tried to pinpoint the target from the direction of her lens and, after searching the waves for a few seconds, saw it. The unmistakable disturbance of a diving submarine, the shape of its conning tower still visible for a split second until it disappeared. I screwed my eyes up to see more, but the spray had gone, the boat now fully covered by the waves.

"What was that?" Sarah gasped, dropping her camera to let it dangle around her neck.

"A sub I think, Sarah, but what was all that by the cliff. I thought I'd lost you."

"Oh no, there was a ledge. I was perfectly safe."

"You screamed."

"That was gorse. Look, cut through my jeans." She placed her finger inside a rip in the denim of her trousers, withdrawing it to show me droplets of blood.

"Does it hurt?" was all I could say.

"A little, darling. Nothing that a cream tea in that café wouldn't make better though."

"Another healthy lunch?"

"Oh Jack."

"We had a cream tea instead of lunch yesterday as well. You'll burst."

"Don't be such a spoilsport."

*

"Can you pop the camera back in its case, darling? It's in the boot, inside that carrier bag." She pulled the camera strap over her head and passed it to me. "I'll go and get this cut cleaned up in those loos. See you in there?"

"In the ladies?"

"No, the café, silly."

"Sure," I said, walking back to the parked car and still a little bewildered from Sarah's mock cliff fall and frenzied pursuit of the submarine in the bay (the sight of which had also caused me some disquiet).

*

"Were you limping to the car?"

"A little, twisted my bad knee when I pulled you up from that cliff."

"What cliff?"

"The one that wasn't."

"Sorry. You still running most mornings?"

"Mmm…" I nodded.

"Don't overdo it, Jack."

"Will try not to," I said, indignant she hadn't asked more.

"So, darling," Sarah went on, my knee seemingly forgotten. "Remember, jam before cream."

"Isn't it cream first, then—"

I leaned towards the cream dish only to have my hand slapped.

"Naughty, Jack," Sarah laughed. "When in Rome, do as the Romans, I mean the Cornish do." We sat munching the scones and sipping the tea in silence for a good few minutes before she spoke again.

"So, well you know how they work…"

"Sorry?"

"The navy, I mean, do they often have exercises around here?"

"No reason why they wouldn't, but in my time never this close to shore unless it was practice for the marines or something like that. And anyway—"

"More tea?"

"Please."

"Anyway, what, darling?" she continued, while pouring milk and tea simultaneously into my cup.

"Well, I didn't get a great look at it, but that conning tower."

"The sticky up bit?"

"Yes, the sticky up bit. It had the look of one of the new generation Soviet boats."

"Are you sure?"

"Not completely. If we were at home, I could look in Jane's."

"Hmmm… I knew that white elephant you insist on buying every year would come in handy one day."

I laughed, as my annual purchase of Jane's Fighting Ships, an expensive and massive volume, was always a bugbear of Sarah's. I didn't strictly need the modern Jane's for my work as a part-time naval historian, but it was something I liked to have to hand, and the outline of the conning tower I'd just glimpsed submerging into the depths of Falmouth Bay was definitely familiar. The previous year's edition of Jane's had included a special feature on the latest Soviet nuclear submarine, the K222 'Papa' class, explaining, amongst other things, how far in advance this boat was of anything in the navies of the West. I remembered an illustration of the conning-tower silhouette, low and long with a particular arrangement of antennae and periscopes, especially the forward periscope, which was hooked over with a splash guard so that it looked like a neck and head (not unlike the famous 'surgeon's' picture of the Loch Ness Monster). That shape seemed identical to the one Sarah and I had just seen and, as far as I knew, could never have been mistaken for any active Royal Navy boat.

"So I think, Sarah," I said slowly, "that that was more than likely a Russian sub we saw." I looked out of the window as I spoke, eyeing the twin castles guarding the harbour, and wondered whether I'd been a bit premature in wanting to retire these silent bastions from guarding against foreign foes. "And only a few hundred yards away from the shore as well. I'll call Phil at the Admiralty tomorrow and ask about it."

"Do they still put you through to him. I know he's your friend and all that, but after all these years?"

"Oh yeah, as long as I use my rank. Commander Sangster will get me through to Phil, even if he is an admiral now, I… Oh." I slapped my forehead. "Those people in the choir last night, in the bar."

"Sorry?"

"They must have thought I was a copper, Sarah."

"So Morwenna said."

"Commander. That's a police rank, maybe one below assistant commissioner."

"Did you tell them you are an ex-naval commander?"

"No, but Morwenna called out to me in the bar a few times when someone was on the hall phone asking for a Commander Sangster. Must have been overheard, you know how things get about in a village."

"Well, as I said last night, darling," laughed Sarah, leaning forward and wiping a mix of jam and cream from the side of my mouth with her napkin. "Your erect military bearing makes me feel quite weak at the knees."

*

"That'll be six shillings please," shouted the waitress over the noise of a motorbike revving outside in the carpark. I handed over the coins. "And your wife's poor leg. Is there anything else we can do?"

"Oh, no thanks," Sarah answered, as the engine noise subsided into the distance. "I'll have a better look when we get back to our hotel, but it feels like it's not too deep."

"That's alright then, my lovers, well goodbye."

I dropped a sixpence in a tip bowl to a nod from the waitress, and we left, walking across the car park, the wind now strong enough to chill.

"Are you cold?"

"A bit, but I'd still rather drive back without my jacket on."

"Give me your coat then, and I'll put it in the boot… Oh my God." I looked at the car boot to see the lock forced and the lid lying half open.

"My camera's gone," shouted Sarah, then ran back to the café. I followed, to find her talking frantically at the waitress.

"Now calm down, dearie. It'll be them bikers. Always a bad lot."

"Did you get any descriptions, registrations?"

"Well, there were two young lads, then there was a couple in a combination bike and sidecar, but they all left before you came."

"No dammit." Sarah banged her fist on the counter. "When we were in here. That's when it happened."

"'Fraid not, dearie. There was a bike outside, you heard it, but the rider never came inside."

"Have you a phone?"

"No dearie, nearest one's about a mile up the—"

"Oh, never mind," said Sarah. "Thief's probably miles away by now. Come on, Jack, we'll report it when we're back at the hotel."

"I guess you don't want to drop in and say hello to the Flimwell's now?" I said as we drove out of the car park, boot lid now lashed to the bumper with elastic.

"No."

"I'm sorry, Sarah, but we should be able to get the money back on the company insurance."

"That's not the point. You ordered me all that Japanese gear for Christmas. Latest Canon Flex SLR with FL telephoto lens," Sarah went on, true to her habit of clinging on to facts and details for comfort when distressed. "It was, well it was…" she sniffed. "Special. Replacing it will feel dirty somehow. Maybe I'll stop taking pictures altogether."

"Of course you won't, it's a hobby, almost a passion. You love it and you're good at it. And someone probably realised the gear was valuable and took their chance while we were having tea. Just bad luck."

"Or realised I'd snapped a Russian submarine."

I felt a jolt as she said this. Had someone seen us, deliberately broken into the car, and taken the camera?

"They've taken our road atlas as well," Sarah added. "It was in that carrier bag."

3 PM

With the thought of being watched in mind, as soon as we returned to the hotel, I called the police and reported the theft. The officer who finally took my call, reached via a central switchboard I was diverted to that covered a wide area on Sundays, spoke wearily, unable to disguise his boredom. As he gave me a reference number for the insurance, I very much felt as if we were going through the motions, and that he was all too aware of this as well. As we spoke, I remembered the angry shepherd's words ('police don't do nothing!'), but nevertheless, decided to also mention the big cat.

"Did you take a photo, sir?" he asked in an even more wearisome voice, then added. "Don't suppose that matters now your camera's been taken though, does it, sir?"

The constable was, he then said, aware of recent sheep killings and confirmed there were no reports of a big cat on the loose, so assumed it was likely a large dog we had seen. He thanked me for calling in and said my report had been filed and there would be checks made to see if a camera like ours was offered for sale, and enquiries with owners of large dog breeds in the Bodmin area. I hung up feeling I'd got what I needed to make an insurance claim and, unidentified predator-wise, at least done my duty, then went to find Sarah in the taproom.

"Hear you've seen a Dandy Hound," said the familiar voice of Pasco, as I walked into the bar.

"Pasco says we've seen a ghost dog, darling," said Sarah, now apparently in much better spirits. "How exciting."

"Drive you mad if you look him the eye," Pasco shouted from behind her. "Dandy Hounds, that's what we call 'em here. Cursed to roam the moors at night, part of a wild hunt led by the Devil himself."

"Have you ever seen one?" I asked Pasco, deciding not to contradict him by mentioning that our sighting was in broad daylight, the animal was alone, and as far as we could tell, not part of a pack driven by Satan.

"Pasco sees all sorts after a few hours in here," said Morwenna.

*

Sarah and I spent the afternoon resting in our room, then enjoyed a quiet evening in Truro, dining at the town's one and only Chinese restaurant (Nob had his night off on Sundays, so the hotel was unable to offer hot food). As we dined, and although I didn't feel an overt atmosphere between us, conversation was nevertheless subdued. Perhaps because of the lost camera, and perhaps also due to fatigue after what had been a long and eventful day, but mostly, I suspected, because we were about to be parted again.

MONDAY,
MAY THE 25TH
7:30AM

I t was a tearful Sarah I put onto the train back to Chester that Monday.

"Oh Jack," she suddenly sobbed out loud. "It's been such a short weekend. How can I—"

"I've got you in my pocket," I said, pulling out the Polaroid photo. "Now go on."

I watched the back end of the guard's van pull away into a grey morning, which, along with the weekend sunshine having disappeared, the sky now being overcast with a light drizzle, and Sarah's sudden outburst, compounded my feeling that her visit had somehow changed things, so that I no longer relished the single life I had found quite comfortable for the last six weeks.

And it occurred to me as the train finally disappeared from view that my job had somehow morphed into administration and project management, with little of the direct work with troubled children that had inspired me to join the Granville Institute in the first place. Perhaps it was now my lot to contribute indirectly to that cause by establishing the academy and others like it, leaving individual investigations to other, maybe younger people. As I walked back to my car, anticipating another tedious week behind a desk, I felt saddened at the thought of no more individual case work, no excitement out in the field, no more conundrums to solve for Sir John, no more children who (I always hoped), might look back one day and say, 'Jack Sangster helped me once, when nobody else could'.

How wrong I was.

TUESDAY,
MAY THE 26TH
8:45PM

There are some moments we all remember, and for me, receiving the call from Velinda Flimwell to say that Angel was missing was one of those moments. I'd spent long hours during the Monday and Tuesday holed up on my hotel room, preparing the phase-two plans, then tidying up those plans ready for another visit to London and the eagle-eyed Prendergast.

"Call for you, Jack, I've put it through to the phone on the hall table by the front door," Morwenna had said, just as I sat down in the taproom to what I'd felt was a well-earned supper and the first meal I'd taken outside of my room since Sarah had left. "A Mrs Fullwell the caller says she is."

'You mean Flimwell' I cursed under my breath, looking at the clock. What could she want at this time in the evening?

"We've got the police here, Jack," was Velinda's opening line.

"Why, what's happened?"

"One of the pupils is missing, Angel Blackwood. Last seen at about three on Sunday afternoon." I was tempted to ask if it might be a mistake, if the girl had simply gone home or something like that, but the presence of the police, Velinda's worried tone of voice, and the lateness of the hour made me think better of it.

"Why in thunder wasn't I told at the time?"

"Well, er…" She stumbled for a moment almost, I thought, as if she was hiding something. "Fell through the cracks, we've all been running around, working with the police, I'm sorry, I—"

"And Sir John?"

"Yes, we reported it immediately." I wondered how I would explain my not knowing for two days to him. 'Ignorance isn't innocence in the eyes of the law', I'd once heard him shout at a cowering underling.

"What are the police doing about it?" I eventually asked.

"Searching the building, the grounds, talking to the children and staff, that sort of thing. They've set up what they call an 'incident room' at the school." I heard the sound of barking in the background. "They've got dogs as well, that's them finishing for the night."

"Runtle see anything?"

"No, and he swears the front gates were closed all day Sunday, except for when he let me through to drive to Truro that is. Says nobody else has been in or out that he didn't know, and no other vehicles but mine."

"Is there anything I can do right now?"

"Not for us here, thanks, but perhaps you'd appraise Sir John of the current situation."

"I will try. Can you call me back here at the hotel if there are any developments?"

"Of course. Otherwise, we'll see you in the morning, shall we?"

"Yes, first thing."

In fact, I didn't go to the academy until the following afternoon. Sir John, who I finally tracked down at his club in London, was less upset about me not having been told than I expected but did insist on coming down to Truro on the first available train to personally supervise the situation (a nightmare in the making for me, the police and the Flimwells, I thought to myself as he blustered in my ear).

"Meet me at the station, Sangster, and book me a room for tomorrow night at that little billet where you're staying, the, er…"

"It's called the Watersmeet Hotel, Sir John."

"That's the place. How's the grub there?"

"Good," I answered, knowing that I would need to be both truthful and detailed on this subject so dear to my employer's heart. "Country dishes, plain and simple. Pasties, pies with local fish, meat and so on. Home-made puddings."

"Hmph…" I heard him snort down the phone. "Not sure I like the sound of it." He snorted again. "May have to make contingency plans and all that," he added cryptically. "Can't starve to death, and my secretary will tell you when my train arrives. Be there."

"I will, Sir John."

"Very well. Now then, the local MP owes me a big favour, and I've already been in touch, but I'll get onto him again pronto. Make sure the rozzers down there really have put their best man on the case."

"That's good to hear," I said, wondering why he had already contacted this 'MP' when I'd only just told him the girl was missing.

"And, Sangster."

"Yes?"

"I'd have thought the girl would have turned up by now." Again, I wondered at his choice of words, which sounded as if he'd already known for some time that Angel had disappeared, but I said nothing and let him continue. "This business could ruin all our good work if it goes pear shaped, so whoever the top man is that the police have assigned, I'll still be counting on you."

I heard the phone click as he hung up, and questioned, for the first time but not the last, Sir John's priorities and judgement (other than just his distrust of the local food). Yes, the scandal might damage the institute but, more importantly, somewhere, perhaps not too far away, was a terrified girl, possibly suffering an ordeal which I could only too easily imagine. And even that ordeal was a better scenario than some.

WEDNESDAY, MAY THE 27TH
12 MIDNIGHT

Staring up at the bedroom ceiling, and still none the wiser for recalling the events of the weekend and being told of Angel's disappearance, I punched the pillow in frustration. If only I could find the one clue that would show the way to Angel. There must be such a clue, I thought and, feeling wide awake, decided to go over everything once again.

But my wakefulness was an illusion, and before I could even recall Sarah and I meeting under the Paddington Station clock, my eyes closed and sleep was upon me.

THURSDAY,
MAY THE 28TH
6:30AM

I stood on the hotel terrace in the dawn light, the screeching chorus of birds that had woken me early in the first place now silent, allowing clarity of thought on what would have seemed a glorious morning if there had been no shadow cast by the ever-present spectre of the missing girl. Towel around my neck and skin still sweating from my morning run, I sipped a cup of tea, gazed across the river (which in different circumstances would have soothed the mind), and listed the few facts I did know about Angel Blackwood's disappearance.

Firstly, she had disappeared on Sunday not long after three o'clock in the afternoon, so almost four days ago. Secondly, police investigations of staff and pupils, plus search officers and tracker dogs, had failed to shed any light on her disappearance, despite the police being called in quickly, and despite more than the usual police resources being allocated due to Sir John's influence with the powers that be. And it seemed to me they had no real reason to actually suspect their one 'concrete suspect', the anonymous old man with the beard, who was anyway apparently able to elude all of their enquiries. Thirdly, the academy was a relatively secure facility, and no apparent way out of the grounds for the girl, let alone a would-be abductor, had been identified.

But Angel was nevertheless missing, so I added other elements into the mix; the children, with (as my wife had seen), their almost superhuman abilities, the police (apparently diligent but painting by numbers), plus the age of the academy building itself (why I included this last factor I didn't know, but intuition told me it mattered).

Different thinking was definitely needed.

And as I looked at the creek, the brightening dawn across the calm and reflective water touching the hopeful parts of my mind, and despite the near certainty of the previous evening that the girl was lost, I now felt Angel still to be alive. Then I shook myself. How could I know, especially now that it had been several days since her disappearance? I was talking out loud about this in an attempt to be more rational when I felt a large hand clutch my shoulder.

"A bit moist, Sangster," said Sir John. "Your shoulder that is. Want to have a wash before you drive me to the station?"

"Morning, Sir John," I laughed. "Yes, better had do, give me ten minutes, then…" My answer was cut short by the sound of furious revving, which in turn prompted raucous cawing as a mass exodus of birds flew up from the river. It was the motorcyclist priest, dressed in a long leather coat and goggles, starting his machine, then tearing off down the road, long hair flying in the wind.

"Infernal noise," huffed Sir John, as the sound eventually tailed off into the distance. "Shouldn't be allowed in a place like this. Chap had a dog collar on as well."

*

"So, Sangster," said Sir John as we stood on the station platform about half an hour later. "Just waiting for… ah, here he is."

I turned around to see a middle-aged man, perhaps not quite of Sir John's epic proportions, but nevertheless tall and well built, and wearing a wide brimmed fedora hat and what looked to me like an ankle length Australian cattle drover's raincoat (under which I could see a suit, shirt, and tie).

"Tremayne, good of you to come."

"Granville," he answered in a richly melodious, deep, mild but (it seemed to me) nevertheless super-confident Cornish accent. Here, I thought, was a man who would give Sir John a run for his money if it came to dominating the room. "Always a pleasure, got my surgery this morning so not too much time to talk. How's this awful business going?"

"This is Sangster," said Sir John, clapping his hand on my shoulder. "Sangster, Charles Tremayne, Member of Parliament for Truro, Liberals you know." I nodded. "And Tremayne's been helping me mobilise the local rozzers."

"No, no, no," said the MP with a wave of his hand. "Just a few suggestions in the right ears."

"Piffle," Sir John replied, making the MP wince a little. "You got the ball rolling. Made sure they sent Pentreath and his crew down here."

"Local force no good then?" I asked.

"Truro lot are very competent," Tremayne replied quickly. "Very competent indeed, but Pentreath's the best in Devon and Cornwall by all accounts. Heads up our CID." He looked uncomfortable, which I could see by the way he shuffled from side to side, despite the coat and hat largely providing cover. "I, er... anyway, when John asked, I spoke to a few people and, well, Pentreath was assigned."

"Aye, Tremayne," Sir John almost shouted (his Lancashire accent always grew stronger when he shouted). "I knew I could rely on you."

"Well, Granville, you know I believe in your academy." Tremayne then looked at me. "I'm a great supporter, Sangster."

"What is it you like?"

"Why, to bring the cream of our country's youth down to Truro and invest in the facilities, staff and so on the way the Granville Institute has. What's not to like, Sangster?"

"When you put it like that I—"

"Anyway, Granville," Tremayne interrupted, pulling his coat collar up. "Nothing else you need for now?"

"Nothing for now."

"Well, just tip me the wink if something comes up and, Sangster?"

"Yes?"

"I hear good things of you, very good things, and a happy ending to all this is as important for Truro as it is for the academy." He stared hard. "Make it happen."

"If I can, for the girl and her family."

"Of course, now goodbye."

He turned, walked down the platform and, as I watched him go, I wondered how Tremayne had mobilised Pentreath so quickly. After all, it had only been about thirty-six hours since I'd been told of Angel's disappearance, so presumably Sir John hadn't known before that either. This thought played on my mind for some minutes before being displaced by other, more immediate concerns.

*

Sir John and I stood alone on the platform.

"So, the local MP pulled strings with the police, got their best assigned?" I asked, and Sir John nodded. "How did you get him to do that?"

"Known the chap for a while, met him, er…" Sir John looked over my shoulder in the manner I'd become used to when his ever-active mind was focused on multiple ideas so that he lost his thread of thinking.

"You met Tremayne where?"

"Oh, in London at the Liberal Club. Tremayne's made of the right stuff. Trust the man."

"And he trusts you?"

"Course," said Sir John with a snort, that told me the MP's reciprocal trust had never entered his mind. "But his ideas, his morals, Sangster – we can trust the man."

"Such as?"

"Well, he's against nuclear power but right behind the nuclear deterrent. Shows common sense."

"I suppose so, Polaris submarines and everything, I mean—"

"Course. This buffoon of a Labour prime minister Harold Wilson and his cronies have no idea what they're doing."

"Perhaps," I said, wondering why Tremayne's general morals and politics mattered, but nevertheless trusting Sir John's instincts, which I'd never seen fail in the past (as he spoke it occurred to me that pressure on Pentreath from such a high level certainly explained the chief superintendent's defensive, self-justifying manner). "But anyway, Tremayne supports our academy project, so he'll help again if we need him to I take it?"

"Quite, Sangster. Now then, it's some minutes until the train arrives, so long enough for you to tell me about those instincts you mentioned last night. Come on, spill it please?"

"I need to do more checking."

"Nonsense, tell me what you think, our work is on the line here. I didn't set up the Granville Institute for nothing. I was a problem child too you know."

"Yes, I know."

"By the way, Sangster, never asked you. Were you, er…?"

"Was I what, Sir John?"

"A problem lad. You know, unhappy, difficult teens, couldn't establish empathy and so on?"

"No, sorry, model school pupil, model naval cadet. Followed all the rules. Thought you knew all that."

"Perhaps I did once. Can't remember everything we check up on our people. But you don't now, do you. Follow rules that is. Not always?"

"I follow what I think to be the right rules," I answered, irate from both the grilling and plain fatigue. Sir John nodded.

"Very well, and I suspect this case needs someone who doesn't follow all the rules. But anyway, tell me your ideas thus far."

"I can't give you facts, but my instinct, well, I'm not sure…"

"Go on, man, go on."

"Oh, it's somehow a combination of the children and the place itself."

"You're talking in riddles, Sangster."

"What I mean is, that due to their intellects these children, and from what I hear, Angel especially, are capable of doing things outside of our understanding. Incredible things, so that the police are applying procedures that might work for, say, a child missing from a standard environment like their own home, a boarding school or even a care home. But," I paused, wondering whether I was about to say too much, "DCS Pentreath's approach simply won't work for the kids at the academy."

"And?" said Sir John, as the approaching train made the rails click beside us.

"The place itself. As we've said many times, the layout is actually super secure, but somehow more importantly for me…" I struggled for words.

"Yes man?" shouted Sir John as the noise of the train grew louder.

"Many things," I answered, suddenly feeling a flow of ideas. "It's antiquity for a start, then the building being right by the creek, and the very dense woodlands, the strangely warm climate, the site's isolation, the er… history and general ambience of the place I suppose."

"That's still riddles to me."

"Well, they have some very odd ideas down here you know, it's hard to know what's real and what's imagined."

"How do you mean?"

"Oh, nothing really, people here just have different ways I suppose."

"No, come on, Sangster, you must have meant something by that remark, I mean…" Sir John was stopped from telling me what he 'meant' by an announcement over the tannoy.

'Eight-fifteen London Paddington service arriving Platform One. London Paddington service.'

"Well… okay," I said, now finding it hard to talk over the noise of the approaching train. "Here are just a few things I've heard in the last week alone. Locals are convinced there are ghostly dogs roaming the moors and woodlands, that you can find old lost Roman trackways using a lead weight on a string, and, last but not least, that Jesus visited this area, as a boy, to the very place where our academy now lies. I mean, Jesus, here."

"Superstitious poppycock. Just ignore it all, Sangster," yelled Sir John, as the train pulled up beside us.

"Guess so," I said, thinking perhaps he was right, and also that I was letting myself get a little bit too immersed in the locale.

"And use that intuition of yours, Sangster, get me a result," he added, climbing into the carriage. "And please, man, keep me posted."

"I will," I called as the train pulled away, then turned and tripped, realising too late Sir John had left his picnic hamper on the platform. Guessing Sir John would only have brought the very best in victuals. I picked myself up, brushed gravel off my knees and smiled in anticipation of some leftover treasure trove. I then bent down and opened the basket, only to find empty space where the food and wine had once been, plus dirty plates and cutlery. I dropped the hamper in a dustbin by the ticket office and strode to my car.

8:45AM

"So," I said to the Flimwells, as the three of us sat in their study at the academy. "I need to be circumspect, as I'm fairly sure the police see me as interfering, but Sir John's given me carte blanche to do whatever I can to find Angel."

"I know," said Velinda. "He told us that as well, and I think there may have been some political strings pulled."

"I couldn't possibly say," I answered with a smile.

"Well," Velinda continued with a nod. "DCS Pentreath said to me this morning that he'd just had another call from his superiors telling him to, and I quote, 'pull his finger out'. Seems Sir John has been wielding his influence and it's not appreciated by the local force."

"As I say, couldn't possibly comment, but if that were the case, I'd need to tread carefully with the police."

"So how can we help you, Sangster?" Cyrus asked.

"First off, I'd like to look in Angel's room if I may."

"Of course. She shares with two other girls by the way."

"Has anything been moved since she disappeared?"

"No. Room hasn't been touched, other than the police search of course."

"And Simon Founds, I'd like to talk to him."

"Spider, why yes. Anyone else?"

"Jonny Waites. And any background material you have on them. Upbringing, previous schooling, that sort of thing."

"Very well," said Cyrus. "I'll get the two boys down to the study and fish out their files. Vi, in the meantime could you take Sangster to Angel's dormitory please."

*

"Here we are," said Velinda, as we entered Angel's dormitory, equipped, as I saw, for three pupils, with beds, wardrobes and desks. The walls were adorned with posters that any fifteen-year-old girl might have in her bedroom, reflecting very usual teenage contradictions, such as pop stars, horses, dogs, and kittens.

"So, this would be Angel's bed," I said to Velinda.

"Yes, how did you guess?"

"Elementary, my dear Flimwell, the cleaners haven't been in yet and it's the only one that's made." I immediately realised the inappropriateness of my remark. "Sorry, couldn't help that," I then said, looking at the bed and the desk, and realising Angel's corner was somewhat different to the others. Along with the pop and film stars and animals (the stars, all male, outnumbered the animals significantly), various drawings were pinned to the wall, with more lying loose on the desktop. Even at first glance, to me they seemed to have a theme, show a pattern, tell a story in some way linked to the locality. I then noticed that the shelves in Angel's corner, which stretched over the bed and the desk, were empty.

"Police took all her books, study work and so on down to the incident room," said Velinda, following my gaze. "Just left these sketches."

"I see, so tell me what you know of Angel."

"You've met her haven't you," Velinda replied.

"Fleetingly."

"Then you know she's a beauty, but that's the least of it. She has an interest in everything and the skills and drive to back it up. That's as much as I can say unless you want to go into detail."

"Is she…" I remembered Sarah being obsessed with Leonardo Da Vinci some months before, so that I heard all about his insatiable curiosity, and his abilities in everything from art to anatomy. "Like Leonardo Da Vinci. Gifted at everything?"

"Hmmm… good analogy, but no."

"Then what?"

"She's gifted, but by no means gifted at everything. She can sketch but she's not our best artist by any means. And she can sing but she's not our best musician. No, Angel's uniqueness lies in her analytical mind and her ability to absorb the information she needs to make that analysis. And an amazing ability to pick up languages. Never seen anything like it."

"Inherited from her parents?"

"Adopted. We don't know who her birth parents were."

"Ah."

"And always precocious. Comes from a stable but very humble household in rural Essex, Brightlingsea. Angel won a scholarship to Roedean when she was nine. Normal intake age for the entrance exam she took is thirteen."

"Did she go?"

"No, her mother, rightly in my opinion, kept Angel at home. Local school in Colchester."

"And academics aside, er… how is she with boys, that sort of thing?"

"Ah." Velinda went silent, clearly considering her next answer. "She's a true genius, Jack, but also a teenage girl with all the normal urges and uncertainties that go with it." I looked at the posters on the wall and Velinda followed my eyes. "Yes Jack, I would say Angel is definitely on the cusp of womanhood."

"Hmmm… in my line of work, with a teenage girl missing, especially a pretty one like Angel, and when there are no family issues to take into account, a boy is the first place we look."

"No. I know some of the lads at the school were interested, but I got the idea Angel was keener on older boys."

"Why's that?"

"Don't have much to go on really, more a feeling. I saw her looking at men when we were out on trips, especially in London a few weeks ago, and I did overhear one of the school lads saying Angel didn't care for the likes of him. Wanted someone more mature."

"Who was the lad in question?"

"Spider."

"Anything else?"

"No."

"Can you leave me here for a while then?" I asked. "I need some time to look over all this."

"Of course. Shall I get the two boys to come to the study a bit later?"

"Please. And Velinda, I'd like to see Spider first, then Jonny Waites afterwards, both on their own if that could be arranged."

*

As soon as Velinda left the room, I sat down in Angel's chair and closed my eyes, trying to imagine the girl spending time at her desk. A beauty with a rare mind and an interest in everything, on the edge of womanhood, dreaming of things to come.

And I knew I wouldn't be able to match Angel's academic train of thought, so decided to keep things simple. She was a teenage girl.

I looked again at the pictures on the wall. All of the photos were men not boys, so lads of her own age surely weren't enough. Had Angel run away with an older man?

It seemed physically impossible she'd run away at all given everything I'd been told about the academy building's security and the circumstances of the disappearance. I also had to wonder where she could have possibly met this phantom lover, given she was in a closely monitored boarding school environment. But for all that, from what I already knew of Angel's intellect, it would have been easy enough for her to outwit the likes of Runtle, and even the Flimwells, if she set her mind to it.

The drawings pinned on the wall were mainly sketches, mostly scenes of the river, including one line drawing that I recognised as the view from my hotel across the river to the point and Pasco's cottage.

'*Bad crossing over the River Fal at high tide, April 1970*'

…was written underneath, followed by the initials '*AB*'. Looking down at the desk, I saw scattered papers that seemed to be related to Angel's lessons, with some written in different languages, including French, German, Latin and even a paper in what looked to me like Russian Cyrillic script. One sheet, however, particularly caught my eye, entitled 'Granville Challenge Number 1'. Below this heading were printed four lines of what looked like, as far as I could tell, Cornish language:

> *Me a moaz, a me a moaz, a me a moaz in goonglaze,*
> *Me a clouaz, a clouaz, a clouaz, a troz, an pysgaz miniz.*
> *Bez mi a trouviaz un pysg brawze naw losia,*
> *Olla boble en Porthia ne mi nôr dho gan zingy.*

Below this text, Angel had done a stylised pen and ink drawing of a fish, but her fish looked somehow wrong. I stared at its downturned mouth, exaggerated spiky fins, and curved form for a moment before realising it had multiple tails, which when I counted them up (three times as they were tangled together and hard to tally), totalled nine. The underlying handwritten English text explained why.

> *As I was going out on the green downs,*
> *I heard the sound of little fishes.*
> *But I found one big fish with nine tails,*
> *And all the people of St Ives couldn't catch it.*

Below the translation, Angel had written in block capitals...

OCTOPUS!

... and someone, Velinda I assumed by the initials 'VF', had then scrawled next to the drawing.

Winner, but how did you do it?

'How did you do what, Angel?' I asked myself.

Then, folding the paper and placing it in my pocket I looked around the room, under Angel's bed and finally in her wardrobe. It was full of the usual clothes, undergarments, and shoes of a teenage girl, as well as some cosmetics and hygiene products, but held little else of interest. I was about to leave when I noticed a draw underneath the desk. It clearly wasn't intended to be secret, the desk design merely needing it be set well back from the front to make space for knees. Nevertheless, this draw could be easily overlooked, so that I only noticed it myself while moving my head back from the odd angle need to look under the bed.

Pulling the draw open, I found a rolled-up sheet of tracing paper inside, held together with an elastic band, which when stretched out on the desktop, showed what looked like brass rubbings of either side of an ornamental dagger. The lower part of the handle was shaped to be gripped, with indents for the user's fingers, and there was a broad knob on the top to stop the dagger slipping (the 'tang' and the 'butt' I seemed to recall these parts of a knife might be properly called). But it was the blade that really caught my eye, curved like a scimitar, and embossed all along either side with literally hundreds of tiny symbols of a type I'd never seen before. All in all, the dagger imprint was around a foot long, with handwritten notes around it (presumably Angel's), each linked by arrows pointing to different parts of the weapon. What the notes meant, I couldn't have said, as they were in the same incomprehensible script as the symbols on the blade, all swirls and squiggles, (the closest thing I'd ever seen to this was secretarial shorthand).

Rolling up the tracing paper as carefully as I could (the soft pencil used for the rubbing had already starting to come off on my fingers), and replacing the elastic band, I bent and picked up a visiting card from the floor that had fallen from the roll of paper.

'Prof. Josiah Polkinghorne, PhD, CEng'
Cambourne School of Metalliferous Mining
Laboris Gloria Ludi

I pocketed the card, then pushed my hand to the very back of the draw, where I felt another piece of paper. This turned out to be an envelope with Angel's name written on the front (in what appeared to me a familiar hand, although I couldn't recall where I'd seen it). The top edge was torn open to reveal a note inside, on which was written a single line, probably done in a hurry as the punctuation was wrong.

'I, must see you. Boathouse at 4. Your devoted T'

There was no date or other clue to tell me more about the note (which joined Angel's fish poem sheet in my pocket), or who this mysterious 'T' might be. 'Boathouse at 4' I said to myself out loud, remembering Angel was last seen on the front lawn around 3pm on Sunday. And the boathouse, which lay to one side of the lawn behind a screen of hairy-trunked, leafy dracaena palm trees, would have been easy enough to get to without being seen, so one of the few places inside the academy walls suitable for a clandestine tryst.

But a clandestine tryst with who?

*

"Did you find anything else in the room?" Velinda asked as I entered her study.

"Yes, a few things actually."

"Sir John was right."

"How so?"

"He said you'd find things the police missed."

"Have you any idea what this is?" I said, rolling out the dagger etching.

"No idea, Jack, and what weird symbols. Angel was keen on that sort of thing though."

"I saw this on her desk as well." I unfolded the sheet with the translated poem about the fish with nine tails. "Recognise it?"

"Ah yes," Velinda laughed. "We do a challenge for the pupils every week. This was the first one I think, back in April, and Angel, well, she just astounded us, especially Cyrus."

"How's that?"

"Well, the challenge was to translate the text, which we thought was enough on its own, but Angel, well…" Velinda then explained how Angel, having just arrived at the academy and with no prior knowledge of Cornish and precious few resources, other than an amateur and privately published English Cornish dictionary, mastered the basics of the language in a few days. Angel, she said, not only accurately translated the poem, but also realised it must be some kind of riddle.

"Even Cy hadn't understood it was a riddle," she said. "We were quite shocked at Angel's perspicacity."

"Is Cyrus interested in Cornish folklore and so on then?"

"Oh yes," she laughed. "It's one of the reasons he was keen to take this job. Cy would give up teaching to study folklore full-time if he could. Be like a pig in clover, don't think he'd even notice I was there." She laughed again.

"And the octopus?"

"The answer to the riddle. A fish with nine tails."

"Sorry, I'm being a bit dim."

"Oh Jack," she sighed. "Eight legs equals eight tails, then add a body and you have nine tails. So… the big fish they couldn't catch in St Ives that day must have been an octopus."

"Ah, slimy," I said wiggling my hands like tentacles, before quickly withdrawing them behind my back when Velinda didn't react.

"And that's what Angel worked out, in an unknown tongue, in a few days, without really trying, and without even being told there was a riddle to be solved in the first place."

"Remarkable," was all I could say.

"And, Jack, one other thing. Not sure it's important though."

"You never know."

"Well, that fish drawing."

"Tattoo?"

"Yes, Angel went to a backstreet tattooist in Falmouth. Had it done on her leg."

"You let the pupils have tattoos?"

"No, of course not, it's illegal if you're under eighteen.

"But she got it anyway?"

"'Fraid so," Velinda nodded. "Said something odd to me when I challenged her about it as well, now what did she say again..." Velinda scratched her head. "Yes, that she'd felt driven to draw the fish, and didn't know why, which was even odder coming from Angel, who usually always knew why." Velinda carried on scratching her head. "And d'you know what, Jack?"

"No."

"All the other kids loved that tattoo. Wanted one the same. Was if the whole school went, well... fish mad."

"Did you let them?"

"Pardon?"

"All have these tattoos."

"Once again, no, but several children managed to get one all the same. We informed the parents of course, but there were no complaints, so please don't mention it to Sir John." Velinda wagged her finger at me and winked.

"May I continue?"

"Mmmm..." She nodded.

"Alight, well lastly, at the back of a draw under her desk, I found this." I handed the note in the envelope to Velinda.

"Yes," she said as she opened it. "Those desk draws are very awkward, set well under the desktops, always jamming, I—"

She stopped talking and stared at the note for a moment, then continued. "Yes, looks like Angel was meeting someone at the boathouse. One of the, er... other pupils I suppose."

"Maybe, but would a teenage boy use the word 'devoted'?"

"Perhaps, Jack." She coughed. "Ahem... the, um, youngsters here don't always speak like their less gifted contemporaries."

"Okay, well let's see how they do speak. Did you manage to round up Spider and Jonny?"

"They're waiting in the hall. It was Spider you wanted to see first, wasn't it?"

"Yes. Can you ask him to come in five minutes, and wait with Jonny while I speak with him, please?"

"Of course."

"And these are the boys' files?"

"Yes."

"You're sure you don't mind me stealing your desk?"

"Yes," she laughed, and left the office.

I opened the first of the files, to see Jonny's photograph staring out at me. There seemed nothing remarkable, the notes telling of a gifted boy from a poor background in Newcastle upon Tyne, recommended to the institute by his local teachers mainly due to his exceptional skills in Greek and Latin. The file on Spider described a boy, highly gifted in a number of areas, especially modern and classical language, as well as biblical history, and educated by Christian Brothers. Besides a tendency to suffer occasional fits, again the profile showed nothing else out of the ordinary.

*

"Spider?"

"Eight limbed animal, surprisingly close relative to the little-known horseshoe crab," answered the gangling youth in front of me, standing well over six foot, with greasy, black shoulder-length hair and disproportionally long limbs that had no doubt given him his nickname. "Phylum Arthropoda, order – Araneae, class – Arachnida, okay?"

"Simon, then," I said, in no mood for cheek, the precious morning hours already racing on.

"Simon Founds."

"Sit down then, Mr Founds." I gestured to the chair opposite. "I'm—"

"Jack Sangster, I know."

"Yes, you did the same trick on my wife."

"She wore that Hebrew bracelet."

"A gift from me, bought in Jerusalem. Now then, I'm looking for help anywhere I can, anything at all that might shed light on the whereabouts of Angel Blackwood."

"I'm sure you are," smirked the boy.

Trying to ignore the dislike I was beginning to take to this 'Spider', I decided to treat him as I would have done an errant seaman hauled up before me on board ship.

"I've read your file, and I'll be taking notes," I said, bringing out a pad and pen. "And these may be passed to the police, so try and answer concisely and clearly."

"I'm sure you'll tell me if I don't, sir," he retorted, in a voice that said with every inflection, especially the way he said 'sir', that he didn't acknowledge my authority. "Like you would have done in the navy, sir," he then added to my complete surprise, although I managed (I think), not to give him the satisfaction of showing it.

"So, when did you last see Angel?"

"Sunday. We were sitting on the lawn after lunch, talking."

"Just you and her?"

"No, Jonny Waites as well."

"Talking about what?"

"You really want to know?"

"Yes, lad," I said slapping my palm onto the desk with a thwack that made him jump. "Take this seriously, Angel's missing."

"Koine Greek influences on Judean Aramaic script," he said, with a look that implied he expected me to ask what that meant. I decided to note it down and ask Sarah rather than give him any satisfaction.

"Did Angel bring that subject up?"

"I think so, but maybe not." I watched him look sideways for a moment, a sure-fire sign of discomfort.

"I thought you were certain about everything, Mr Founds. So did she or didn't she bring it up?"

"Yes, she did," he sighed. "She's been talking about it a lot lately, that particular dialect."

"I see. Now I'd like to ask you an important question."

"I thought they were all important," he smirked. "But please, go ahead."

"Did you have a relationship with Angel?"

"Ah, what's the definition of 'relationship'," he answered, feigning exaggerated concentration by touching the top of his head along the (rather greasy) centre parting. "Now let me see. 'The way in which two or more people or things are connected, or the state of being connected.' So, I suppose, as we were both at this school, yes I did."

"You know what I'm talking about."

"Then no." He looked at me flatly. "Sir."

"And did you want to?"

"Yes, I did," he answered quietly. "But she was interested in older boys, 'real men' as she called them." Looking at this awkward, know-it-all, insolent and (to my eye), somewhat unwashed specimen, I couldn't help admiring Angel's taste.

"And was she seeing anyone?"

"No, I don't think so. I'd have known."

"No doubt you would," I said, imagining he would be the last person Angel would confide in. "Does she, or do you for that matter, know anyone whose first name begins with a 'T'?"

"Well, we all do don't we, know someone whose name starts with T, for example I—" He stopped himself, now realising (I hoped) that sarcasm wouldn't help. "Someone special I guess you mean," he then said, sounding for the first time reasonably genuine. "No, I don't think so. There really aren't too many opportunities to meet people for any of us cooped up here. Place is like a fortress." He thought for a moment. "Doesn't mean she couldn't have met someone elsewhere though I s'pose. She was allowed out more than most."

"Okay," I said, passing him my card and scribbling the hotel number on the back. "Any other ideas let me know or pass a message via the Flimwells." Again, he looked defiant, this time at the sound of the principal's surname, and I decided our talk should end. "Thank you for your, er... cooperation, you can go now, Mr Founds. And ask Jonny Waites to come in would you please?"

With that, Spider lifted his long limbs and left the office. As he did so, I looked at his left ankle, which was exposed, his trousers pulling up well above his socks.

There it was, the nine-tailed fish tattoo.

*

Waiting for Jonny, I sifted through Spider's answers for clues, but found none. Even his comment that Angel was allowed out more (why?) and might have met someone outside the school seemed insignificant. After all, whoever the mysteriously devoted 'T' of the note was, he (or she) was to meet her inside the school grounds.

"Mr Sangster?" came a voice from around the door.

"Come in. Jonny Waites, isn't it?"

"Yes, sir," Jonny replied.

"You can drop the 'sir' Jonny. Just Jack or Mr Sangster will do nicely."

"Er, thanks Mr Sangster." Jonny, whose Geordie twang matched the back story in his file, was easier on the eye than Spider, shorter and more normally proportioned, with a mop of black curly hair and an altogether friendlier countenance.

"So, I'm trying to find out more about Angel, Jonny."

"Spider said you were."

"Yes, well he's told me what he knows, so just try and tell me anything you think he might not know." Jonny looked awkward and stared at his feet. "Nothing you say need go beyond this room, unless I have to tell the police of course."

"Well, you know Spider fancied her, Mr Sangster."

"Yes, he told me. Said she didn't fancy him though."

"That's right. She's always dreaming of film stars, pop singers and so on. Seems like real boys of her own age don't interest Angel." He paused for a moment, then looked up and spoke more brightly. "But Angel is my friend. We talk about all sorts of things, go canoeing together." This confirmed to me that Jonny was the other kayaker Sarah and I had seen from the ferry.

"Anywhere interesting?"

"We've been up most of the creeks on the Fal now."

"Anywhere special on this creek?"

"Near here, not particularly. There's some ruined jetties, old mine workings and things, but nothing much. Far more interesting further upriver, towards Truro, where those ships are moored."

"Yes, I've seen them. Huge." He nodded. "And did Angel go out of the school on her own much, at weekends say?"

"No, I don't think so. We had an exeat weekend recently, but she didn't use it. Parents live in Essex she said, so too far to go."

"Any idea what she did do that weekend?"

"I think she said Prin took her out sketching, but maybe she went into Truro on the bus or something."

"Yes Jonny?"

"Um… I remember Angel mentioning she went up to Camborne one Saturday as well, and she'd have had to change buses in Truro to do that. She could, er… do that because Prin had given her permission to go out more than the rest of us."

So, I thought, plenty of opportunities for a determined girl to meet someone.

"Was there anything she would ask you about, any subject where she wanted to know more?"

"No," he laughed. "Angel could do most things better than anyone."

"You all seem to be really good at something here. What is your speciality, Jonny?"

"I like old myths, and the languages that go with them. Latin, Greek and so on."

"Aramaic?"

"Yeah, a bit," he said, nodding slowly. "But that's more Spider's thing. I think it annoyed him Angel knew more about it than he did though, and Aramaic wasn't even her special thing."

"What was her special thing, Jonny?"

"Nothing." He paused for a moment. "No, I mean, practically everything."

"I understand." I handed him a card with my number on, as I had Spider. "Thank you and call me or let the Flimwells know if you remember anything else." He stood up to leave.

"Oh, and Jonny?"

"Yes?"

"What does Laboris Gloria Ludi mean?"

"Ooh, er..." His eyes suddenly lit up. "It's not exactly the same in Latin, but we would say, work hard, play hard."

"Thank you, Jonny, and sorry, one other thing."

"Yes sir."

"Please roll up your left trouser leg."

"Sir?"

"You heard, lad."

He then complied, and sure enough, I saw the sad looking nine-tailed fish.

"What's that, Jonny?"

"Just something Angel drew sir, and we had the tattoos done in Falmouth."

"What made you want that?"

"I'm not sure sir, I just wanted it... got in a bit of trouble for it as well, but there's no harm done, is there?"

"No harm done, Jonny."

"Let's go through to the incident room, Velinda."

"Did you find out anything more from the boys?"

"Not much I'm afraid. I need to tell the police what I found in the desk draw though."

"Alright, Jack," she said, her voice seeming a bit flustered. "Can you go on without me, I'm already late for a class. Still got the day job to do."

"Of course, must be difficult juggling everything at the moment."

"Thanks," she said, almost running away from me down the corridor.

"I'm going to make a few calls after this so I may not see you again today," I called as she went. "Will let you know if I have any news."

"Me too," came the reply as she disappeared, not into a classroom as I would have expected, but back into her office.

I walked on to the school gym, where the numerous uniformed police officers and clerks bustled, and the telephones were busy as ever. Pentreath was standing with his back to me in the corner by the blackboards.

"Morning, Sangster," he said without turning around, in a way that slightly took me aback. "Don't worry, haven't got eyes in the back of my head."

"How d'you know it was me then?"

"Reflection." He pointed to a glass board behind the others which was scrawled with black felt pen, parts of which had clearly been wiped clean several times.

"Any news, Pentreath?"

"No, and I might ask you the same. Been interviewing the kids yourself I hear, and you've been searching in their rooms."

"Yes, and I didn't learn much from talking to the boys, but I did find this." I showed him the etching of the dagger.

"Interesting. May we keep it?"

"I've someone who may understand it, so was wondering if you could somehow make a copy for your files."

"Woon," he shouted before I could finish, whereupon the WPC I'd seen the day before comforting the Blackwoods came running. "Take some photos of this would you, wide angle." The policewoman trotted over to a cupboard at the double, returning with a massive camera which she then clicked over different parts of the paper, each time with a blinding flash.

"One moment, sir," she said, as the camera whirred, producing several large, fully developed photographs from a slot in the underside after less than a minute. WPC Woon then picked the photos up by the corners and waved them in the air. "Just drying the acetates off."

"That's amazing," I said, looking at the detail of the sketch on the photos. "My wife's got one of those instant cameras, but nothing like that."

"Latest industrial Polaroid from America, Sangster," said Pentreath, with pride judging by the way he held his chin up as he spoke. "We're not the yokels some people think down here you know. And we get our fair share of murder, abduction, violent crime."

"I'm sure you do, and I never thought for a minute you were 'yokels', as you put it."

"Your boss does."

"He thinks that about almost everyone," I laughed. "Anyway, I did find out that the script on this drawing is likely…" I pulled out my notebook. "Judean Aramaic, so if you know anyone who can translate as well, we can both try."

"Hmmm…" Pentreath scratched his chin. "Maybe Exeter University. We'll have a look into it. Anything else?"

"Found this card. Camborne mining school."

"Ah yes, heard of this chap, Jos Polkinghorne, featured in the newspaper a few weeks back. Came from a local mining family, now lectures all round the world. May I keep it?"

"Of course. And I also found a note, it says—" I felt in my pocket, but the envelope wasn't there. "I could swear I…"

"You lost something, Sangster?"

115

"A note I found in an envelope in the girl's desk. I can remember roughly what it said though."

"Woon, take this down." The WPC duly took out a notebook and pencil.

"Er... 'I must see you. Boathouse at 4. Devoted T'. I think that's it."

"Sure?"

"Pretty much."

"We'll look for Christian names and surnames beginning with T then. Sounds like a lead."

"And that old man you mentioned, the one the kids call the tramp?"

"Disappeared off the face of the earth, Sangster. Not a trace. We're continuing our house-to-house searches though. Done quite a wide range now, almost down to Helston, up as far as Redruth, and over to St Austell." Once again, he sounded proud, while once again, I felt he was looking in the wrong place, and should be focusing closer to home.

"Pentreath," I then said quietly. "May I have a word?"

"Of course, over here." He gestured to one of the larger notice boards. "Behind this screen. Now what is it?"

"Well, firstly, I think Angel has quite an interest in men."

"Normal enough for a teenage girl."

"Yes, but more so than the average teenager. And she's a real beauty, so equipped to do something about it. Just thought you should know."

"Thanks, I had wondered, and that could certainly have a bearing on the case. You've er... done well here, Sangster. Found a few things we missed."

"Thanks."

"And between you and me," he whispered. "That's good to know. I, er... I'm not so used to being out in the field these days. As a DCS I tend to be a bit more desk-bound, let the more junior officers do the hands-on detective work if you know what I mean."

"Really?"

"Yes, but I was given a three-line whip to head up this investigation personally, so what I'm trying to say is, well... we need each other. Your boss is counting on you, and mine on me." He clapped me on the shoulder, and after a few moments' silence (being used to the police disliking the Granville Institute's involvement in cases this didn't immediately register as a sign of friendship), I realised I had an ally in this Pentreath. "And," he went on, "I have to say being this hands-on is a little daunting. I've not personally led an investigation for some time, and given my rank the personal consequences of failure, well…" He looked me in the eye, and for a moment I saw a genuine anxiety that went some way to explaining the undertones of discomfort I'd detected as he spoke earlier. "Don't bear thinking about."

"Um…" I then said, wanting to make the most of the newfound comradeship. "You took most of Angel's books and her notes from the dormitory. May I look over them?"

"Of course, Sangster, WPC Woon has filed them all. Far corner of the room. Go over now and she'll show you."

"Thanks, and one more question if I may."

"Yes?"

"You say you're a little rusty but you do have the experience with this kind of thing." He nodded. "So, tell me, what do you really think Angel's chances are, now that it's been four days?"

"Honestly, Sangster, unless she's run away up-country, which is always possible I suppose, then not good. Not good at all."

*

"Now listen up everybody, a moment of your time," shouted Pentreath, emerging from behind the screen as the room gradually went silent. "This is Commander Sangster, here at the specific request of no less an authority than the chief constable himself, so you will, and I repeat will, give him any and all help he needs. Any questions?"

The room remained silent.

"Carry on then." The bustle recommenced, and I walked over to the corner Pentreath had indicated.

"WPC Serana Woon," said the officer by the filing cabinets, a trim and pretty young woman with dark brown hair piled up in a bun, and (at least I found it so), a very attractive Cornish lilt. "Ana for short," she added, pronouncing it 'aar-na', slowly but slightly self-consciously I thought, in a way said that she half expected me to make some joke at her expense.

"That's a very pretty name." She smiled at this, and the self-conscious look passed. "I'm Jack Sangster. DCS Pentreath said you had catalogued all Angel's books and so on."

"That's right, and here are the books." She gestured to two piles of volumes, both stacked precariously on a tabletop. "They're really of two kinds, academic and er... ahem." She reddened. "Romantic, and we found those all stuffed behind the academics. The girl clearly didn't want them seen by the teachers."

"I can imagine," I said, looking down the spines of the left-hand pile of titles, at least some of which I knew were certainly not 'romantic' in the popular women's fiction sense of the word. "And Angel's notes, her exercise books?"

"Here, in bundles on the desk. I arranged them by date as best I could. Angel had a habit of dating every sheet she wrote on, which helped."

"All looks very neat. I'll have a browse through and let you know if there are any questions."

"Alright, sir."

"No saying sir, please. Just Jack, and if I may I'll call you Ana, I'll make sure it's with a long A."

"Okay, Jack," she said, now with a broad smile. "And I'll be right over there if you need me."

I watched her walk away, past a group of desks where, amongst others, a uniformed officer sat (I recognised him as the sergeant who had taken my statement). The young officer put his leg out.

"Fetch us a cup of tea and try not to 'Swoon' when you bring it."

The WPC kept her nose in the air and tried to pass the sergeant, whose leg remained firmly blocking her path.

"Guess you're about to 'Swoon' at the sight of my trousers. Why don't you come for a drink with me, and I'll show you what's inside."

"I don't think so, Bolitho," she answered, deftly stepping over his outstretched limb. He whistled after her and called out.

"You know you want to."

Then he turned to his colleagues and made a fist gesture. The group all laughed for a few seconds, adding some more whistles and whoops before resuming whatever it was they were doing at their desks.

Show over, I turned to the matter in hand, and noticed that, as WPC Woon had said, some of Angel's books would indeed have been worth hiding from the teachers.

The Passion Flower Hotel,
Lady Chatterley's Lover,
The Story of O,
Nana,
Venus in Furs...

...the pile of 'romantic' books went on, merely confirming, if it were necessary, that Angel was very much 'on the cusp of womanhood'.

I then perused the academics, to see that WPC Woon had topped the pile with a number of classics in the author's original languages. It seemed the likes of Tolstoy, Moliere, Boccaccio (whose *Decameron*, I felt, might have sat as easily in the 'romantics' pile), and even Hans Christian Anderson had all graced Angel's shelves in their unadulterated form. Below that were books on Cornwall itself; the county's myths and legends, the locale around the River Fal, metallurgy of Cornish natural resources, and one heavy (and judging by its cover, quite old) tome entitled *Cornish Castles, The History of Mine Workings from Bronze Age to Steam Age*. I noticed something sticking out of the pages, which turned out to be a pressed leaf, marking a page that showed an old photo of the Bethadew Well mine. The accompanying text explained that this small working, which had begun as an open cast mine and was already operating when written records began, had been abandoned in the nineteenth century after its tin lode ran dry.

The picture was clearly important to Angel as next to it she'd drawn an exclamation mark in turquoise blue ink.

My eyes then fell on a medium sized paperback published, according to its cover, by the University of Michigan, and entitled: *Lake Superior Copper and the Indians: Miscellaneous studies of Great Lakes prehistory.*

This rather nondescript looking volume also seemed to have been important to Angel, as she had inserted a bright-red book mark inside. I opened the book at the marked page to find a fold-out map, detailing an island. 'Archaeological expedition of 1929 and 1930' was written at the top, with the island named as 'Isle Royale'. Besides towns and roads, numerous mines were noted, and by one mine, next to a small lake, Angel had scribbled, in the same turquoise ink used for the exclamation mark, 'He lies here'. I folded the map back and closed the book, then picked up the next, which bore the incomprehensible title *Iron Age Fogous of Cornwall.*

Clearly Angel was researching archaeology, but why Lake Superior or Iron Age Cornwall?

I carried on looking through the stack of books, coming upon a volume on *Phoenician Ceremonial Artefacts*, and another on *The Charts of Ottoman Cartographer Admiral Piri Reis*. There then remained just a few books that dealt with Aramaic dialects, so that, all in all, the academic book pile seemed less in number than the romantics, and I assumed Angel had supplemented the front of her shelves with exercise books and sheaves of notes to disguise her private library. In any event, there were plenty of notes, piled high on an adjacent table.

And in front of these was a typed inventory (the work of WPC Woon I assumed), which was, as she had said earlier, arranged by date. Picking a date at random, I easily found the appropriate pile of notes, and having read through these, repeated the exercise several times before realising the notes (which were loose leaf sheets designed to fit in the standard ring binders which all of the pupils at the academy used as exercise books), didn't seem to hold anything pertinent to the case.

Below the list of dates, however, WPC Woon had handwritten:

Notebook is of interest.
Shows some location nearby?
Impossible to decipher.
Dates may be significant.
SW.

I waved across the room, and she waved back, setting off to run the gauntlet past Sergeant Bolitho and his gang, where sure enough, the officer's leg once again blocked the aisle. This time the harassed WPC said nothing, jumping over the leg and proceeding on her way.

"Bet I could make you jump higher than that, Swoon," Bolitho called after her. "Just you see if I couldn't."

"Sorry about that Command… Jack, I mean."

"Nothing to apologise for. Now what did you mean when you wrote this line about a notebook?"

"Angel kept a notebook, a small leather-bound one."

"Like a diary?"

"That's what you'd expect from a teenage girl isn't it, but not Angel." She opened a filing cabinet and produced the notebook, leather-bound and threadbare, its spine torn and held together by an elastic band, its dimensions making me think it might have started life as an autograph album. "Nearly fell apart when I opened it, must have been very well used, but it was worth seeing nevertheless, look."

I turned back the cover and leafed through the pages very carefully, seeing diagrams and symbols similar to those on the dagger etching. These were seemingly directions for finding some sort of location, or perhaps more than one location, although it was hard to understand exactly what the directions meant. I fancied some were very local to the academy and small scale, while others could have been on an epic intercontinental scale, showing oceans and coastlines.

At the bottom of some pages were scribbled lines I could at least read (if not understand their meaning), all in Angel's trademark turquoise ink and more in the manner of a diary, and each with a date, in line with Angel's habit…

> 19.4.70 – *What have we found in the mud?*
> 21.4.70 – *London*
> 21.4.70 – *For the first time, a man worth meeting!*
> 25.4.70 – *Sketched the Bad Passage today. Imagines he's Tristan and me Iseult. No fool like an Old Fool.*
> 27.4.70 – *JP will analyse it.*
> 8.5.70 – *Eureka! J brought J, J brought M, J moved J far away.*
> 9.5.70 – *Should I tell him?*
> 10.5.70 – *Why am I being watched?*
> 22.5.70 – *He's coming for me at last.*
> 24.5.70 – *Old fool persistent. I'll be gone anyway.*

Then finally, on an otherwise blank page, with no dates, I read:

> *Bethadew Well Mine – Beth a Dhu Hwel – leave out the mine.*
> *Beth a Dhu – tomb of black? No!*

Below this she had added:

> *Did he cause me to find the dagger?*
> *Does he really wander the Earth for ever, this FK?*

"Those are interesting dates, Ana, at least some of them. Did you show this notebook to Pentreath?"

"Yes, of course. He wasn't sure it was really relevant."

"Well, that last entry was dated last Sunday, when she disappeared. Tells us something, surely?"

"I guess," she shrugged. "But unless we could find out who these people are, JP, the Old Fool, the wandering one, the FK she just mentions as 'him' and 'he', if that refers to a different person, then I don't see what more we can do."

"Can I take the book?"

"Yes, I suppose so, just sign in the register here."

"Oh, and Ana?" I said as I scribbled. "Are you a local?"

"Born and bred in Gerrans, by Portscatho. Mum runs the post office there."

"I remember seeing signposts."

"That's right, just a few miles up the road, by the coast, so yes, I'm very local."

"You're Truro police then?" I asked, remembering that MP Tremayne had arranged for detectives outside of the locality to work on the case.

"That's right again, but they didn't assign anyone from our local CID. Sent Chief Superintendent Pentreath. No idea why."

"Politics I suppose. Anyway, on another subject, and given you are a local." Here she smiled. "Do you know if there are any mine workings around here, really close by?"

"Not much at all. There's the old Bethadew Well, but that's mainly tumbled down."

I jolted as she said the name.

"It's near here then?"

"Oh yes, in the wood, the one they call the Plantation. Used to play there as a kid. Went up to Bethadew on summer evenings courting a few times when I was older as well," she added with a twinkle.

"And I suppose the mine has an old well?"

"No," she said, pausing to think. "It doesn't come to think of it. There's a closed-up entrance to a fogou next to the building where we'd, you know, snuggle up, but there was never a proper well that I saw."

"Fogou?" I asked, remembering the curiously titled book in Angel's academic pile.

"Yeah, an old prehistoric tunnel thing."

"What was it used for?"

"I don't think anyone knows. There's a sign up next to the entrance, tells you about it."

"Okay. And I suppose you would have seen this academy building when you were growing up too."

"Oh yes, of course, Jack."

"And?"

"Well, it was a hotel right up until your institute bought it, although…" She thought for a moment. "It's owned by an old Cornish family, and I think my dad said it was used by the Ministry of Defence during the war, hence the high walls and fences."

"I know who the owners are, and the MOD thing wasn't on the records I saw but makes sense," I laughed. "I mean, you don't get many hotels with unscalable fences that stretch all the way down to the low tide mark." We were both silent for a moment. "And that's what makes Angel's disappearance so hard to fathom."

"It does," said Ana, shaking her head. "It does."

"Alright, well you've done some great work here, Ana. I'll be sure to mention that to Pentreath."

"Oh, it's nothing," she blushed. "You don't need to…"

"Oh, but I do. Your filing system's immaculate. By the way, once the case is over what happens to all this lot?"

"Oh, all these papers will get stored somewhere and forgotten about, but we never throw anything away."

"Okay, but good work, really."

"Just doing my job."

"Perhaps, now one other thing if I may…" She nodded, cheeks still flushed. "That sergeant over there," I said quietly.

"Nick Bolitho?" she replied in similar tones.

"Does he bother you?"

"I can handle the likes of him."

"I know you can, but should you have to?"

"That's what my fiancé says. And Bolitho's a lot worse when nobody's looking, there was one time when he touched me and… no, I shouldn't say more." Her eyes welled up with tears. "Richard wanted to wait outside the station and have a go at him."

"Did he?"

"Richard wouldn't last a second with Bolitho. Nick's a rugby captain, and Richard's, well, he's not..." She dabbed her eye. "He's brave and he's my fiancé. I begged him to leave it, told him I'd get a transfer."

"I see. Well, sterling work on the Angel Blackwood case, Ana. Truly sterling work. You'll be mentioned in despatches, as they say."

"I like you, Jack. You're not like other Commanders I've met. Maybe it's because you're out of uniform."

"We're all different," I said, my mind beginning to turn over. Pentreath hadn't thought to make the distinction, so that they all clearly imagined 'Commander' meant a senior police officer, not an ex-naval rank. Alright, I thought, it had worked in the taproom at the Watersmeet with calming down the male voice choir, so maybe it would work with a bullying sergeant.

*

"Bolitho, is it?"

"That's right," said the sergeant, standing up. "And you are Commander, er..."

"Sangster," I answered, thinking I would name-drop the chief constable of Devon and Cornwall, but then realising I didn't know his name. "Now tell me, what are you and your team working on here, sergeant?"

"Collating all the house-to-house search notes, sir. Piecing it all together."

"Any luck?"

"Sir?"

"Shed any light on this affair, have you?" He looked to the ground.

"Oh, er... no sir, we just collate. Get the data from the search officers, sort through it, hand the sorted data over to the chief super."

"Four of you?"

"Yes sir."

"Well, Bolitho," I said, putting my hand on his back. "Come along with me would you, I may be able to help." We walked through the incident room and into the corridor, where, once out of earshot, I stopped.

"Been a sergeant long?"

"Three years, sir."

"Ripe for promotion I shouldn't wonder, a talented chap like you."

"Hope so, sir. Not really for me to say."

"You must have an idea."

"Well, my chief inspector said a few times I have it in me to make inspector before too long. Thought I might have to take a post up-country though."

"I'm afraid I can't make promotion happen, but here's how I can help you, Bolitho." I stared him hard in the eye, and he looked back at me, a little confused but still, I sensed, hopeful to hear something to his advantage. "I know that you wouldn't want to go back on the beat, now would you?" He shook his head. "Well, it could happen, but luckily, er... I can stop that happening. Only if you help me, mind."

"How's that, sir?"

"Well, it's come to my attention that some officers have been, how shall we put it, taking liberties with WPC Woon."

"No, you don't say." He feigned surprise, making such an effort to be convincing that I wondered how this Bolitho imagined I could have missed his behaviour in the incident room.

"Yes, hard to believe isn't it, but I have a solution."

"Sir?"

"Oh yes. I've been looking for a guardian angel, a tough copper who will make sure it never happens again. Use force if needs be." I clapped him on the shoulders (he was almost exactly my height, six foot one, so that our eyes were entirely level as I spoke). "And I've chosen you."

"Oh, er... yes sir, be an honour, sir."

"And we'll keep this between ourselves eh, Bolitho? No need to burden an already busy DCS Pentreath?"

"Oh no, sir."

"Good, now off you go." He turned away. "And..." I said after him, "if I were to get even a whiff of anything happening to WPC Woon

126

from now on, who by the way is the best of the bunch of you, someone will find themselves back on the beat faster than you can say 'Swoon'. Got it?"

"Got it, sir."

*

Feeling rather smug (although I knew Sarah would have laughed at me for playing the knight in shining armour quite so theatrically), I walked on down the corridor, past the Flimwells' offices, where I could hear raised voices through the door. I thought nothing of it (most married couples argue now and then) and continued out into the entrance hall. I felt my heart miss a beat when I saw Mr and Mrs Blackwood there, standing close together and looking visibly aged (especially Angel's mother), since we had last met two days before.

"Hello," was all I could say.

"Mr Sangster," Mrs Blackwood asked with desperate eyes. "Have you any more news on our daughter?"

"We're all doing everything we can, Mrs Blackwood, and you will be kept right up to date, I'm sure. Are you staying close by in case we need to reach you?"

"A bed and breakfast in St Mawes."

"Well, I do hope you're comfortable."

"We're waiting for the Flimwells, have you seen them?" asked her husband.

"I heard them in their office just now, so I'm sure they won't be long. Anyway, I'll say—"

"I'm still counting on you, Mr Sangster," Mrs Blackwood implored, grabbing my arm. "I know my Angel's still alive, and I know you can find her."

"Somehow," I said, quite genuinely. "I think the same. At least about her being alive."

12 NOON

I walked out to the front lawn, wondering to myself why I'd felt so
certain Angel was alive. I had no idea, but I didn't subscribe to gut
instincts or intuition, except when they were kicked off by some real
event, subconscious or otherwise.

Thus, lost in thought, I bumped (almost literally) into a very
flustered Runtle, doing the nearest thing to a run I could imagine.

"Got three cars just come though the main gate," he blustered.
"Want to take their kids away they do. Got to tell the principals." With
that he waddled on, and I looked over at the driveway to see the cars
now parked, and figures walking towards the main entrance, suitcases
in hand.

Angel's disappearance had been on local and national news, so I'd
thought it would only have been a matter of time before this happened.
Nevertheless, I was still surprised at how quickly some of the parents
had reacted and made the trip down to the academy. Sir John would
not be pleased.

I walked on, towards the row of palm trees on the right. I'd looked
at the boathouse on plans many a time, and even approved the budget
to kit it out, but never had occasion to go there before. Now I was

keen to see this boathouse first-hand, where someone whose name began with a T had arranged to meet Angel. Coming close, I could see why the place was suitable for people who didn't want to be seen, the matted hair-like foliage on the palm trunks and the broad cascading leaves making for an impenetrable screen, behind which the grey stone boathouse hid. Pushing the door open, I entered, to see two rows of small boats, dinghies, tied up against the sides of the building which was built around a backwater so that a channel ran up the middle. Two wooden doors, which were padlocked shut, opened out onto the river. On one side wall I saw a rack holding two sea kayaks, one bright yellow, long and lean, with upward curving bow and stern, and a small keel at the rear (a 'skeg', I seemed to remember this was called). The boat had elastic straps around it (presumably for carrying luggage of some kind on top), and two round, black plastic waterproof drainage hatches, one fore and one aft. Across the top, someone had stuck large black lettering that spelt *Morgawr*. The other boat, unnamed, was smaller, painted a brilliant scarlet, and built along similar lines. Twin bladed paddles rested on hooks next to the boats, and on the floor below were a pile of orange life jackets and plastic skirt-like spray decks, the latter I guessed fitted around the canoeist's waist and the cockpits. Looking up, I saw more canoes resting on rafters, most in a bad state of repair and none with fresh paint or polished hulls. And to one side, taking up the full length of the same rafters and slung on ropes, lay a wooden racing gig with the name *Igraine* in gold lettering on its stern.

'We're encouraging the kids to take an interest in the water, and gradually doing up the boats we inherited', I remembered Cyrus Flimwell saying.

I imagined Angel and Jonny, perhaps even Spider spending evenings in this boathouse, getting the boats seaworthy, smoothing joints, filling holes, painting, laughing, and even telling personal secrets as they worked.

I also remembered watching these yellow and red kayaks from the ferry with Sarah, on what had been a sunny afternoon only a few days before, but now seemed an age ago, when the two canoeists, who I now knew were Angel and Jonny, paddling upriver from the academy, had suddenly disappeared amongst the trees of the Plantation.

*

"It means sea giant."

I jumped at the voice behind me and looked around to see Spider standing by the doorway.

"Spid... I mean, Mr Founds. You surprised me."

"That name on the kayak, *Morgawr*, it means sea giant. Angel named hers after a sea monster that's supposed to live in Falmouth Bay."

"She did, did she?"

"Yep. She and Jonny fixed up those two canoes, and I helped. Don't think he named his anything though."

"Did you follow me here?"

"Yes," he said, looking at his feet. "Wanted to tell you something."

"Alright, lad, spit it out, come on."

"I didn't have to come." He took a sullen pace backwards. "I just, well... I didn't trust you when you called me into the Prins' office, but I do want to help, sir."

"Sorry, it's been a long day. I do appreciate you coming."

"Thanks," he said. "You saw I didn't want to talk about the Flimwell's, didn't you, sir?"

"I saw you looked uncomfortable when I mentioned their names."

"Well, it's one name. Cyrus, the Prin. He, er..."

"Go on," I said, waving my hands in encouragement.

"Well, he took more than a healthy interest in Angel."

"How do you know?" I said, feeling all my vague suspicions now vindicated.

"Angel told me, and she's not one to make it up. He was infatuated with her. Imagined all sorts of romantic rubbish, like they were lovers from the myths of old."

"Really."

"Laughed at him behind his back she did, used to say about him, 'There's no fool like an old fool.'" Exactly, I thought, what was written in the notebook.

"And you think he might have something to do with her disappearance, Spider?"

"I don't think so, Mr Sangster. You see, I was with him when she was last seen, around three, out on the lawn. We'd both come out of a debating class. Pengelly was holding a service in the chapel straight afterwards and the Prins were both there as well."

"You're religious?"

"You read my file, so you know my parents and how I was brought up to it, went to a church school," Spider laughed. "Give me the boy and I'll give you back the man. That's what they say."

"And afterwards?"

"Well, Mum and Dad were alright, just didn't know what to do with me, they…"

"No, on Sunday."

"Oh, you mean now, when the service finished. I came here looking for Angel, but the boathouse was empty."

"That was when?"

"Around four, and Prin also happened to turn up at the same time. We both walked back across the lawn together, and Angel was already gone by then."

"Do we know that for sure?"

"Nobody had seen her since three o'clock, Mr Sangster, so yes."

*

"So how did you first come to the academy, Spider," I asked as we left the boathouse.

"Someone came to my school and interviewed me, then my parents got the offer. Teachers recommended I come, said they hadn't anything else to teach me. And," he said, looking wistful for a moment, "I got,

131

well… picked on at school for being different, but don't tell Jonny or the others that, please."

"I won't, but do you like it here?"

"Love it, but I do still get overload sometimes."

"What's that?"

"Doctor told me I sometimes take in too much of the information around me, all the detail, and it gets overwhelming. I sort of shut down, I can't…"

"Don't worry, we all go through things we can't control."

"Yeah, but this puts me into a trance. Takes hours to come round." We walked on.

"Look, I came to find you at the boathouse for something else as well," said Spider, as we arrived at my car.

"Something else?"

"Did the police have anyone who could translate Angel's notes?"

"Well… not here. Mentioned they would check with Exeter University, and my wife specialises in—"

"That probably won't get done quickly then," he interrupted. "But I can do it now."

"Hmmm…" I said, wondering whether I should be handing over evidence I'd personally signed out from WPC Woon's files. "I'm not sure, I—"

"I want to help, and I can. They're Aramaic script aren't they, so I'm your best bet…" He looked straight at me, eyes pleading, and I suddenly felt convinced he was right. I'd already discounted my original idea of Sarah looking at the symbols. There simply wasn't time.

"Okay," I said, undoing the elastic on the car boot and passing him the notebook. "And take this as well." I gave him the rolled-up etching. "Be careful with that one, the charcoal rubs off on your fingers."

"I won't let you down, Mr Sangster."

"Good, now this stays between us, tell nobody else. Understood?"

"Not the cops, not even Prin or Prinny?"

"Especially not Prin or Prinny. Alright?"

"Got it. I can cut a few lessons this afternoon, and in the morning, so should have most of it done by tomorrow lunchtime. See you again then?"

"Later in the afternoon, please, I've got a lot on between now and then."

"Okay," he nodded, turning to leave. "And, like I said, Mr Sangster," he added over his shoulder. "I won't let you down."

"Oh Spider," I called after him. "How did you know I was ex-navy?"

"Your blazer. RN officer's brass buttons, right?"

"Right," I laughed.

With that he went back into the school, and I climbed into the car, driving slowly down the driveway to negotiate several cars coming the other way (doubtless more parents withdrawing their children) waved on at the gatehouse by Runtle. I pulled up and wound the window down.

"Afternoon, Runtle."

"Is it?"

"How many cars is that now?"

"Seven so far today. School'll be empty in a week or so at this rate, and I'll be out of a job. What are you doing about it, Mr Sangster?"

"Everything I can, along with the police and the principals."

"Well, I do hope so. Is there anything I can help with?"

"I did wonder. That mine in the woods, the—"

"Bethadew Well?"

"Yes, what d'you you know of it, Runtle?"

"Been closed a tidy few years, that's for sure."

"And I heard it has no well, despite the name."

"That's right, Mr Sangster, always wondered about that myself." This began to feel like trying to get blood out of a stone.

"Is there anything special about the mine that you know of, anything at all?"

"Ooh," he said, rubbing his beetroot-coloured chin. "Couldn't say, except I was told by the old caretaker when I first got the job here back in '38 that Bethadew's old."

"How old?"

"Further back than anyone can remember."

"Thanks," I said with a smile, realising the futility of asking any more questions about the mine, although the Bethadew was still niggling at the back of my mind.

"And Runtle," I asked, remembering I had no road atlas. "What's the best way to Camborne?"

"Well…" He rubbed his chin again. "There's some as would say go up via Tregony, then round to Truro and take the main road to Camborne."

"And others?"

"Ah, well others would say go by St Just, and take the left turning after Gerrans, a few miles up the road here."

"And what would you say?"

"Well…" More chin rubbing as he considered. "St Just is shortest, but I—"

"Thanks," I said, winding up my window before he could confuse me further. "See you tomorrow, Runtle," I mouthed.

And as I pulled out of the gatehouse and to the right, into the narrow lane that led away from the school, I noticed a figure watch me from the trees of the Plantation, then retreat when I stopped the car. I couldn't be sure, I thought to myself as the figure disappeared through the leaves, but this woodland watcher looked very much like the tramp.

*

I drove up the lane, which was too narrow for more than one car at a time so had passing places every now and again. I luckily met no oncoming traffic except a farm tractor which forced me to squeeze my car into one of these laybys, the vehicle rumbling past me without slowing, missing my wing mirror by a whisker. One such passing place also had a sign that caught my eye so that I slowed down.

'Bethadew Well Mine, National Trust'

An arrow pointed to a track that led through the woods to the left.

Carrying on, I passed Gerrans village and came to the junction as indicated by Runtle. 'St Just-in-Roseland, 2 miles,' said a signpost ahead, and I took a sharp left turn down a narrow lane not much wider than my car. I drove on, taking care not to catch the wheels on the 'Cornish hedges' at the side of the road. I'd experience of these 'hedges' (which were actually vegetation covered stone walls where the lanes were set slightly below the ground), from a puncture in the first few days of arriving in Cornwall. A few minutes later I turned left again into a wider road and that took me to St Just. The village comprised a T-junction where houses clustered close by a tidal creek, along with a church, its tower visible from the road through surrounding lush, semi-tropical plants that gave the place (in my mind), an odd, almost out-of-place feel. Runtle hadn't said there was a choice of roads, so I stopped the car and walked over to speak with an elderly couple placing a poster on a board by the church gate.

"Good afternoon."

"And good afternoon to you," they replied in unison. "Fine day," added the woman.

"I'm heading to Camborne and wondered which way I should go."

"Ah," said the man, gesturing along the road past the church. "That'll be to the right, down there." I looked behind him to where his wife (I assumed), was finishing pasting the poster to the board.

'Jesus Christ's first steps in England', it read. 'A talk by Canon Simeon Pengelly, St Just-in-Roseland Church, Saturday May the 30th, 7:30pm'. I recalled this was one of Pengelly's churches, and also remembered his story about Jesus coming to Cornwall.

"Thanks, that talk looks interesting."

"We're looking forward to it, you should come," said the man.

"I, er... do know the canon actually."

"Ah," said the woman, her pasting now finished. "You'd be the chap from the academy in St Anthony then, staying at the Watersmeet."

"Um... yeah, that's right, news travels fast."

"Canon Pengelly mentioned that car of yours. Very nice."

"He told me the story of Jesus here as well."

"Oh, you already know the legend of St Just then?" The man pointed to the poster as he spoke.

"No, not St Just exactly."

"Well, we've a stone down by the creek in front of the church, upon which our Lord first stepped ashore when he came to this green and pleasant land."

"I see." I wondered how many more places in the neighbourhood claimed Jesus as their own. "Anyway, I must get on. Nice to meet you."

"And you." They waved as I drove away, with the road narrowing by the minute, until I feared I'd have to turn back. Then, after a particularly hard to negotiate bend, a sign came into view.

'King Harry Ferry Bridge,'

The sign boasted that it saved a twenty-six-mile round trip and warned of an unspecified toll charge. Of course, I thought, this was the chain ferry I'd seen from the steamer with Sarah. It would be the shortest way to Camborne alright, but by no means the best, which must have been what Runtle was trying to tell me when I cut him off. It was too late to turn back now, so I resigned myself to a wait, pulling up behind another sign indicating a parking area for vehicles waiting to cross. There was a cyclist in front of me, along with several foot passengers, but otherwise the road was deserted.

Sun shining, I stepped out of the car and lowered the hood. There was a fresh breeze, but I felt it would be warm enough to drive top down as far as Cambourne. Then I heard a grinding noise and, looking across the water, saw the ferry; a flat, square, barge-like machine with raised sides and a small tower with windows on one side that housed the bridge, slowly start to cross from the far shore, pulled by two enormous chains from engine houses on either riverbank. It edged closer, and within a few minutes was docking below me, the front lowering to let several cars drive off. Once these passed, a boatman waved to me to proceed, and I drove slowly across a ramp and onto the ferry.

With the roof down, I had an excellent view ahead, and after taking in the scenery during a wait of around ten minutes, the grinding started again, and I felt this strangest of vessels begin to move forward, first imperceptibly, then faster. As it crossed to the far terminal ('one way, sir? Half a crown then', said the boatman when visiting my car), I heard a familiar ship's hooter, and looked up to see the *Kernow Belle* sweep by, its passengers standing on the top deck waving to us, just as Sarah and I had done. I waved back.

Rolling off the front of the ferry, I pulled up a steep hill and drove on through more impossibly narrow lanes, before the road widened out to pass strangely named places; Come-to-Good, Playing Place, Perranaworthal, Carne Brea. As I passed the last of these, I heard a clunk, and realised my boot lid had flown open. Ahead lay a filling station, so I pulled in and parked next to the pumps. An old man appeared from a prefabricated hut and leaned over the car.

"Fill her up, sir?"

"Er… yes please."

"Five star I suppose?"

"Yes please." He undid the petrol cap and inserted the pump nozzle.

"Did you know your boot's up?" he asked over the sound of the flowing petrol.

"Er, yes, I had noticed. My temporary elastic broke, do you have anything you could fix it with?"

"Yes sir, hold on." He left the nozzle in the car and walked back to his hut, reappearing a minute later with a ball of string. "This'll do the trick, sir. One moment." He set to work on the boot, eventually patting it, before recommencing with the filling. "That'll hold, but you need new parts there. Tried Stocker in Truro?"

"No, where is he?"

"Trafalgar Roundabout. Does Jags, I think. Main road into the town, can't miss it."

"Thanks. Do you have any food for sale?"

"Cheese or ham sandwich."

"Can I have cheese and ham?"

"Nope, one or the other or buy one of each."

"Cheese please, now what's the damage?"

"That's a shilling for the sandwich, and two pound ten for the petrol, so, er… he began to count on his fingers."

"Two pounds eleven shillings?" I said brightly.

"Sounds right, sir," he laughed as I handed him the money. "And the string's free."

I drove on, coming to a layby with a phone box, just outside of Camborne town itself, and pulled over to eat the sandwich (which was almost rigid with staleness, so that I took one bite out of it before discarding the thing into a bin). I looked at my watch. Two thirty, so half an hour before my appointment at the mining school. Time to update Sir John.

"Yes… if you could put me though to him… yes I'll hold…"

"Sangster, you've called at last. We're haemorrhaging kids at an unsustainable rate, parents taking 'em out left right and centre. The girl, what news?"

"Getting close, Sir John," I said, going on to tell him what had happened since he left the day before, albeit without some of the theories I was forming.

"You said yesterday you had instincts."

"So I do."

"Well spit it out man."

"I'd rather not for now." I heard him splutter down the phone, then shout some ripe language at whichever unfortunate persons were in the room.

"This Flimwell," he finally said to me. "Do you think he's sound?"

"That's what I wanted to ask you, Sir John."

"Well, he must have passed muster on the references. We usually look into that sort of thing very carefully."

"Perhaps you could do a bit more digging?"

"Consider it done and call me back tomorrow on that one. Now then, are the coppers cooperating?"

"Oh yes, very much so. DCS Pentreath's been extremely accommodating."

"Good stuff. Chief constable's given him a three-line whip no doubt. I made the necessary arrangement with Tremayne, you remember, MP you met on the—"

"Yes, I remember him."

"So, Sangster, anything else?"

"Not really, but I'm hoping to get to the bottom of things by tomorrow. Not sure what the outcome will be though."

"Whad'ya mean?"

"I mean it may not be a happy ending, Sir John. It's four days since Angel Blackwood went missing."

"Academy's counting on you, I'm counting on you, girl's family's counting on you. Get a result, Sangster or…" He coughed down the phone.

"Or what, Sir John?"

"Don't come back."

*

I put the phone down, feeling less than inspired, and immediately called Sarah.

"Darling, how is it all?"

I explained everything to her, including Sir John's threat, and she listened intently until I had finished.

"Don't worry about Sir John, he's worried sick and full of bluster. You know that."

"If you say so, Sarah, but those dagger markings. Would you be able to read them?"

"Perhaps, but you'd need to post me a copy, so it wouldn't be for a few days."

"No time for that. Any ideas?"

"Well," she said slowly. "There is a machine at the university. Called um… a Xerox Facsimile I think, sends pictures long distance, but you'd need another Xerox your end."

"I could ask the police, but I really doubt there's one down here. I've got someone translating anyway, just wanted a second opinion."

"Oh, I see," she said, sounding a little ruffled. "By the way, did you ring Phil Anson about the submarine?"

"Ah, no I didn't. Can do that in a minute."

"Alright, darling. If you can keep your head when all around you are losing theirs and blaming it on you, If you can…"

"Yes, I know that poem. Doesn't help much."

"Well keep a level head anyway, and do what you're good at, but don't overdo it, Jack, if you see what I mean." She paused for a moment. "And darling, you wouldn't, I mean you couldn't…"

"Yes?"

"Well, I was reading a piece on the lone male under pressure the other day, and…"

"Yes," I said again, recognising Sarah's tone would lead to some worry, some issue I hadn't even considered.

"It's just that there's strong evidence that a man like you, on his own and with the weight of the world on his shoulders, will often seek solace in whoever's arms come along."

"If that's very long-winded way of saying I might stray due to the difficulties of this case while you're still in Chester…" I asked incredulously. "Then stop being silly."

"I'm not being silly, I'm here on my own—"

"And so am I, down here," I said, raising my voice. "And I've got a missing girl to try and find, her family is in despair, a thousand threads to follow, most of which don't seem to lead anywhere specific and, to cap it all, my job and perhaps the whole academy are on the line."

"But—"

"No, and just when I'm getting somewhere, you start imagining things for no reason whatsoever." I then said something I immediately regretted. "Pull yourself together and…" I raised my voice to a shout. "Grow up!"

"Jack," she cried. "How could you, I just wanted you to… Oh." I heard the phone slam down.

"How did that happen?" I shouted into the air, then put my head in my hands and thought for a moment. Perhaps there was some reason why Sarah seemed to have become so insecure, but I couldn't think what it might be. Most of the time, with the exceptions of a few recent episodes like this one, everything had seemed fine. But were we truly happy together?

"I think so, or until a few days ago I did think so," I whispered to myself, then, with a heavier heart than before talking to Sarah, took a deep breath and dialled again.

"Hello… Admiralty House… yes, this is Commander J.G. Sangster, can you put me through to Lieutenant Joyce Yorke please… yes, for Admiral Anson."

"Jack, what a lovely surprise."

"Joyce, how are you, your mum still well?"

"Oh, she's bearing up, Jack. And you, still in marital bliss with wife number two?"

"Er, yes," I replied, thinking the call with Sarah just now was anything but blissful.

"Want to speak to the old man?"

"If I may."

"Putting you through now…"

"Jack," came the measured tones of Admiral Philip Horatio Frobisher Anson, long-time friend, fellow Dartford cadet, ex-shipmate from the war years, and now one of the most senior naval officers in the land. "Joyce says you're calling long distance, so let's get to it, what can I do for you?"

"Thanks Phil. Look, this is an odd ask, but any idea if there is Russian sub activity in the area around Falmouth Bay?"

"You in a call box?"

"Yeah," I said immediately, realising he meant are you being listened to. "Random one, nobody would know I'm here."

"Okay, Falmouth Bay's a bit off the Ruskies' usual patch, but I can easily check. Can you hold?"

"If it doesn't take too long."

"Half a minute at most." I waited, actually about ten minutes, the phone box rapidly consuming my coins, so that I almost thought the call was lost when Phil came back on the line.

"Still there, Jack?"

"Mmmm."

"Not sure how you found out, and not sure I want to know, but yes, a minesweeper picked up a likely hit on radar a few miles south of the Dodman Point. Certainly not one of ours."

"The Dodman's not far away from Falmouth, is it?"

"No, just up the coast."

"And was this sub, by any chance, a Papa class?"

"My goodness yes, we think so, but you mean 'The' Papa class."

"Do I, Phil?"

"Yes, the Ruskies only ever built one Papa sub. Better than anything we've got mind you, so they'd have to have a jolly good reason to deploy it. Something really important."

"Stealth I guess, Phil. Can stay under indefinitely, is still small enough to get close in shore, only surfaces when absolutely needed, and really fast."

"You always could figure stuff like that out in a trice," he laughed. "But I wonder when it might surface, and why?"

"I can't say why, but I know when. I saw it."

"Did you now, Jack. Date and time, location?"

"For your records, St Anthony Head, just round the point on the seaward side, by a place called the Battery, around noon last Sunday. About two hundred yards offshore."

"Photo?" I explained the theft of Sarah's camera from the car. "Coincidence, eh? Let me look into that one, Jack, sounds like they've someone there locally, watching."

"One other thing," I suddenly said, and not quite sure why I did. "Not directly in your bailiwick, but a Monsignor Jude Slevin, would you be able to ask some of your more, er... shady contacts to check the name out?"

"What, Monsignor as in Catholic priest?"

"The same."

"Say the surname name again."

"S-L-E-V-I-N."

"Assume he's a bit more than some local villain?"

"Attached to the Vatican no less. Irishman."

"Will do, Jack."

"Okay, Phil, got to go now."

"Call me tomorrow, same time?"

"Will do."

*

"Hello, Camborne mining school... yes... this is Sangster calling, from the Granville Institute... yes, could I possibly speak to Professor Polkinghorne...? His secretary Miss Trimble... yes fine."

"Hello, Sangster here, from the Granville Institute. I was wondering if the professor would be free for a meeting this afternoon?"

"I'm afraid the professor's a very busy man."

I mentally kicked myself for not having called earlier, and decided a little melodrama might help.

"It may be a matter of life and death." I then explained the situation, including the card in the drawer, and especially mentioned Angel Blackwood by name.

"I see, one moment."

"The professor says he will see you at three if that's convenient."

"That's very kind. Thank you."

3 PM

"Excuse me, am I in the right place for Professor Polkinghorne's office?" I asked a young woman sitting behind the reception desk at the mining school.

"D'you have an appointment… ah yes, Mr Sangster, is it?"

"It is," I nodded.

"We spoke earlier on the phone."

"You'd be Miss Trimble then?"

"That's right my 'andsome," she grinned. "Now just go through those double doors and along the corridor there, on the right,"

"Thanks." I walked as instructed, entering the first door I came to.

"Good Afternoon," I said to the young man sitting inside, who was poring over documents on his desk. He had long, dark brown hair and wore a white t-shirt and jeans. One of the professor's students I guessed.

"Hi," he said without raising his head. "What can I do for you?"

"Oh, sorry wrong door, was looking for Professor Polkinghorne, I—" The young man looked up at me, and I saw that he was older than I'd first thought, perhaps mid to late thirties.

"You've found him. You'd be Sangster, from the Granville Institute?"

"Jack." I held out my hand. "Sorry, I was, er… expecting—"

"An older man?" he asked, shaking with a firm grip.

"Well yes, you don't look like a professor."

"Not sure what a professor looks like," he said, in a more grammatically correct but otherwise identical way of speaking to Pasco, with long a's, 'o' pronounced as 'u' or 'a' depending on the word, and 'I' as 'oy'. "But call me Jos."

'Camborne born and bred' Pasco had said when I asked where he was from.

"Your call today intrigued me, Jack. I'd seen on the news that girl Angel was missing, and I already had a call from the police about it this morning. Not sure how they knew I'd seen her though."

"Me, I'm afraid. Found your card in her desk."

"No problem, and I'll give them a full statement sooner or later. I was in Bristol last weekend by the way. You got an alibi?"

"Ahem, er… yes I do."

"Anyway, when Miss Trimble told me you mentioned the dagger, I wanted to see you pronto." He opened a draw in his desk and brought out a copy of a printed form. 'Imperial College of Science and Technology, University of London – Earth Sciences Laboratory Requisition Slip' the title stated, followed by several boxes filled with what to me was mainly illegible scribble. It was signed and dated by Polkinghorne himself, with the stamp of the Camborne mining school over his signature. The date was April 27th.

"This is what I'm waiting for."

"I'm sorry, I—"

"Analysis of the bronze in that dagger the girl brought. I tried, but I've not got the equipment to do the job here." I felt myself getting confused to the point of losing the conversation, and decided to slow things down.

"Maybe we're getting ahead of ourselves." I leaned backwards in the chair. "Let me explain who I am and what I'm doing, then perhaps you could let me know more about Angel's visit and the dagger.

"Alright then, Mr Sangster, go on."

I told him about the institute, the academy, and my role in setting it up and as a special investigator. Professor Polkinghorne then explained that Angel had seen an article in the West Briton telling his story ('"Son of a miner from Camborne turned world's foremost expert in copper," went a bit over the top without asking, the journalist did, embarrassing'). She had telephoned the mining school and asked if she could bring an interesting artefact for appraisal ('she didn't say exactly what, Sangster, but she let out a few hints about the thing that told me it would be worth my while'). When Angel brought her 'artefact', he immediately suspected the dagger might be very old ('but how old I didn't know, I'm a metallurgist, not an archaeologist'). Angel claimed she found it in the mud of the Percuil River at very low tide and had recognised the dagger as likely Phoenician. But, he said, it was the metal itself, not the dagger, that had really seemed to interest her.

"'The bronze was of a hardness I hadn't seen before, around Mohs eight point five to nine.'"

"Mohs?"

"Ah, sorry, that's a one to ten scale we use to determine mineral hardness. One is soft, like talc, ten is hardest, like diamond. To get an idea, a tooth is around seven, so this thing was much harder than that even. Maybe even up to the hardness of a corundum."

"A corun... what?"

"Amethyst."

"Okay."

"And that dagger looked almost die-cast, rather than beaten into shape as I'd have expected. But it was the sharpness that truly shocked me."

"Aren't knives supposed to be sharp?"

"Not bronze ones, not knives that have lain in mud for centuries. Why, I cut my myself just running my fingertip lightly along the blade, and it took a diamond drill bit before I could get a proper sample." He then pointed to a bench in the corner of the room, where various items of laboratory apparatus were laid out, including Bunsen burners and complex glass tubing erections I couldn't have begun to identify, along with a large binocular microscope. "That's a petrological microscope, also good for viewing most metals. Plane polarised light, you know?"

"No," I laughed. "But I suppose I get the idea."

"I asked Angel if she only wanted non-destructive tests, but the girl said no. 'Do whatever you like,' she said, 'to get the best result.'"

"What's non-destructive test mean?"

"X-ray fluorescence and so on if you don't want to damage the artefact. Cutting out an actual physical sample is much more effective, hence the diamond drill, but it's also destructive to the specimen."

Polkinghorne then went on to say that once he'd finally managed to collect some of the metal from the blade, he ran a few chemical tests as well as looking at the sample in the 'scope. With all that information he would typically be able to tell not only the component parts of the alloy, but probably where they came from as well ('I know I said that article in the West Briton went too far, but I'm not boasting when I say I know as much about copper as anyone in England or around the world, Mr Sangster'). The bronze in the dagger, he discovered, was only made of two metals, tin, from Cornwall and, most importantly to Angel it seemed, copper, whereas he had expected more trace metals, like zinc and lead.

"Like I said, she wanted to know where that copper came from," he said. "And that girl knew an awful lot."

"I bet she did."

"Did Angel study metallurgy at your Granville Academy then?"

"Not especially."

"Well," he said whistling. "She's better than any of my post-grads, that's for sure."

"And what did you tell Angel?"

"That's the problem, with all my experience I still couldn't say where the copper was from. And that's me, with Cousin Jacks all around the globe."

"Sorry?" I said, wondering if he was talking about me in some way.

"Oh, that's what we call Cornishmen who've gone out of the county, maybe even the country looking for work, especially mining engineers. You're not Cornish, are you, Jack?"

"Not as far as I know."

"Sorry for that, but anyway, we get samples from all over. I can tell Cornish copper from, say, South African, Australian, and so on. But," he said, shaking his head, "this stuff, it was the purest I'd seen and new to me."

"So, you sent it up to London."

"That's right," he said, holding up the form. "To my old alma mater, Imperial College. If they couldn't say where it came from, I thought, nobody could."

"Hmmm... so they're your last resort."

"'Fraid so." He folded his arms in resignation.

"And when do you expect an answer?"

"They should have come back last week, so literally any time now."

"Okay," I said, handing him my card, and going through my now familiar ritual of writing the Watersmeet number on the back. "If you hear anything, please do let me know. This is a serious situation."

"Of course." He stood up and offered his hand. "Well, thanks for coming, and I'll be in touch. In fact, I'll ask Miss Trimble to chase the Imperial lab up today."

"Goodbye then, and thanks for your time, Jos."

"Oh, Jack," he called to me as I got to the door.

"Yes."

"This girl, Angel. What are the chances d'you reckon?"

"Slim. It's been four days."

"Shame. Pretty little thing, and I never met a brighter one."

5 PM

Arriving in Truro, I kept my eye out for the body shop the garage attendant in Camborne had mentioned, but to no avail. At the Trafalgar Roundabout, where the road to the hotel branched off along the river, I pulled into a petrol station.

"Fill her up, sir?" asked an attendant, appearing instantly.

"Not today, thanks, just need directions. Is there a mechanic called Stocker near here?"

He jerked his head to one side of the pumps and there it was, a hand painted sign proclaiming, 'Stocker's Body Shop – all makes catered for,' nailed above a set of double doors leading into what looked like no more than a wooden shed. Outside these doors, two men in blue boiler suits were talking, both waving wildly at each other.

"Thanks," I smiled to the taciturn attendant, before driving slowly to where the men stood and climbed out of the car.

"Good afternoon."

"Oh, er… hello, what can I do for you?" asked one.

"I tell you it's real," said the other, oblivious to my presence. "There's a TV crew and everything driving around here."

"Hmm…" said the first. "We'll never settle it this way." He pointed at me. "You, sir."

"Me, sir?" I replied, pointing back at my own chest.

"Yes, you look like an educated man, sir."

"Well, I try to—"

"Then tell me this. Do you believe in sea monsters?" I took a deep breath.

"Er… not a question I was expecting, but I'd have to say no, and I was in the navy for over twenty years. Never saw a single one I'm afraid."

"There you are, Ted," the man said. "Been in the navy he has."

"Then how does he account for this, Pete?" said Ted, thrusting a newspaper into my hand.

"That's a bloody elephant swimming, isn't it, sir?" Pete retorted.

"Perhaps," I said, now trying not to laugh as I looked at the photo on the front of the broadsheet, positioned under a headline stating, 'Multiple Morgawr sightings in Falmouth Bay'. The picture showed a grainy outline, with no points of reference, of what at first sight could have been a hump-bodied long-necked monster, but on closer inspection was surely a swimming elephant. "Was this taken recently then?"

"Ah, no," said Ted, pointing to some very small print at the bottom of the page. 'Picture shown for illustrative purposes only, sent to the newspaper's offices anonymously in 1967, Falmouth Packet does not guarantee authenticity', this small print disclaimed. "The reports from this weekend were all interviews with eye-witnesses, so newspaper's got no photos. But still, no smoke without fire, eh?"

"Sorry, sir," said Pete, wiping grease from his hand then offering it to me. "Don't mind my brother, now where are my manners." I accepted his hand, feeling immediately he'd missed much of the grease on his palm, and wiped my own hand on my handkerchief, which quickly went from white to grey. "What can we do for you?"

"My car was broken into. I need a new boot lock."

"Ah, Series 2," he said, looking admiringly at the car. "Let's have a look." Carefully unravelling the string (muttering the words 'granny'

150

and 'knot' several times), Pete then peered around, inside and outside the boot lid. "Needs a complete new locking mechanism I'm afraid, sir," he eventually said, shaking his head. "Course, we don't carry Jag parts here. Nearest concession is Plymouth, and that'll take a while to deliver, I'll—"

"Hold on, Pete," said Ted, brandishing his now rolled-up copy of the Falmouth Packet. "Is Bob going back tonight?"

"Dunno, Bob?" called Pete, to nobody in particular, it seemed.

"Yar," came an invisible voice.

"You going back home tonight or staying at Rita's?" Pete shouted back, then whispered to me. "Bob's got a girl here in Truro, Rita Penberthy from over the chip shop in Lemon Quay, and a wife and kids in Plymouth. Takes turns with them, like."

"And they don't mind?"

"Oh no, both women glad to see the back of him every other day I shouldn't wonder. I would be."

"Yar, Plymouth tonight," came the reply, and I looked down to see a pair of booted feet protruding from beneath a Transit van.

"Could you pick up a delivery from the Jag garage first thing then, Bob?"

"Yar, Pete."

"That's settled then, sir, now just let me call the garage in Plymouth to make sure they've got the part."

He walked into the shed, coming back out a minute or so later with a beam on his face. "Good news, they got one. Going to cost you mind, about seventy quid with labour, that okay?"

"Yes, as long as that price is fair, and I get a proper receipt. It's on the insurance."

"Good, now can I take some details." I gave him my card (hotel phone number scribbled on the back), along with a five-pound deposit, took a receipt and went to leave.

"Till tomorrow then Mr Stocker. Any particular time?

"Oh, Bob'll be in around ten, won't you, Bob?"

"Yar, I should be," came the reply from under the van.

"And it won't take too long once we've got the part, you're lucky," said Ted with a broad smile, as he tied the boot back down using elastic.

"How's that?" I asked, looking at the mangled lock in Pete's hand.

"Whoever did this was a pro. Minimum mess, clean triangular cut in the metal under the lock. Now if it had been kids out for a lark, well, could have taken who knows how long to fix..." He shook his head, and Pete shook his head solemnly in agreement. Then a grunting sound emanated from under the van, and I suspected Bob, whatever he looked like, was shaking his head as well.

I smiled, then lowered the hood to take advantage of the last rays of evening sun and drove off.

*

I went deliberately slowly along the road to the village, looking out to my right as it wound past the Truro River. The water was at low tide, mud flats exposed, the narrow course of remaining water in the centre of the channel almost invisible from the bank, so that the uninitiated might have imagined it was possible to cross to the other side on foot.

My sluggish driving was in part to enjoy the view on this beautiful late spring evening, a view which I never tired of seeing, but also to collect my thoughts.

It seemed to me that an older man might well be involved in Angel's disappearance, but that Cyrus Flimwell, despite clearly being infatuated with the girl, wasn't that older man. The dagger also seemed at the heart of the matter, but how or why I couldn't yet tell. The translation of the script on the blade and in Angel's notebook would surely help, and I suddenly wondered if I'd done the right thing to leave all this in the hands of a seventeen-year-old boy prone to fall into cataleptic trances if he felt the whim. After all, not only was the life of the girl hanging in the balance (I still felt she could be found alive if only I knew where to look), but the academy, which we had set up with such high hopes only a few months before, was rapidly falling apart.

And then there was a heavy-hearted nag in the back of my mind about Sarah, which right now, no matter what else happened, was never far away.

*

"Nice evening, squire," I heard a rich, deep voice almost whisper in my ear as I climbed out of the car and looked up to see Monsignor Slevin standing next to his motorbike.

"Certainly is," I said, holding out my hand. "Jack Sangster."

"Jude Slevin, and I know who you are, Jack. Canon Pengelly mentioned you're looking into the disappearance of that girl from the place down in St Anthony."

"And I've seen your bike around and about as well. You came down on the same train as I did, I think."

"Sure, I did. Here on secondment to exchange ideas with the bishop and his staff."

"Secondment from where?"

"Ah, the Vatican of course." He laughed. "Well, indirectly via London."

"Of course." We both looked over the river, which was as calm as a mirror, reflecting the trees on the far bank almost perfectly.

"Beautiful place this, Jack," he said, spreading his arms out wide and looking upwards in an almost ecstatic manner. "Wouldn't you say now?"

"My wife loves it."

"She'd be the dark-haired one I saw you with in the Pullman car then?"

"That's right."

"You two make a handsome couple, could almost be Tristan and Iseult."

"I'm sorry?"

"Alright, a bit old," he laughed. "Yourself anyway, but you know."

"No."

"I see, then let me enlighten you. They were part of a love triangle, an old style ménage-a-trois if you will."

"Will I?"

"Yes, when you know that you are looking at the very place where they tried to make good their escape. You see, the third party, King Mark of Ireland, was after catching them (first and second parties), and they made their escape across the waters of this river, over the other side there."

"And then?"

"The boat sank, they were caught, and this place, this crossing, in whatever language was used over the ages, has translated to 'Bad Passage' ever since."

I remembered the title of Angel's pen and ink sketch with a jolt. And then there was the note, which I now realised wasn't badly punctuated at all. The 'I' with the comma after it clearly meant Iseult, and the 'T' stood for Tristan, doubtless Cyrus Flimwell's fantasy names for himself and the object of his infatuation, Angel Blackwood.

"You look a little distracted, Jack," said Slevin, perspicacious as ever. "If I may say so that is."

"Not at all." I shook my head, perhaps too vigorously I wondered.

"Mind you," Slevin went on, stroking his beard. "It might have been named because Henry the Eighth and Anne Boleyn lost their baggage here, I never can remember."

"Not a solid bit of history then, Slevin."

"Not really, but where's that divine wife of yours now? Doesn't worry her, you being down here and so on. Temptations of the flesh?"

"Phhh…" I spluttered, taken aback by his directness and change of tack. "Er… trusts me implicitly, a quality I admire in her almost as much as her unique ability to mind her own business."

"Oops, sorry there. Said a bit too much."

"And what ideas…" I then said to change the subject, "are you exchanging with the bishop?"

"Ah," he said, pointing at me. "Very good, changing the subject, so I'm honour-bound to answer." He laughed again, an infectious laugh, so that I understood why his charms had struck with Pengelly. "Well, I specialise in the first century AD, founding of the church and so on. Studied all that at Trinity, PhD and all. Could ask that you call me Doctor Slevin if I'd a mind."

"Fascinating."

"It is, to be sure. We've been debating the possibility of Christ visiting these shores you know. Bishop certainly finds it fascinating, and Canon Pengelly just lives for the idea."

"And you?"

"Oh," he laughed again. "I'm sure it's what people might like to think, but we've yet to show the world a shred of real evidence, so I wouldn't pay the idea any credence." As he said this, I noticed an uncharacteristically serious look suddenly pass over his face, disappearing again almost as quickly as it came. "Course," he then smiled, "if the man upstairs wanted to send his only son somewhere around the British Isles, then it'd surely have been Ireland. Far more civilised place in those days."

I laughed with him and was about to ask more about his Triumph Bonneville, when a van, followed by a convoy of cars, pulled up next to us, people spilling out, filling the evening with noise and bluster.

From the rear of the van, I saw two men jump to the road, carrying equipment that included a camera on a tripod and a long microphone boom, the mic itself covered in what looked like a woolly mop head. A woman followed them, carrying a box the size, shape, and texture of Sir John Granville's picnic hamper.

"I'm out of here," said Slevin, beating a hasty retreat to the hotel door. "Good luck, Sangster," he called over his shoulder as he disappeared inside.

"There he is," said the holder of the mop, pointing in my direction. I looked around to see who he was talking about.

"Sir, can you just say something into the mic?" he asked me, now thrusting the mop in my face. "We're not recording."

"I think you've got the wrong—"

"You are Jack Sangster, owner of this green E-Type?"

"Yes, but how did you…" I saw Pasco climb out of the van.

"Sorry, Jack, they gave me a lift from Truro, and I just may have mentioned you'd seen a Dandy Hound."

"May have?"

"Did."

"Thanks a lot, Pasco."

"Now sir, hold still." The woman brushed both of my shoulders then held both of my cheeks. "That's got rid of any dandruff," she then said, opening her basket to reveal rows of cosmetics; jars of cream, powder brushes, eyeliners, mascara, lipstick, and face paints, all crowded together, so that she seemed to have an entire portable beauty parlour to hand. "And you know, I think we'll leave powdering your skin. Not much shine at all."

"That's, er… very good to know." I felt rooted to the ground, completely confused as the crowd from the cars gathered around.

"In fact, I think you've got quite the natural look we want, all that lovely grey hair and a nice upright stance," the woman went on to say. "Don't move from here please. Light still okay, Jimmy?"

"All ready, Nora," the cameraman answered, giving a thumbs up.

"Sound right, Clip?" Clip also gave the thumbs up, waving his mop headed microphone.

"Right, I'll get Sue. Now don't you move, Mr Sangster."

"The witness is there, Nora?" came a deep female voice from the cab of the van.

"Jack Sangster, all ready for you, Sue."

"Let's do it then," the deep voice replied, and I watched as a stiletto heel at least four inches high, followed by the shapeliest of legs, appeared from the van. The owner of both was then revealed, a statuesque woman, perhaps just less than forty years old, with shoulder-length dark hair and a heart-shaped face, not perhaps classically beautiful, but nevertheless as striking as I could remember seeing. Her eyes met mine, and mine met hers, both of us staring for an instant.

"You must be Jack Sangster," she said, her voice sounding even deeper than it had in the van cab.

"Er, yes."

"I'd like to interview you."

"Here?"

"Of course. Here and now."

"Alright," I shrugged.

"I'm Sue Driver by the way, Harlech TV." We shook hands, she maintaining her grip just a second or so longer than was necessary. "And we're mainly here because of the Morgawr sightings, but we also heard you might have seen a cryptid on the moor." As she spoke, I noticed a Harlech TV logo on the side of the van, along with a complicated arrangement of antennae on the roof.

"I'm sorry, a what?"

"A cryptid, an unknown animal, or a known animal that shouldn't be where it is."

"Ah."

"Now we'd like to start filming, if we may, Jack."

"Okay."

"Nora," Sue shouted, voice suddenly becoming shriller. "Move these people to a distance, would you?" Nora shooed the crowd backwards, which now numbered at least twenty, then waved to the cameraman. "And pass me the book and newspaper, would you?" Nora ran to the van and returned with a small hardback volume and a rolled-up newspaper which she passed to Sue, who stepped closer to me and began to talk into the microphone.

"I'm here this evening, just outside the Watersmeet Hotel on the beautiful banks of the Fal, and once again on the track of unknown animals." She held up the book, which had a red and white dust cover with line drawings depicting various apes and other odd-looking creatures.

"And, as ever, I'm trying, in my own small way, to add to the work of Bernard Heuvelmans, author of this ground-breaking work." She pointed to the volume, which was titled ''.

.'This evening, I'm lucky enough to be able to speak to an eyewitness from a strange animal encounter, right here in Cornwall a few days ago.

This is Commander Jack Sangster, RN, surely as sober and credible a witness as one could ask for. Hello Commander Sangster." Nora jerked her head at me and mouthed 'say hello'.

"Hello."

"Now, Commander Sangster, Jack, if I may?"

"You may."

"Jack, tell us in your own words what you saw on the moor."

"I'd say it looked like a black panther."

"And what makes you qualified to judge that?"

"Seen one in India, during my time in the navy. This animal moved like a panther."

"So not only credible, but qualified," said Sue, now facing directly into the camera.

"Did you see any other evidence this might have been a panther?"

"I came on a shepherd who'd lost one of his sheep, and we found the carcass torn to pieces."

"Now the locals here have legends of giant black hounds from hell roaming the moors at night, Dandy hounds they call them. Could it have been a dog you saw?"

"No, I'm—"

"So, it couldn't have been a dog," she interrupted (I'd been going to say 'No, I'm not expert enough to have an opinion'), then looked straight at the camera again. "So, there you have it. An eyewitness of the highest provenance, sighting what can only have been a big cat loose on Bodmin Moor, and in broad daylight. Now then..." I felt a hand pulling on my shoulder and saw Nora behind me.

"Get out of camera, we're finished with you now," she whispered, still pulling me.

"This," said Sue in the meantime, holding up the same copy of the Falmouth Packet I'd seen at Stocker's garage, "is the hot local headline for the week. There've been sightings of a marine dinosaur-like animal, christened Morgawr by locals, for decades, centuries even. Cornwall's own Nessie." She pointed to the picture of the (probable), elephant. "Now this is an old photo, but there've been several sightings in

Falmouth Bay over recent days. Too many to discount." She turned and looked out over the creek, then began to speak in wistful tones, voice lower, quieter, and slower for dramatic effect (Clip held the mop microphone close).

"Yes, this is a truly mysterious country, and perhaps it holds its mysteries close, but at Harlech we intend to get to the truth if we can." She turned back, smiled, and resumed the commentary in her natural voice.

"So, for now, it just remains for me to say that we'll be back on air when we have more news, and to thank our witness. Jack, come and say goodbye to the viewers." Nora then tugged me back within range of the camera, then thrust me towards Sue, perhaps a little too hard so that I fell against her.

"Oh, you're very forward, Jack," Sue said, grabbing me around the waist before I could escape, and smiling at the camera. "And a personal thanks for your…" She gave me a slow kiss on the cheek. "Help," she then said, pulling away again and addressing the camera close-up. "This is Sue Driver in Truro, for Harlech Television, on the track of unknown animals."

"Cut," shouted Nora.

"Did we get that alright?" Sue shouted to Clip.

"Yes, Sue, and just in time for the network news if we're really quick."

"Then get to it."

Sue was then mobbed for autographs, so that I was swept aside, pushed towards the water's edge. I leaned over the railings at the side of the road and regarded the creek, wondering what had just happened, as the noise of the crowd began to subside, and I heard the sound of motors starting (people driving home now the show was over I supposed).

Thwack.

I felt something hit my backside and jumped up straight then turned to see Sue Driver, holding two glasses in one hand and a rolled-up newspaper in the other.

"Sorry, you presented too good a target bending over the railings there. Did we bushwhack you just now, Jack?"

"Well just a bit. Hadn't a clue what was going on for a minute, Sue."

"Peace offering." She passed me a gin and tonic. "Friends?"

"Of course," I said. "I just like to be asked nicely."

"Don't we all," she said with a wink. "Cheers." We clinked glasses and stood, arms resting on railings overlooking the water.

"So, is that all genuine?"

"What?"

"The unknown animals and so on."

"How do you mean, Jack?"

"Well, do you do it for, what is it you people say, ratings?"

"Yes, but it's also a passion."

"You don't look like an unknown animal-tracker."

"Not sure what an unknown animal-tracker looks like," she replied, reminding me of Professor Polkinghorne, and making me wonder if I tended to judge books by their covers.

"Well, it's just that…" I felt my cheeks redden and she sensed my embarrassment.

"Poor boy. No, it's a long-time passion of mine. I read the first edition of that book of Heuvelmans' while I was still up at Cambridge, and it really did it for me."

"You studied that cryptozoology stuff then?"

"No," she laughed. "College didn't approve, it's not even considered mainstream science. I read English and became a journalist, then a newsreader, but cryptozoology's always been my thing."

"How d'you get into it then, through that book?"

"Oh no. It was an article in a kids' magazine about a fish called a coelacanth. Said to have died out with the dinosaurs but they found one alive. Look." She opened the inside page of the newspaper to show a photo of a large and very ugly fish.

"You wrote that article in the Packet, didn't you?"

Sue smiled, and we both went back to staring across the creek.

"So, what's your thing, Jack?" she asked after a few minutes.

"Naval history."

"But you're what, a school inspector?"

"Not exactly. I'm a special investigator." I immediately wished I hadn't used the 'special' prefix, although she didn't seem to notice. "I write about naval history, but my day job's finding missing children, trying to help troubled kids, that sort of thing. Also did a lot of the set-up work for the Granville Academy near St Mawes."

"If I may say," she said, placing her hand on my arm and laughing, "you don't look like an investigator."

"Touché," I laughed in return. "Teenage naval cadet if you want to know, made it to commander, served in the war, then worked all over for National Oil. The investigator thing's quite new. A bit over a year old."

"Ah, then you're brave, successful, experienced, travelled and have a conscience as well. Is there anything at all about you that isn't perfect?"

"Plenty wrong with me, you really don't want to know?"

"Oh, but I do, Jack," she said with a grin. "Anyway, I'll leave you to it. Take this copy of the Packet as well." She handed me her newspaper. "Limited sea monster edition. Memento of your interview."

With that she drained her glass, turned, dark hair swinging about her shoulders in the most alluring manner as she did so, then crossed the road and walked up the steps back to the pub.

I couldn't help but watch her go.

Once Sue was out of sight, I looked at the Falmouth Packet again, and decided to call the only person I knew who might be able to cast light on the veracity of the witnesses' claims.

That person was Sam Youd, long-time friend, head vet at Chester Zoo, and invaluable source of information about anything weird and wonderful in the animal kingdom. I'd tapped into that source more than once during my case work, and I was fairly sure it wouldn't fail me now. I looked at a red call box next to me, then crossed the road to the hotel.

"Morwenna, can you change up a pound note for the phone box please?"

"Why not use the one in the hall, love, and we'll put the call costs on your account?"

"I need a bit of privacy," I shouted over the noise in the bar.

"Right you are, my lover," she said, reaching into her cash register. "Ten-shilling note, and ten shillings. That alright?"

"Wonderful." I took the change, handed her a pound note, then negotiated my way through the crowd in the bar and crossed the road to the phone box.

Dialling, I heard tell-tale pips, pushed the money into the slot, then waited the pre-requisite few seconds, after which the familiar Cheshire tones of Sandra, Sam's wife, echoed faintly out of the receiver.

"Hello, 625 7701."

"Sandra, it's Jack," I shouted. "How are you doing?"

"Jack, you're very loud," she said, as far as I could tell also coming closer to the mouthpiece herself.

"Sorry. Bad line, quiet one minute, deafening the next."

"No, it's wonderful to hear from you, and I'm fine thanks. Saw Sarah the other day and she told me about the weekend. Sounds lovely where you are."

"Yes, you two must come down to Cornwall at some point."

"Just you try and stop us. Now is it Sam you want?"

"If you could get the old ball and chain to come to the phone, I'd appreciate it. Need his advice."

She laughed, and I heard her calling out to Sam.

"Jack, how the devil are you?"

"I'm well in myself, Sam, but I've got a bit happening down here." I went on to give him a short version of the last week's events. "So, I'm just a little bit tense." I then also explained that Sir John was petrified we would be closed down if Angel wasn't found.

"You do fall into these things, lad," said Jack when I'd finished. "But why do you think she'll be found? I mean, of course we'd all want her to be safe and sound, but four days missing, it's not—"

"I feel it in my water, as they say, Sam. Don't ask me why, but I'm sure she's alive."

"I won't. You have good instincts for things like that, whereas I don't have instincts about anything, unless it's to do with animals."

"Well as it happens…" I told him about the animal we saw on Bodmin Moor, the dead sheep, and the recent sightings of Morgawr. "What do you think?"

"Right up my street, it really is," he said excitedly. "So, Jack, let's talk about the Bodmin Moor sighting first. I take it there are no known big cats on the loose, escaped private pets, or from circuses or zoos?"

"Cops didn't think so."

"And no hard evidence, like photos, paw prints, scat or anything?"

"Nope."

"So just eye-witnesses?"

"Yep."

"And you say what you saw looked like a leopard?"

"From a distance."

"Well, leopards can easily hide from people, and some do live in climates harsher than Cornwall. And they're occasionally melanistic."

"Sorry?"

"All black rather than spotted, you know, like panthers."

"Oh, yes."

"And if someone owned a big cat illegally and wanted rid of it, they might not say if they released it into the countryside."

"Interesting."

"The sheep carcass you saw, how had it been killed?"

"Ripped to pieces around the neck, and disembowelled."

"Hmmm…" Sam went silent for a minute. "You see, a leopard will usually despatch its prey neatly with a killer bite, two razor teeth puncturing the victim's neck. Then it will hide the carcass if it can, maybe even up a tree."

"And if it can't?"

"Um… it'll generally eat the fleshiest parts like the rump as fast as possible. Wouldn't tend to go for the guts unless it had a few days to finish a meal uninterrupted.

"So..."

"I reckon your sheep was killed by a dog, or if it was a weak animal, sickly or injured, then maybe even a couple of foxes could have done the job."

"Certainly made a mess."

"Yes, I've seen dog-kill on farms before. Dogs don't have the best table manners."

"And the sea monster, Sam?"

"Ah," he laughed "Now that's a very different matter. Again, any photos?"

"There's one on the front page of the local paper, but there's no background, the sender was anonymous, and anyway, I'm pretty sure it's of a swimming elephant."

"Yes, likely. We get sent this kind of thing to us at the zoo most months, and I'm always very sceptical. There's lots of ocean still to explore, but the big sea animals have all been found I think."

"The TV reporter was very compelling, she was really believable."

"She?"

"Yes, she."

"I hear that tone in your voice, Jack, so exactly how was 'she' compelling?"

"Stop it right there, Sam," I said, the exquisite form of Sue Driver immediately flashing into my mind.

"Likes an older man, does she?"

"She's a professional newscaster and reporter, and I meant her arguments were compelling. She's a crypto... what did she call it?"

"Cryptozoologist, Jack, someone interested in animals unknown to science."

"That's it, and she mentioned this enormous fish, showed me a photo, it's called a—"

"Whoa Jack." Sam cut me off immediately when I said the word 'fish'. "It was a coelacanth, wasn't it?"

"How d'you guess?"

"All these people, these cryptozoologists who want to believe in living dinosaurs and so on, bring out the old coelacanth before too long."

"She said it was thought to have died out with the dinosaurs, but it looked pretty real to me."

"It's just a fish, Jack. Amazing discovery, sure, found in deep water off Madagascar just before the war."

"Oh."

"And if people have really seen something I'd bet on some kind of whale, maybe a fin. Huge thing, very rare for those waters but could look just like a monster from a distance."

"A fin whale?"

"Yeah, but if you really want to dazzle her, tell this woman that the coelacanth is what we call a 'Lazarus taxon'. She'll love you for it."

"A what?

"An animal thought to be extinct, that came back from the dead as it were."

"Well, you really are a font of useless information, Sam. I'd never have known that."

"Sarky."

"No, sorry, that's all actually really useful, I mean it. Anyway, what's your verdict on the cat and the monster?"

"Well, cat's unlikely by the way you describe the dead sheep, although just possible, but put it this way about the monster. When I was an undergrad, I remember what my old professor said when they had all that fuss in Loch Ness with monster sightings during the thirties." The pips went again, and I thrust several more shillings into the slot.

"What did he say?"

"Sorry, Jack, say again?"

"You mentioned a professor."

"Yes. He said that if there were enough dinosaurs in Loch Ness for a breeding population of monsters then we'd have a forest of necks sticking up out of the water."

"The sea is bigger than Loch Ness though."

"True."

"Anyway, Sam, odds?"

"Well, if I was a betting man, and I had a hundred quid, I'd put half a crown on the sea monster, a fiver on the big cat, and keep the rest for myself."

"Thanks Sam. And I'm pretty sure I already know what this Morgawr really is."

"Do tell."

"No, I need more proof first, but I'll bet you the rest of your hundred quid it ain't no dinosaur."

"Mysterious as ever, Jack, and it sounds to me as if your lady newsreader is out to catch an altogether different kind of dinosaur tonight. You guard your honour, my lad."

"Goodbye, Sam, and thanks for the advice. All of it."

*

Sam's talking about Sue catching a dinosaur took my mind back to my call with Sarah, which had been eating away at the back of my mind all afternoon. I resolved to ring her immediately and took a draft of air in through my nose for courage before dialling. There was one ring, and then the pips went.

"Hello, Sarah. It's Jack. I—"

I was immediately met by a barrage of screaming, the gist of which told me she had seen my interview on network TV news, especially the part with Sue kissing me (I cursed Clip's comment 'just in time for the network news if we're really quick'). The phone at the other end was then slammed down, and despite me dialling back several times, not picked up again. What could I do?

Taking several more deep breaths, I determined to call Sarah's sister in the morning. Perhaps she could cast light on all of this, I wondered, feeling a new sensation when I thought about Sarah, a slight frustration. None of this recent discord felt as if it had been of my doing, but if she wanted it that way, then perhaps I just needed to give her some time. Not letting myself think further, I walked back to the hotel, entering the taproom to see Pasco grinning in front of me.

"Reckon you owe me a pint, Jack. Made you a star."

"No, you've dropped me in it with my wife, so it's you who owes me the drink, Pasco," I snapped. "G and T, Morwenna, make it a large one."

"Sorry for I don't know what," muttered Pasco, lowering his shoulders like a slinking dog. "Put it on my slate, Morwenna."

"If there's room on your slate," she snarled back at Pasco, then passed me my drink with an exaggerated smile.

"Anyway, Sangster," Pasco said. "Me and the lads are out tonight, wanna come?"

"Out tonight," echoed Stocker and Jackson.

"Out where?"

Jackson explained that the landlord (one Jem Treburden), of a local waterside pub, the Cassandra Arms, was being evicted at midnight by the Devenish brewery for, and here he lifted up a newspaper clipping and held it at length from his nose before reading out loud. "'Brawling, pilfering, serving minors, running a house of ill-repute, fencing smuggled goods, failing to pay excise on same, keeping pigs without a permit, brewing and distilling beer and liquor without due license, illicitly gathering and selling Duchy owned oysters, and harbouring known ruffians and criminals', at least that's what the judge apparently declared."

"Was there anything this Treburden character didn't do?"

Jackson admitted that there wasn't much Treburden didn't do, but also noted that the court order didn't question the apparently disreputable landlord's own brewing skills, or, most importantly, his intellect. In fact, it seemed that not only did he brew the best ('you mean strongest' shouted Stocker), rough cider in Cornwall, but had also identified a loophole in his eviction terms.

"You see," Jackson continued, "the landlord of a tied pub like the Cassandra can charge what he likes for drinks, and if he makes a loss that's his problem providing the brewery gets its share. But Treburden's already been evicted, so he figures he can serve what he likes until midnight, and the whole loss'll be on the brewery."

"Clever, eh?" said Stocker.

"I don't quite see."

"To spell it out," shouted Pasco. "He's giving free drinks, it won't cost him a penny, and there's nothing the law can do about it. We're all off there tonight, as is half of Truro, Penryn and Falmouth. Coming, Sangster?"

"You know," I said, thinking of my most recent call with Sarah, as well as the apparently insoluble case of Angel Blackwood. "I believe I will."

"Then meet us down here at eight," said Stocker. "The wife's agreed to drive us."

8PM

I went out to the car park just before the appointed time to see a long, blue Land Rover next to the phone box.

"Going out on the raz?" I heard over my shoulder. It was Slevin, kitted out in riding leathers and standing by his bike.

"I suppose you could call it that."

"Well enjoy and, as I say, don't give in to those earthly temptations that beset the best of us." He bowed low and I walked on, climbing into the back of the Land Rover, where Jackson sat. Stocker and his wife were in the cab.

"Where's Pasco?"

"Took his boat, just after you went upstairs," said Jackson. "Had Pengelly on board, with his bike strapped to the front and all." Jackson's words conjured up a vision of the canon as Jenny, the ship's figurehead at the Fo'c'sle Chandlery, lashed next to his bicycle on the bows of Pasco's dinghy. "The Cassandra is only a few miles down the river, and it's got a landing stage, so they'll both be well settled in by now. Promised to save us places by the bar."

"Good evening, Mrs Stocker," I shouted through a tightly meshed metal grill that separated us in the back from the cab. "Very nice of you to take us."

"It is, isn't it. Maybe a bit too nice, eh Stocker?" David Stocker very wisely neither agreed with his wife nor contradicted her. "Hold tight, and we'll be off."

I then felt the clutch lurch us forwards and the Land Rover begin its journey to the Cassandra, bouncing along, almost as if it had no suspension. Mrs Stocker seemed oblivious to the bumps, and sat clenching the wheel, peering ahead through thick glasses.

"My cousin Pete just redid the shocks," shouted Stocker from the cab. "Smooth as a feather bed, eh?"

"Are they your cousins at the Trafalgar Garage then?"

"Yeah, Pete, Ted and Bob. Best in the business, Sangster."

"I'm sure," I said, jolting as Mrs Stocker drove over a particularly harsh pothole, barely acknowledged by the Land Rover's shock absorbers.

We passed Truro, and then took the main Falmouth road, before negotiating narrow lanes every bit as tortuous as those by King Harry Ferry, the difference tonight being that Mrs Stocker didn't really care about Cornish Hedges (and neither it seemed, did the Land Rover's tyres), so that more than once I was thrown sideways as the wheels hit the stone edgings. For all that, we survived, eventually driving down a frighteningly steep slope to see water beyond.

"There's many an emmet took that hill too fast and ended up in the creek," Jackson laughed. Mrs Stocker then turned a sharp ninety degrees to the right and the pub came into view, illuminated by strings of lightbulbs that already shone in the twilight, and with music blaring outside ('Morgan's Mobile Music Machine' was painted in psychedelic lettering on the side of a van parked next to the pub doorway).

I stepped out, stretching my joints, which ached from the Land Rover's constant buffeting, to see what could definitely be called a 'party' underway. The pub had a large terrace at the front laid out with wooden picnic tables (on top of which people were dancing) and leading from this was a very solid looking pontoon, perhaps stretching one hundred feet out into the creek, presumably so boats could tie up at any time of the tide.

The music was coming from two enormous speakers on tripods (both had 'Morgan' painted on the front), with the DJ ('that's Alfie Morgan, Sangster, did my niece Alice Jackson's wedding'), sitting at a table below, frantically changing discs and shouting into a microphone as he introduced the next record. "This is number three in the charts from Christie and *Yellow River*." A tune with a catchy rhythm then struck up, only for the song to be drowned out by the foghorn of the *Kernow Belle*, which swung alongside the landing stage to disgorge about a hundred people, most of whom ran towards the pub door and the promise of free beer.

"Now come on," Jackson said, "let's go and find Pasco inside. Stocker, you with us?"

"In a mo, in a mo," came the answer, and I looked to see wild gesticulating between Stocker, standing by the open Land Rover door, and (presumably), his wife, still in the cab.

"We'll see you in there," Jackson called.

If the terrace had seemed quite crowded, then the inside of the pub was doubly so and could only be described as heaving. The building comprised impossibly low beams, a network of numerous tiny rooms and several ('narrower than you'd like' as described by Jackson), passages in between them. The nearest to a usable space, given this night's throng of people, was the main saloon, which boasted a long, curved bar with a very broad wooden counter on which were lined up numerous glasses of beer, constantly being emptied by the revellers, with full ones replaced just as quickly by the bar staff.

The lucky few people who had arrived early occupied bar stools, and the rest jostled for an opportunity to take one of the filled glasses. It was a veritable (and literal as beer was being given away) free for all, and fortunately for Jackson and me, one of the 'lucky few' was Pasco, who sat at the end of the bar, having 'reserved' several stools by putting basket covered glass flagons upon them.

"Sangster, Jackson," he shouted. "Come here." He removed two of the flagons, groaning at the weight, and banged them down on the bar. "Where's Stocker?"

"Having a word with the missus," said Jackson. "He's asking her to hang around so she can drive us all home."

"Ah, good luck to him then." Pasco pulled the glasses from mine and Jackson's hands, then shouted behind the bar. "Jem."

On the other side of the saloon, I saw a ruddy faced man of about fifty hold his hand up. He was tall and round, sandy haired with a handlebar moustache and full set of side whiskers and sporting a white apron (which seemed to have suffered from several spillages during the evening). He also wore a peaked yachting cap with a stuffed parrot attached to the side.

"Don't mention the parrot," Pasco whispered to me.

"Why ever not?"

"Makes old Jem sad. He loved that bird. Over a hundred years old when it croaked."

"It was," nodded Jackson.

"You can joke with Jem about most things, but not Nigel."

"He had her stuffed and the bird's feet sewn onto that hat," Jackson added.

"Her?"

"That's right, Sangster." Pasco raised his mug. "Here's to Nigel. Great little talker she was."

"The parrot?"

"That's right, Sangster, African Grey," said Pasco, banging his tankard back down in frustration at my questions. "Ah Jem, let me introduce you to my good friend Jack Sangster. Jack, Jem Treburden, our host and the finest cider maker this side of Saltash."

"Either side of Saltash," said Jackson.

"Evening, Jack."

"Evening, Jem." I offered my hand, then immediately regretted it as a bone crushing grip almost flattened the palm.

"This'll be the Cassandra's last night, so let me give you something to remember the old place by." He passed me a matchbook with a picture of the pub on the front.

"Oh, er, thanks very much." I slipped the book into my coat pocket using somewhat numb fingers.

"Weren't you the chap I saw on TV a bit earlier?" he then asked, squinting sideways at me as I clenched to get some blood back into my fingers. "Talking with a newsreader, Sue Driver?"

"Yes," I sighed.

"Tidy bit of crackling is that Sue Driver, and you know what, Mr er..."

"Jack Sangster."

"She's outside this pub. Tonight."

"What, here?"

"She is, came with her film crew. Now Pasco, you got everything you need?"

"Need some more mugs, Jem," said Pasco. "And by the by, we got one more coming." He pointed to the other stool, still occupied by a flagon.

"Course," said Jem with a good-natured grin, and produced four stone tankards, before expertly pouring flat, greenish-yellow cloudy liquid from a basket flagon into each, somehow leaning the narrow flagon neck across his forearm in a sort of 'backhand' style. This deft trick, Jem said, let him serve with one hand from a vessel weighing thirty pounds or more when full.

"Gents," said Pasco, raising his mug. "Now down in one, to Jem Treburden." We drank, and I felt my throat burn and my eyes water, almost gagging before I emptied my tankard.

"Whad'ya think?" asked Jem.

"Oh, very fine," I said hoarsely while nodding seriously.

"Enough of that and girls'll be all over you."

"How much do I need to drink to make it 'enough'?"

"Not you, them. Get the girls to drink some, open's 'em up. There's a baby in every flagon you know."

"Is there?" I said, coughing over another mouthful.

"Oh yeah, it'll put lead in your pencil as well, and it gets easier to drink after a few, trust me." Jem recharged our tankards, then excused himself.

"We'll take this next one slower, lads," said Jackson. "Don't want to overdo it, eh Pasco?" Pasco nodded, just as Stocker arrived.

"Alright, Stocker?" he said laughing. "Escaped from your own sea monster I see. Now, drink this down."

"Is it all your first pints of cider as well?" Stocker asked, looking at our empty mugs as he appraised his own brim-full tankard.

"No."

"We're on our second," said Jackson. "So easy enough for you to catch up. Just get it down you."

"Second?" said Pasco. "Speak for yourself."

*

After two more of the lethal tankards, I felt it best to, at least temporarily, excuse myself as well.

"Just away to the ablutions," I said to Pasco, before sliding off the bar stool.

"Got your stool covered." He plonked a flagon on top of it almost before I had stood up.

"Thanks." I walked through the saloon, pushing past the occupants as best I could, before coming to the passage that I guessed would lead to the toilets. Before I could find out, however, there was a tap on my shoulder, and I turned to see Canon Pengelly.

"Sangster, fancy seeing you here."

"Pengelly."

"Like a drink? It's free, after all."

"Light beer would be great, but I need the loo. See you back here in a minute?"

"I'll set 'em up."

I walked down the passage and found the appropriate door, which suddenly opened, slamming into my face.

"Oh my God, Sangster." It was Monsignor Slevin. "I'm so sorry, you okay?"

"Okay," I said, rubbing my nose.

"Sure?" I nodded. "Enjoying the evening?"

"I am, Slevin. Didn't expect to see you here."

"Why ever not?"

"Well, you a man of the cloth and everything. Although..." I was about to say that he didn't look like a priest but thought better of it. "Why not?" I said instead.

"Why not indeed. See you later." He walked back up the passage, and I into the gents, emerging a few minutes later to find Pengelly standing by the passage entrance and holding two glasses of beer. He was staring intently across the room, so didn't notice me at first, and I followed his gaze to see Slevin standing deep in conversation with a familiar figure, Professor Jos Polkinghorne.

"Hah," Pengelly eventually said to himself, then turned to see me. "Sangster, I got you a beer. Saw you on TV this evening as well. Not sure anyone else did mind."

"Oh, everyone else did, rest assured."

"You sound like you're carrying a burden. Care to share?"

"Well, no, I..."

"It's alright, we can talk without me insisting you sign up to attend evensong."

"I'm not, how shall we say, getting on with my wife," I then heard myself blurt out. "Thinks I'm going to be unfaithful to her, and I don't know why. It's not my fault though, that's for sure."

"Isn't it?"

"Course not, Pengelly. I'd know, I've never strayed, I'd—"

"Matthew, Chapter 5, Verse 28," he almost shouted. "But I say to you that everyone who looks at a woman with lustful intent has already committed adultery with her in his heart."

"What?"

"Well, have you?"

"Perhaps, but it's only natural to look, I didn't do anything."

"Your wife doesn't see it that way."

"Then what do I do? Wear a blindfold in front of other women."

"Perhaps she has been hurt, in the past maybe?"

"I don't know."

"Then find out, and if you love her, keep your head, no matter how she behaves. That's what she needs from you."

"Sound advice," I nodded. "Sound."

"I do hope so, Sangster, I... ugh." Across the room, Slevin now had his arm across Polkinghorne's shoulders, the two engrossed in deep and close conversation. Pengelly banged his glass down and went to walk towards them.

"No Simeon," I said, holding him back by the shoulder.

"You're right," he muttered. "Do as I say, not do as I do. But..." he added, looking with anger at the two men who were now openly embracing. "That's enough, and I'll not be made a fool of. I want to see you tomorrow, can you come into Truro?"

"Sure. I've a car mechanics appointment at, er... about ten. What do you want to see me about?"

"Never mind for now and meet me at the Three Spires Café."

"Where?"

"In Cathedral Lane. Just be there and I'll tell you some things you need to know."

"But about what?"

"Until tomorrow, eleven sharp?" He left down the passage, and I didn't see Pengelly again that evening (presumably he went home on his bike). I did see Slevin though, as a moment later he passed me.

"Weak bladder tonight," he said, winking as he walked in the direction of the gents. "Yet another piss."

I laughed, then decided some fresh air might be good, and squeezed my way to the outside terrace, where the music had temporarily stopped, making for a relative calm.

"Sangster, well fancy meeting you out here."

My immediate instinct on hearing this was that Pasco had come to find me, but I turned round to see Jos Polkinghorne, smiling, pint in hand.

"Professor."

"Do I still look like one?"

"Oh, entirely."

"Good, because I've news for you. Was going to call you tomorrow but seeing as we're here."

"Yes?"

"That dagger. Your girl's going to be disappointed."

"If we ever find her."

"Of course, Sangster, I didn't mean it to come out that way. Point is though, dagger's a modern replica."

"Really?"

"Yes," said Polkinghorne. "Miss Trimble chased up Imperial College this afternoon and it seems they hadn't understood the urgency. Did all the tests a while ago and were going to send us a full written report." He sipped his beer then put the glass down and held up his hands. "And to be honest, I never actually said to the guys at Imperial it was urgent either."

"And what did they tell you? On the phone that is."

"That the copper comes from America. Great Lakes region. Unmistakable."

"I thought you claimed, well…"

"Well, what?"

"Well… that you could identify any kind of copper."

"Any kind we use today. This stuff was mined by Indians, thousands of years ago."

"But you… you…," I stumbled in my words, the cider beginning to catch up with me. "Think the knife is modern."

"It is," he said with the kind of sigh that said he was having to explain as he would to a child. "Look, you often get stuff made in America using existing bronze melted down from old Indian statues and so on, which were made of a simple alloy of just copper and tin. And I believe that's what we have here."

"Are you sure?"

"Pretty much. I mean, this Great Lakes copper source was mined out more than a thousand years before Columbus discovered America, so it can't have been fresh copper, can it. Ergo…"

"Ergo…" I copied.

"Dagger's modern. Might be a hundred or more years old, but still pretty new compared with the Phoenicians."

"What about all that old writing on it?"

"Like I say, a modern replica, perhaps a fake antique, but made by who I couldn't say. Not my department."

"Okay."

"I'll post you a copy of the report when I get it, but for now, I'll leave you if I may."

"Thanks Jos, that's useful stuff, even if I feel I've gone one step backwards now."

"Good evening, Jack."

*

I went back into the saloon, not sure if I felt better or worse for my talks with Pengelly and Polkinghorne, but definitely feeling pain for Pengelly, and Angel still never far from my thoughts. I was also still off balance from my spat with Sarah, and I had to admit, the thought of Sue Driver disturbed that balance further.

Pasco was still holding court at the corner of the bar, so I returned to my stool, and took another tankard of cider. The conversation was disjointed, with Stocker and Jackson now well on the way to catching up Pasco.

After about twenty minutes of this I began to lose concentration. Looking vacantly around the room, I noticed a collection of framed photographs on the adjacent wall, clearly very old by their sepia hue and the dress style of the subjects, which were either miners or fishermen. One photo particularly caught my eye, as the title underneath was 'The closing of Bethadew mine, AD 1859'. A line of men, dressed in mining helmets and smocks, posed in front of the pump house building, and beside them were several figures dressed in frock coats and stove-pipe hats, presumably the mine owners. But what struck me most of all was a figure to the right of the main crowd. He stood watching the proceedings, and I had to shake myself when I realised the man looked exactly like the tramp, even down to the staff and the long, buttoned-up coat. The picture was faded though, and as with most very early photos it was hard to tell detail, so I squinted for a moment then looked away, to see someone I recognised on the far side of the saloon (at least semi-recognised). It was Ana Woon, standing amongst a large group and now dressed in jeans, sneakers and a blue and white striped jumper, hair in a ponytail and looking (to me), years younger than she did in a police uniform.

"That's someone I know, Pasco. Save my chair please."

"Guard it with my life, Jack," he yelled as I walked across to the group.

"Jack," said Ana, waving. "How lovely to see you."

"And you, Ana. A bit crazy in here, isn't it?"

"Yeah, but all legal, at least for now."

"Landlord found a rather nice loophole in his contract I hear."

"This is Richard," she said, thrusting a slim, blond-haired young man towards me. "And Richard, this is the man I was telling you about."

"Commander Sangster," he said, holding out his hand. "It's a pleasure."

"All mine," I answered. "And if your young lady here tells you anything other than she's destined for great things in the force, then don't believe her." He said nothing, and I wondered if I (or Treburden's cider), had said too much. Luckily, the awkward silence was broken by none other than Sergeant Nick Bolitho.

"Hello Serana, Richard. I've brought you a couple of drinks. Pint of Saxon for you isn't it Richard, and Serana, you're on rum and coke?"

"Well, er…" Ana stuttered. "Yes, that is what we're drinking. Thanks a lot."

"Just wanted to pop over," he said, handing over the glasses. "By the way," he winked. "Make yourselves scarce by about half eleven."

"Why's that?" Richard asked.

"Dot of midnight there's going to be a raid. Brewery have enlisted the police to help reclaim the property. Anticipating trouble, that's the rumour, so they'll come ready for it, armed and dangerous."

"Thanks, Nick," said Ana.

"And Commander Sangster, nice to see you, sir." I nodded, and Bolitho left.

"He didn't bring you a drink, Jack," said Ana.

"Good thing. I've been drinking Jem's cider."

"Heard of that," she laughed. "But let me at least get you a beer." I acquiesced with a nod, and she reached out to the bar and grabbed me a glass. "There we are, Jack, a half of Saxon. Now cheers." We raised our glasses, and I watched as Richard, clearly devoted to this lovely young woman by the look in his eyes, stood guard as she sipped her drink. I asked him about his job, and he explained he worked with computers, which meant little to me.

"Richard's working for Carrick District Council at the moment," said Ana. "Biggest computer in Cornwall."

"Computers are the only thing I'm good at," Richard added. "But I don't know if computers'll really catch on enough for me to make a career of it. Probably have to live off Ana when we marry."

"And that'll be just fine," Ana said, placing her arm tightly around Richard's waist.

"Ahem… you never know, computers just might catch on," I said, finding the cuddle a little embarrassing. We stood and made more small talk for a few minutes, then Ana jerked her head towards Richard, who muttered something about going to the gents.

"Jack, can we go outside, we need to talk."

"Sure," I said, and took her by the arm, weaving through the throng in the bar, eventually getting out into the fresh air to find the terrace leading down to the pontoon similarly packed with people, and it seemed even more revellers had arrived in the short time since I'd left Polkinghorne on the terrace.

"And now, for all you lovers out there," said Alfie Morgan in hushed tones down the microphone. "And as a thank you to Jem Treburden for putting this night on." An enormous shout went up. "And for the ever-thoughtful Devenish brewery, along with the ever-generous Launceston County Courts, for paying for our beer and not being able to do anything about it." An even bigger shout went up. "It's Elvis, and 'Can't Help Falling In Love.'"

"Tell me over a dance," I said to Ana, the cider behaving exactly as Jem had foretold.

"How could I refuse, Commander."

The rich tones of the 'King' then echoed through the evening air, as we held each other and turned around the waterfront, in a close-but-not-too-close manner appropriate (I felt) to the nature of our relationship.

"So Jack, I spoke to my mum…"

"I can't hear you, Ana."

"Then let's move." We twirled across the terrace, away from Morgan's PA and towards the edge of the water. "So, I spoke to my mum this afternoon, just on the off chance, and I think I struck lucky."

"How?"

"Angel's been sending telegrams from her post office."

"You sure?"

"Yes, Mum recognised her picture. I'll give the details to the chief super first thing tomorrow."

"Did you learn anything?"

"Angel was communicating with someone in London, that's all I can tell. Very careful what she said. Reckon it was in some sort of code."

"What, odd symbols?" I asked, thinking of Angel's notebook, and wondering how these could be sent via a wire.

"No, just weird sentences. Mumbo jumbo, so I think it can only have been code, like I say. That's what I'd do if I was her."

"You're a bright lass." We returned to dancing. "And I mean it. You've been thinking out of that box, just as I suggested you should." She said nothing, we continued dancing until the track stopped, and then said our goodbyes. I went to walk back to the bar, but she caught my arm.

"Come on, Jack, one more dance for me."

"Alright, one more. Let's see what they…"

"This is Fleetwood Mac, girls and boys," crooned the DJ, "and 'Need Your Love So Bad'. If you can't feel your love in this song, you don't have a heart."

I sensed my mind falling, the antiquity of this waterside pub, the perfume of this young woman dancing with me, my separation from Sarah, the racing mystery of Angel Blackwood that surrounded everything I did, and even the wildness of the revellers as they caroused at the brewery's expense, the voices, the lights, the water, the music, all merging into one spinning dream. And as I dreamed, the music played, and I swayed with Ana.

"What does your name mean?" I asked her.

"Well," she said, looking up at me. "Serana was a saint, who gave her name to Zennor."

"Who's Zennor."

"Not who, Jack, where. It's a Cornish village. Serana was a Breton princess, maybe even a mermaid."

"That's nice."

"At least I think she was, but Jack…"

"Yes."

"Nick Bolitho's been strangely nice to me."

"What do you mean," I said, pulling away from her, ready to go back into the pub and face the sergeant.

"No, 'nice' nice. He brought me a cup of tea this afternoon, took me into a corner and said if I needed his help, anything at all, to just let him know. And you saw this evening in the bar, he brought us drinks over."

"Clearly begun to appreciate your qualities."

We then danced in silence, serenaded by a mournful guitar solo.

"I don't think he has, Jack," Ana said as the solo finished, and the verse recommenced. "I think somebody said something." I remained silent, and we danced on until the music stopped. "You didn't need to do that," she then whispered. "Frighten Nick on my account, I mean."

"I'm sorry, Ana."

"Why are you sorry?"

"I shouldn't have got involved, it just incensed me, the arrogance of the man, what he thought he could get away with, and after all the work you'd done, I—"

"No, you have me wrong. I couldn't be more grateful, and I can't imagine anyone but you being able to, oh I don't know…" she went silent, and then threw her arms around me. "Thank you."

I said nothing.

"You don't have any kids yourself, do you, Jack?"

"Is it that obvious?"

"You'd have liked a daughter, wouldn't you?"

"Go and find Richard," I said. "And I'll see you tomorrow."

I returned to the bar, only to find Pasco, Stocker and Jackson deep in a political argument (about what I couldn't quite tell). I picked up a mug and one of the cider flagons then went back outside, sitting down at one end of a picnic table, where the occupants began to eye my flagon jealously. I imagined people felt any booze was fair game this evening and cradled the basket tight with both arms.

"Well, you are a dark horse." I recognised the baritone of Sue Driver over my shoulder.

"Er, am I?" I answered, quickly releasing the flagon.

"Dancing the night away with that young thing."

"She's a policewoman I'm working with I'll have you know, Sue, and anyway, the night's not 'away' yet."

"Well, it will be away if you keep drinking that rough cider," she laughed, picking up the basket flagon. "You'll be no good to anybody, so I'll take that."

"I think my liver owes you an everlasting debt of gratitude."

"Ha. Now come on, let's walk up to the landing stage at the end of the pontoon and look at the moon in the water. On the way you can tell me about all of your innermost torments."

"No pontoon's long enough for that, Sue, but lead on anyway."

And on we went, she stepping carefully, the gaps between the pontoon planks making for a high-heel trap, and the weight of the cider flagon affecting her balance as the floating pier rocked to the tread of our feet.

"Oh, that cider really is rough," she said, eyes watering when she took a swig from the flagon as we reached the landing stage.

"Ciggy?" she then asked, pulling out a pack from her handbag.

"Gave up."

"I don't suppose you could light me?" She placed the cigarette between her lips.

"You're in luck." I pulled out the matchbook Jem Treburden gave me and, using a trick I'd been taught by a petty officer during the course of one very long and uneventful voyage, with one hand, bent a match, struck it still attached with my thumb and held the book open, the flap cradling the flame from any wind.

"Jack, you have hidden talents," Sue said, smoke curling from her mouth, as I suddenly staggered, somewhat spoiling the suave effect of the matchbook trick as well as making the landing stage rock back and forth.

"Not sure if it's the water or the cider, or perhaps you've made the earth move for me, but this decking's quite the rollercoaster."

"How like life," I added, immediately realising that even with the 'Jem's cider' excuse, this wasn't exactly sparkling wit and repartee. "Sorry, talking gibberish."

"S'okay, Jack, gibberish permitted at this time of night, and I heard all about the missing girl by the way. Didn't like to say when we were at the hotel." She was quiet for a moment. "I'm staying there tonight by the way. At the Watersmeet."

"Mmmm…" I nodded.

"I guess it's been a long week for you."

"Yeah Sue, and it's not over." She looked back towards the pub.

"Do you ever get gut feelings, Jack?"

"Sure, all the time."

"Well so do I, and right now they're about this Morgawr. All my life I've wanted to find some animal, some creature nobody else knew existed. This is my chance, I feel it."

"So how come you became a newsreader?"

"Gotta pay the bills, Jack."

We both stared into the darkness.

"I just might have something for you," I blurted out after some minutes, fairly sure I wanted to tell her about the submarine, and that it wasn't just the cider speaking.

"Really?"

"Yes, and your monster's probably not what you think it is."

"Oh Jack, don't keep me guessing…"

"Tomorrow, I think, or maybe the next day…"

"You're a truly sadistic man, Jack Sangster," she said, flicking her cigarette butt into the water then kissing me on the cheek. "Making me wait like that, but for you I'll do it."

"As soon as I know, I'll leave a message at the hotel with Morwenna."

"Alright, now don't go away, I just need to powder my nose."

"Be my guest, Sue, but nobody'll mind if you get your compact out right now."

"Oh, you know what I mean you naughty boy, and you keep this as well." She plonked the cider flagon on the ground by my feet. "Back in a sec, Jack."

I sat down on the edge of the pontoon and looked across the creek. Ahead all was still, with the light of the half-moon looking as if it was indeed 'in the water', as Sue had said. Other than that, the flat, black surface reflected the few house lights on the far bank, with the distant night silent bar an echo from the occasional bird call, while the lights and din of the Cassandra's last night went on. Two different worlds, one behind me and one in front, I thought to myself. Taking out the picture of Sarah from my wallet I stared. What would she think of everything that was happening? She always had a different view, and I missed her voice, her warmth. And my goodness, I thought as I looked at the photo, Sarah really was very pretty. Did I deserve her?

I swigged from the flagon and remembered Pengelly's advice. Perhaps I could speak with Sarah's sister and ask if there was a reason for her distrust that I didn't understand.

Or was that reason me, and that was what I didn't understand?

I'll call Rachel tomorrow morning first thing, and then call Sarah and tell her I love her, I said to myself as the music droned on, now playing some sort of Cornish anthem that, judging by the singing, all the revellers knew. At first, I thought they sang, 'Little Eyes', but then as I listened to the chorus, I realised they were singing about 'Little Lies'.

I tried hard but in vain to follow as the lyrics became more and more incomprehensible, my thoughts wandering back to Sarah until interrupted by a voice from behind.

"You like movies, Jack?"

I looked up to see Sue, returned from 'powdering her nose'.

"Come and sit here," I said, patting the side of the pontoon next to me. Pulling off her shoes, Sue then gracefully lowered herself and slid along the planks until she was sitting next to me, feet dangling over the end of the jetty.

"Got to mind the splinters," she laughed, wriggling so that her short skirt covered the backs of her legs.

"Oh yes, Sue. Splinters. Got to mind those."

"So, you like the old movie stars?"

"Ner, I'm not a great film buff."

"Why do you keep that picture then?"

"What picture?" Jem Treburden's cider was now really baffling my senses.

"That one in your hand. Hedy Lamarr?"

"Ah no, that's Sarah."

"Who?"

"My wife."

"You don't wear a ring?"

"None of the men in my family did."

"Taken when she was younger?"

"A few days ago."

I felt Sue's hand heavy on my shoulder as she pulled herself up and put her shoes back on.

"She's a lucky girl. What's her name again?"

"Sarah."

"Goodnight, Jack." She bent down and kissed me on the top of the head, then walked back along the pontoon.

I sat for a few more minutes watching the dark creek, then went to find Stocker, whose wife had (somewhat implausibly), waited for us in the Land Rover after all.

12 MIDNIGHT

"Jump up, Sangster," shouted Jackson through the rear door, and I climbed in to see Stocker (who it seemed was banned from sitting up front in the cab), and Pasco, who was slumped on the right-hand bench.

"Five to twelve," I said, looking at my watch. "I heard a tip off that the police will be here in a minute. Better get going."

"Mabel," shouted Stocker. "I'm not being funny, now put your foot on it."

The car engine eventually spat into life (after several turnovers where it threatened to start then faded to a halt again, thanks I felt sure, to the recent attentions of the Stocker cousin car mechanics). I was about to pull the door shut when I heard sirens, then saw flashing lights, as police cars careered down the hill, racing past us and screeching to a halt on the terrace, causing revellers to scatter in every direction.

"We got some new guests here, let's give 'em a Cassandra welcome," shouted Alfie Morgan, upping his volume before beginning to play 'Satisfaction' by the Rolling Stones.

A long, blue police van then arrived, and about a dozen uniformed officers sprang out, armed with shields and batons. Then I heard a splash and looked round to see a car landing in the river at the bottom of the hill, water up to the bottom of its windows. 'Devenish Brewery, Weymouth' was printed on the side, and I watched as the occupants began to crawl out, safe but very wet.

"Ha, that'll be the brewery men," laughed Stocker. "Didn't I say emmets can't handle that hill?"

"That you did," said Jackson solemnly. "And look at that lot on the pontoon." He pointed to where an angry looking crowd stood shouting at the stern lights of the *Kernow Belle* as it made a rapid exit down the creek, the skipper presumably deciding to leave quickly and forgetting to tell his passengers.

I watched as the police then set to work, serenaded by the Rolling Stones, and shouting through megaphones for the crowd to leave the pub and its grounds and disperse or face the consequences. The officers with the shields lined themselves in a rank, and waited for a few seconds, before a cry of 'Draw batons' rang out from one of the megaphones, and they charged. I watched revellers go down one after the other, some that resisted being snatched and taken to the vans, others left cowering on the floor. More officers then entered the pub door, where seconds later people emerged, running frantically this way and that. Then a window burst, followed by another, and finally, flames appeared.

"He's on fire, Cassandra is aflame," yelled Pasco (the noise and light apparently raising him from his cider induced slumber), as I suddenly heard my name being called.

"Jack, is that you?"

"Yes," I shouted, seeing Sue Driver running towards us, high heels in her hand, and followed closely by Nora. Click and Jimmy were further behind, both facing backwards as they ran, Click with his mic boom and Jimmy filming with a portable TV camera.

"Jimmy, Click," yelled Nora. "Never mind that."

Jimmy then jumped sideways to avoid a newly arriving police van and took the very sensible decision to stop filming. I pulled Sue up with both hands, then did the same with the film crew, and was about to close the door when I saw Jem Treburden panting along the terrace, holding an enormous carpet bag under one arm.

"Wait for me," he shouted, and we did, pulling him up as well (it took me, Stocker and Jackson to heave him aboard), then, closing the door, Stocker signalling to Mabel it was time to go. She needed no encouragement, and in a few moments, we were in the quiet of the narrow lanes, the pub (perhaps now entirely on fire), merely a glow above the trees behind us.

"Jack, you are my hero for ever," said Sue, leaning her head on my shoulder.

"Did we get all that Click?" said Nora.

"Saved something from it all," said Pasco, pointing to a flagon of cider at his feet.

"Lost Nigel," said Jem, patting his bare head.

FRIDAY,
MAY THE 29TH
8 AM

"Morning Harry… yes, I know it's early but… yes I'm still in Cornwall… is Rachel there… thanks."

I waited for a minute or so as the sound of children's voices echoed down the phone, then heard my sister-in-law's voice.

"Jack, is everything alright?"

"I'm fine, Rachel, and sorry for the early call but I need to—"

"Just hang on." I heard her shout to her husband. "Harry, take Charlie and Ruth into the front room, would you, I need some peace and quiet." The background noise subsided. "Now what's the matter?"

"Does there need to be something the matter?"

"Come on, Sarah called me yesterday in a dreadful state."

"Alright, look, without beating about the bush, it's like this…" I told Rachel that Sarah, no matter what I did, worried about me being unfaithful, about being not good enough for me, about being unable to bear children.

"It's all nonsense, she's out of my league, everyone knows that."

"Some people wouldn't say that."

"But just look at her."

"Certainly always the beauty of the family, Jack."

"And clever, everyone knows that as well."

"Always the brains of the family too."

"And I never gave her any reason to—"

"Well hold on, Jack. Have you ever asked yourself why she might be worried she'll lose you?"

"Of course."

Rachel sighed down the phone.

"Really?"

"Well, maybe not when you put it like that, I…"

"Do you love her?"

"Yes."

"Then talk to her about the reason she can't have children. Now then, I've got kids to feed and a husband to get out of the house, so bye-bye, Jack."

It took me what seemed like an age to dial our home number, and when I did, I felt my heart drop when the pips went.

"Sarah?"

Silence.

"It's me, Jack. I love you."

"And I love you." I could hear her sob as she said this.

"I want you to come down here. Tomorrow."

"Alright," she sniffed. "It was my fault, Jack."

"No, it was mine."

"Don't be such an, oh, I don't know… blithering idiot."

"You sound like Sir John."

"That was the idea, slowcoach," she laughed. We spoke a little more, mainly trivia, then went to say our goodbyes. Then, just as she was about to hang up, I asked her.

"Sarah, is there something I don't know, something you want to tell me?"

"About what, darling?"

"Look," I said. "Cards on the table. I was so worried I spoke to Rachel, and she said that—"

"Did she now."

"That there might be a reason you can't, well, you know, children…"
I heard her cry loudly down the phone and looked out of the call box
to make sure there was nobody within earshot.

"I suppose the phone's not too good a place to tell you, Jack, but
there never will be a good place, or time, so here goes…"

Sarah talked about meeting me on a cruise to Israel and Egypt
when she was still in her late twenties, and I was recently divorced. My
ex-wife, Eileen, who suffered from Huntington's Chorea, the wasting
disease of the mind that gives every generation a fifty-fifty chance, was
still alive at the time, and this had been an emotional burden for Sarah.
I still wasn't sure she'd overcome the guilt (which wasn't justified at all),
and had always thought this burden, as well as her being unable to bear
children, the reasons for the periodic insecurity. After all, Sarah was
a beautiful woman, highly educated and more than twenty years my
junior. Why else would she be insecure?

"You see Jack, with everything to do with Eileen, I never got the
chance to tell you."

"Tell me what?"

"About Frank."

"No, you never mentioned a Frank."

"Then let me tell you now…"

She was, she said, studying for a psychology masters at
Manchester when she met Frank, a senior lecturer who immediately
caught her eye.

"I was twenty-two, he was thirty-seven. Never underestimate the
charm of the older man to the younger girl, Jack, no matter how bright
and logical she thinks she is."

"I, er… won't."

"Well, we dated, and Frank was kind, super clever, funny, took me
to all sorts of places, dazzled my friends, so that within a few days I
was head over heels in love."

"Sounds just like me, except for the kind, super clever, funny,
taking you to places and dazzling your friends parts."

193

"No," she snapped down the phone. "Stop making a joke of it. He's nothing compared with you, nothing."

"Sorry."

"So," Sarah continued, voice returning to normal. "Then I found out, doesn't matter how, just after we first slept together, that he was married. I confronted him and he didn't deny it."

"How did you find out?"

"Stupid really, I knocked his wallet off a dressing table and a wedding ring fell out, and when I asked him if it was his he didn't even try to deny it. Anyway, that was that, until I began to experience symptoms."

"Symptoms?"

"Yes. You don't need to hear the gory details, but it hurt when I, you know…"

"Had sex?"

"Yes, I had a couple of partners after that then gave up. I also had pain in my tummy, which got worse and worse. By the time I was checked out it was too late."

"You were okay when we met, weren't you?"

"I'd been treated by then, and the thing was all cleared up, but the scar tissue on my tubes had already done its worst." She began to sob. "There Jack, what do you think of me now?"

"I think…" I said, for a few seconds lost for any more words, my mind spinning with emotion, not confused emotion, but a tremendous throbbing warmth for Sarah, a throbbing that made me feel twice as alive. "I think, I love you and I want you here for a while."

"Oh Jack, I'll make sure I can get some time off… and you know, there's something in your voice."

"As long as you are okay, then I'm okay, and right now, knowing you're coming down here, everything seems connected."

"Connected?"

"Yes, somehow, although the girl's still missing."

"Then use that. Such feelings don't come calling all the time. Use your instincts to find that girl, as only you can. And you know what?"

"No."

"If you do, I think you'll find her before the day is out."

*

"I've not said anything in the past," said Morwenna. "But I want to say now, it's an odd breakfast that one." She cleared away my plate and refilled my coffee cup. "We never had anyone else ask for an egg white omelette."

"I did have kippers at the weekend."

"Agreed, but Nob don't know what to do with all the leftover yokes."

"You charge me for them I hope?"

"Oh yes, all goes on your bill, but why just the whites?"

"It was a navy cook years ago first made me one that way, and well, I just feel it's healthier, don't ask me why." I raised my coffee cup. "Good way to start the day after a run as well, that and a bit of fruit."

"And running each morning, you'll do yourself a mischief. Mind you, you got a good figure Jack, and…" She placed her hand on my thigh before I could protest. "Your leg muscles certainly seem in shape."

"Suppose you heard about the Cassandra?"

"Oh God yes. Heard it on the radio. Place almost burned down to the ground. Thatched roof caught fire they said, scores of arrests as well. Had to laugh when I saw all those Devenish folks stuck in their car in the river though."

"One up for the St Austell Brewery, eh?"

"Of course, Jack." She looked up at the 'St Austell Ales' sign above the bar and smiled. "But you got back safe?"

"Yes, it was pretty hairy at the end though. I was glad to get away."

"Glad all my boys got home safe then," she said, presumably referring to Stocker, Jackson, and Pasco, as well it seemed, as me, now elevated to be an honorary 'Morwenna's boy'.

"Is Slevin still here?"

"No, that priest left first thing. Paid cash, went on his way, and I don't miss him."

"Okay," I said, watching her trying to pull a pint from a beer pump. "Bit early for a drink isn't it?"

"It's the weather."

"The weather?"

"Just checking the barrels. The proper ale like Hicks, not the lager or the keg bitter with the gas, won't pull properly when there's a storm coming. Hicks don't like low pressure storms."

"We're due rain on Sunday," I said, looking out of the taproom window at the blue sky.

"No Jack, the ale never lies," she said, repeatedly pulling at a beer pump handle. "There's a weather front coming in fast, and 'e's a nasty one. Be here tonight latest, so if you're going out, take a raincoat."

"I'll do that."

"And you know, Jack, it's been a funny spring all round, weather wise. Garlic's really late."

"Garlic?"

"In the woods. Normally smell garlicy in March, but this year, why, I was out walking the other day and the air was still thick with it."

I decided it was time to go.

"May I ask," I said, as I stood up to leave, a comment from Pasco suddenly coming to the forefront of my mind ('Morwenna speaks better Cornish than me'). "What your name means?"

"Ooooh, never thought you'd ask, Jack," she replied, with her tell-tale flirtatious hair adjustment.

"No, really, could have some bearing on the missing-girl case."

"If you want to know then, 'waves of the sea' or more exactly…" She adjusted her hair again. "The white spray you sometimes see on top of the waves."

"Poldhu?"

"Ah, no that's Morwenna."

"So, in Cornish, Poldhu means?"

"Black lake, only the other way round. 'Pol' for lake, 'dhu' for black."

"Impressive. Pasco did say you knew more Cornish than him."

"Taught by my granny," she said. "I couldn't have a long conversation in the old tongue, but I know plenty of words."

"And do you know if there's any other meaning of 'dhu'?"

"None that I can think of. Nearest would be 'duw', which you'd actually pronounce more like 'dee-ooh', but nobody would have that in their name."

"Why not?"

"It means God."

"And 'well'?"

"Like a hole in the ground where you find water?"

"Yes, but a word that sounds like well."

She put her hand on her chin and seemed lost in thought for almost a minute (the longest I could remember Morwenna being silent during any conversation).

"Nearest might be 'Hwel'," she said at last. "What they now say as 'Wheal'." She pronounced this 'Hweel'. "Means a mine and sounds a bit like 'well' in English."

"And 'Betha'?"

"No such word that I know of."

"If we broke it down, 'Beth' and 'a'?"

She put her hand on her chin again.

"Ah, a word like grave, or maybe tomb."

"Tomb?"

"Could be a tomb Jack, but… now what was it… yes, now I remember," said Morwenna. "Granny and I once went to a village church up near Bodmin, and she used that word 'Beth'. To do with Easter it was."

"Easter?"

"Yes, Easter Sepulchre she said it was in English, and now I see."

"What do you see?"

"Something," she said, looking at me with an uncharacteristically serious expression. "I don't know what you're getting at, Jack," she then said, now with no. "But put together, that would all translate as 'Sepulchre of God Mine', but hang on, no it wouldn't." Her eyes lightened and she laughed. "You're talking about Bethadew Well, aren't you?" I nodded. "It would have to be called Bethawhealdew to mean Sepulchre of God, so they're not the same Jack. Dunno why I went on so about it."

10AM

An hour or so later, my yellow oilskin lying on the passenger seat (I didn't dare to remove the elastic holding down the boot lid and pack it in the back), I drove to Truro and my assignation with Pengelly as well as my car's assignation with the Stockers. As when driving home the evening before, I began going over what I knew, the riverside road once again somehow helping my concentration. This, along with a newfound sense of wellbeing after talking to Sarah, bestowed an enhanced clarity of purpose and the lifting of what had started as a stinking cider-induced hangover, eased away by a longer than usual morning run (a scalding hot bath and the egg white omelette breakfast may also have helped).

Cyrus Flimwell was clearly the 'T' in Angel's note, and I resolved to challenge him on this, especially given what Spider had said. Whether I should go through the formal channels of the institute or not I couldn't yet decide, but the fact remained that the principal of the school had made advances towards an underage girl who had now been missing for five days.

Then there was the Sepulchre of God Mine. I'd somehow felt closer to Angel as Morwenna, step-by-step, arrived at this strange

Cornish translation of Bethadew Well, but her last comment had been deflating ('so they're not the same Jack. Dunno why I went on so about it'). I tutted to myself 'you've succumbed to wishful thinking again Sangster, it's a red herring'. Nevertheless, I couldn't help wondering...

*

"Ah, Mr Sangster," said Pete Stocker, as I pulled up in front of the shed that was 'Stocker's Body Shop – all makes catered for'. "Bob'll be along any time now I shouldn't wonder."

"When shall I come to collect it," I said, handing him the keys.

"Two o'clock I'd say. Ted," he called into the shed, "when do you think he should come and collect it?"

"Two o'clock sounds about right," echoed the reply from within.

"There, we're all in agreement," beamed Pete (I couldn't quite see how they knew when they would finish, given there was no sign of Bob turning up with the parts, but said nothing).

"Hey," shouted Ted, "you hear about the Cassandra last night?"

"I was there, with your cousin David."

"David alright, is he? Heard it got a bit wild."

"Yes, he's fine. Mrs Stocker rescued us, just as it started getting really bad."

"Ah, bloody fine woman, Mabel, salt of the earth."

"She certainly saved our bacon last night. Anyway, I'll see you at two. Take a cheque?"

"Cash if you wouldn't mind."

*

I stepped out of Martins Bank onto Boscowen Street, Truro's cobbled main thoroughfare. Patting my inside jacket pocket to make sure the wad of notes I'd just withdrawn was secure, I felt the large bag of silver coins in my trouser pocket (changed up with the bank teller for phone calls) rubbing uncomfortably. Cathedral Lane didn't seem to be in

200

the immediate vicinity, so I walked for at least ten minutes around some back roads towards the spires that rose up behind the parades of shops, eventually finding myself in front of an imposing triple-towered gothic building that proclaimed itself, on a large white sign outside the main gate:

Cathedral of the Blessed Virgin Mary – See notice board for
service times

'Cathedral Lane', said a street sign on the corner of a narrow alley opposite and, turning into it, I saw the Three Spires Café, halfway down on the left. Good timing, I thought, as the cathedral clock chimed eleven times.

Pengelly was already there, waving to me from a secluded alcove, where he sat hunched, a solitary cup in front of him and a maroon leather attaché case leaning against his chair leg. I explained to a waitress that I was meeting the man in the corner and ordered a coffee.

"Morning, Pengelly, I just asked for a coffee. Did you want anything else?" He shook his head. "You managed to get away early last night?"

"That's right, cycled home straight after I spoke to you."

"You missed the fun then?"

"Didn't sound like too much fun to me, pub burning down. Nobody hurt, was there?"

"No, nobody hurt by the fire," I said solemnly, wondering how many had been hurt by the police baton charge.

"God be blessed."

"Coffee sir?"

"Thank you," I said, as Pengelly, apparently oblivious to the waitress's presence, placed his head in his hands and then laid his head down, cheek to one side, on the table.

"Sit up, Pengelly." I tapped him on the shoulder, speaking as quietly as I could. "And please, tell me what's troubling you."

"Remember our talk in the taproom the other night?" I nodded.

"Well, I tried to do the right thing as you said, and it got me nowhere."

"How do you mean?"

"I've been used, Sangster, used. You saw Slevin with that Polkinghorne bloke, didn't you?" I nodded again. "Won't be made a fool of," he then muttered, resting his head back on the table.

"What did you ask me here for?"

"Very well," he sighed, sitting upright once more, to the interest of several other customers who glanced sideways at us until I caught their eyes. "I need to let you know everything I know."

"Then you'd better have another cup of coffee, excuse me."

"Yes sir?"

"Two more coffees please." I turned back to Pengelly. "And we've plenty of time. I'm not going anywhere right now because my car's being fixed."

Once the cups were brought, Pengelly related a story that only a week before would have seemed to me outlandish in the extreme. Very soon after he had begun teaching at the academy, he said, Angel had piqued his curiosity. Her interest in everything, her ability to absorb knowledge, all the exceptional attributes I'd heard about from her friends and teachers, all those that Pengelly had already told me he admired so much.

But it was when he held a lecture at the academy on the legend of Jesus in Cornwall that his bond with Angel really began. His ideas had mainly been met with derision, the gifted children tearing his arguments into shreds, to the point he had stopped the lecture and stormed out of the room. Angel had followed, telling him she wanted to know more and that she had already begun to formulate her own ideas from this single, unfinished lecture.

Angel then showed Pengelly the dagger she had found but, despite his insistence, refused to hand it over to him for analysis. Pengelly nevertheless became very excited after this one glimpse of the dagger, as the blade's markings (which he couldn't translate but recognised as probably first century AD), might just provide the first concrete evidence he'd seen of a connection between Roseland and the Holy Land at the time of Christ.

Over the coming days, Pengelly had spent more time with Angel, giving her access to books at the cathedral and Truro town libraries, even organising for her to spend the day at the Reading Room of the British Museum. And it was there, by chance, as she thought, but actually engineered by Pengelly, that Angel first met Slevin, who also specialised in first century Judea and had long suspected Christ's body had been hidden somewhere in the southwest of England. Slevin immediately realised that Angel was something special and, given the right resources, would stand a better chance of getting to the truth than the most eminent archaeologist or biblical scholar. He then set about using his charms to influence her.

It worked, and she became infatuated with the priest, communicating with him regularly by telegram as to her progress.

"And, as you know, Sangster, Slevin didn't just use his charms on Angel," said Pengelly with a sniff. "Told me almost straight off he had explicit instructions from the highest level to make sure our Lord's earthly remains would never come to light. Told me I was special and that he wouldn't have confided in anyone else."

In fact, such was the sway Slevin held over him, despite knowing the priest was intending to cover up any discoveries, the canon organised a goodwill visit so that Slevin could come to Truro at the invitation of the bishop. What Pengelly hadn't known was that Angel, who never fully explained her thinking to him, was now very close to finding the tomb, and had already told Slevin everything she knew.

The cathedral clock chimed twelve, and Pengelly stopped talking to listen to it.

"Angel loved the cathedral as well, Sangster. Seemed fascinated by the idea of a cruciform church."

"That just means cross shaped, doesn't it?" He shook his head.

"Not quite, if we're talking very technically about church architecture. It's where the chancel's at an angle, like the head of Christ."

"You've lost me."

"Alright," said Pengelly. "You got a pen?" I handed him a biro, and he began to sketch a cross on his paper napkin. "All churches, or most traditional ones anyway, are built in the shape of a cross, yes?"

"I suppose so, I never really—"

"And the top of that cross has to face east, towards Jerusalem."

"If you say so."

"The long part at the bottom is called the nave, this cross part is the transept, and the head is the chancel, which here I've drawn as straight up from the nave." I nodded. "Now then, have you ever imagined yourself crucified, Sangster?"

"Er, no."

"Well, you'd be nailed to a cross, both hands or wrists, and your feet or ankles as well."

"I suppose I would."

"But not your neck or head, so what would happen?" I said nothing. "Your head would loll to one side, wouldn't it?"

"Almost certainly." I wasn't sure whether to grimace or laugh, so tried to do neither.

"So," he said solemnly (it seemed I had successfully contained my emotions), crossing out his straight chancel and replacing it with one at an angle. "Some churches, like this cathedral in Truro, are built cruciform to reflect the true posture of our Lord on the cross."

"I see."

"And this fascinated Angel no end." He handed me the napkin. "You can keep this if you like."

"Thank you." I folded it up and put it in my pocket, next to the wad of notes for the car.

"And there was this." He reached for the attaché case by his chair and opened it, carefully lifting out a cardboard folder and laying it on the table with both hands.

"It's a map of the River Fal, from the twelfth century." He opened the folder to reveal a map, drawn on what looked like some kind of parchment rather than paper with two dark furrows down and across the middle, presumably where it had for a long time been folded into four. The material was yellowed with age, the ink lines and script faded so that in places they were almost invisible. Nevertheless, I immediately recognised the outline of the estuary, not drawn to scale, but still clearly showing the main body of the Carrick Roads and the various inlets and creeks that branched off it. Across each of these branches was a dotted line connecting one bank to the other. The map title, written in a sweeping script, simply stated:

'Ferry transitibus fluvii Fal'

"Well, I recognise the 'Ferry' and the 'Fal' bits anyway."

"It merely says 'Ferry crossings of the River Fal'. And this is old, look at the date." 'Tregony Augusti Prioratus MIIX Anno Domini' was written in a spidery hand at the bottom right-hand corner. "But it's not any kind of esoteric document, more a kind of road atlas for people wanting to travel around the area. Ferry crossings would have saved hours, perhaps even a whole day back then."

"I used King Harry Ferry yesterday. Saved twenty-six miles."

"There you have it."

Pengelly sipped his coffee again, jumping back when a droplet landed on the map, then pointed to a river inlet above the date in the corner. 'Flumen Percuil' was written along it, where a dotted line ran from the St Mawes side to St Anthony, but at an angle, well upriver from the current landing stage by the academy.

"Your friend Pasco discovered this map tucked inside the cover of another book."

"Yes," I said, remembering Pasco's triumphant entry into the hotel bar the previous Saturday. "He told me all about it."

"Well, I'm pretty sure Angel found it before him."

"How's that?"

"Just a throw-away line but makes sense now."

"What was?"

"We were waiting by the landing stage, and she pointed upriver. 'Joseph's Pill' she said, almost to herself. Seemed meaningless but look here."

At the point on the map where the line from St Mawes met the

205

St Anthony bank, faint script that read 'Joseph flumen' could just be made out.

"I don't follow."

"This says Joseph's river, or river of Joseph."

"She said 'Pill' though, so it's a bit tenuous." I felt Pengelly was making a jump too far. "Especially as you don't know for sure Angel saw this map."

"Perhaps," he said, replacing the parchment in its folder then placing it gently back in the attaché case.

"But about Slevin, shouldn't you have said something to the authorities?"

"I had no idea he might abduct her," Pengelly said, once again placing his head in his hands. "No idea at all, how could I?"

"Didn't it seem a bit odd, when we were talking the other evening in the taproom, when I'd first heard Angel was missing."

"Looking back now, yes, but I was blinded by, well… love, Sangster. I've been such a fool."

"You're not the first and you won't be the last." I placed my hand on his shoulder. "But when did you realise?"

"Yesterday. Slevin, well, he didn't care. Told me he had the girl, and that I'd outgrown my usefulness, then said…" Pengelly sniffed again, whether in despair or rage I couldn't tell. "I was a bore and that he wanted a man who he actually fancied. There, I've said it."

"I'm sorry to hear that. I suppose he didn't say where he's holding the girl?"

"Near the academy, that's all I know."

"In the grounds?"

"No, definitely outside the walls, but near."

"But you think she's alive?"

"He didn't say otherwise."

We then sat sipping our coffee in silence for some time and, hearing the cathedral clock chime the half hour, I realised we'd now been together for around ninety minutes.

"I'm going to have to go soon but, Pengelly, I'll ask again. Why didn't you tell me earlier, or anyone else for that matter?" He rubbed his face, then looked directly at my eyes.

"Alright, there was another reason." I gestured for him to tell me. "In fact, I was still in two minds this morning, because, well, you don't know Slevin."

"I'm beginning to know him."

"Remember Leviticus."

"Er…"

"The passage in the Bible I quoted, bit about men with men being an abomination."

"Oh, yes."

"Well, Slevin remembered it as well. Quoted chapter and verse to me and told me he'd speak to the bishop if I said anything."

"The blackmailer's law still going strong," I laughed ruefully. "And you weren't tempted to say something anyway?"

"My official title's 'Canon Pastor and Priest-in-charge, Tresillian and Penkevil, and Rural Dean of Powder'. Bit of a mouthful I know, but I'd have lost everything I've worked for."

"What changed your mind?"

"When I saw Slevin last night, brazen with another man. He knew I was going to be at the Cassandra, so I guess he just wanted to taunt me."

"Okay," I said, standing up. "I need to be getting on. I'm going to call the police straight away, and then I'll be going down to the academy as soon as my car's ready. You?"

"Yes, I'll come down there as well. Later in the afternoon. Help any way I can."

"I'll see you later then," I said, placing some cash on the table. "And again, don't blame yourself, and I'm sorry it turned out this way."

"Oh, but I do blame myself, Sangster. If anything happens to that girl, I'll never…" There seemed nothing more to say, so I walked away, and passing a mirror, saw that Pengelly had placed his head back in his hands and laid his cheek down on the table once again.

The entire café was now staring.

207

The narrow strip of sky visible from Cathedral Lane was beginning to look angry when I emerged into the fresh air, and I remembered Morwenna's warning.

'There's a weather front coming in fast, and 'e's a nasty one.'

Then I remembered another warning, or more accurately a prediction. 'Next week, Friday late afternoon I'd reckon', was the date and time of day I would need to use my new oilskins according to the tramp. How could he have known, I wondered, but then thought his prediction no odder than a cask of ale providing a weather forecast. This was Cornwall after all.

And whether by luck or design, both the ale and the tramp were right, with the wind rising so that I pulled up my collar before continuing on down the lane. After a few steps walking against this wind, I was once again in Boscowen Street, smiling to think that the bottom of the lane was actually only a few yards from the bank where I'd started. Then I shook myself, having found Pengelly's emotions hard to deal with, and wanting to get my mind focused on finding Angel. It seemed ironic that Pengelly, for all his religious ethics, had only given up details that might save a young girl's life when he felt romantically slighted. 'Hell hath no fury like a canon scorned' I whispered to the wind as I walked.

Arriving at the broad expanse of Lemon Quay, where the head of the Truro River met the town, I passed a fish and chip shop wittily named 'The Lemon Sole Plaice' and looked above it to see a window with red curtains drawn across. I wondered if Bob Stocker's Rita was at home, perhaps resting while her every-other-day boyfriend was on family duty in Plymouth. Down the river, the clouds to the southwest were now darkening and, pulling my collar further up around my neck, I squeezed into a call box next to the quay before taking out my bag of coins.

*

"Truro police, WPC Woon speaking, how may I help?"

"Hello, yes, Ana?"

"Jack, you survived last night."

"Just about."

"Good. I've got copies of those telegrams from Mum by the way. They make interesting reading. You could drop into the station."

"You're in Truro, not at the academy incident room then?"

"No, chief super closed it up just before twelve this morning, shut for the weekend, so I'm working out of Truro. Could come down later if you need me?"

"Don't worry, right now I just need you to tell Pentreath to put out, what do you call it, an APB?"

"A what?"

"All Points Bulletin."

"I think that's American, Jack."

"Well, the English for one of those anyway. You're looking for a Monsignor Jude Slevin, if that's his real name." I gave her a full description, and the background of his being seconded to study at the cathedral. "The bishop and his people may have more details, so you definitely need to get in touch with them."

"Anything else?"

"Slevin rides a black Triumph Bonneville."

"Number plate?"

"Sorry, meant to note it down but didn't."

"Anyone you can think of might know?"

"Perhaps Morwenna Poldhu, landlady at the Watersmeet would."

"Okay Jack, I'll check all that out."

"He should be arrested on sight. Knows where Angel is."

"She's alive?"

"Perhaps."

"I'll get right onto it."

"And Ana…" My voice trailed off as my mind struggled to take everything in.

"You sound worried Jack."

"Just make sure..." I shivered and tried to collect my thoughts. "You let the powers that be know that Slevin may be very dangerous."

*

"Hello, Velinda, yes, Jack here... can you find Spider... yes... Simon Founds, that's right... probably in the study room or his dormitory... yes, I'll hold."

I waited several minutes, then heard Spider's distinctive voice shout through the receiver.

"Mr Sangster?"

"Here."

"Look, we haven't finished translating."

"We?"

"I roped Jonny in. Needed Koine Greek as well as Aramaic translation. She'd done a triple translation, with Greek as the intermediary cipher, it's—"

"Who did a whatsit... a triple translation, Angel?"

"Yes."

"How long then?"

"Another few hours."

"Alright, I'll come around five, that okay?"

"Sure, and, Mr Sangster, if we're reading Angel's notes right, this is, well... I can't believe it, Mr Sangster."

"Tell me when I see you and put Velinda back on the line would you."

"Who?"

"Prinny, get Prinny for me."

"Right."

I heard the receiver clatter as he handed it over.

"Jack, what's happening, what have you got our Simon Founds doing?"

"I'm going to need to talk to you, this afternoon."

"About Angel Blackwood?"

"Sort of. It's Cyrus, I need to know a few things." I heard her let out a short cry as her husband's name was mentioned.

"Yes Jack, I understand. What time will you be here?"

"Perhaps four."

"I'll be waiting."

*

"Yes, Sir John, I'm close to the truth, I think. You should come down."

"Impossible today, Sangster, but as soon as I can."

"Okay. And Flimwell?"

"What's that?"

"Cyrus Flimwell. You were going have the team to do some background checks."

"Ah yes. Came back clean as a whistle. No form at all."

"That's good to hear I suppose. And, Sir John?"

"Yes."

"I'll need to make an insurance claim." I explained that the car had been broken into but decided not to go into detail about the submarine at this point.

"Vandals and petty thieves everywhere, Sangster. What's the damage for the repair?"

"About seventy pounds."

"Phhh…" I heard him splutter. "Now then, the local rozzers," he went on after a moment's sniffing, changing the subject in his customary manner. "They still performing alright?"

"I think so, yes."

"And you, Sangster, you say you're close to finding her, well how close?"

"Perhaps today, but no promises."

"Leave you to it then." I heard the receiver click after which the line went dead.

"Putting you through now."

"Thanks Joyce." I waited as the phone clicked several times.

"Jack. Glad you called back. Look, is everything alright?"

"Yes, I'm fine. On a case for a missing girl though—"

"That girl on the news?"

"Angel Blackwood, if that's who you mean."

"Yes, but anyway, I did get a hit on your Monsignor."

"And?"

"They said 'person of interest', and not to be approached under any circumstances."

"Oh."

"Well, that doesn't sound much, Jack, but in intelligence circles it means something."

"Does it, Phil?"

"Definitely. Wanted to know more from me, and I avoided giving your name, but they'll put two and two together. Look Jack, these are serious people, and er... how do I put this?"

"Phil?"

"Well, it sounds dramatic, but people playing at that level sometimes disappear."

"Come on, Phil," I said with a laugh, while at the same time feeling a cold chill down the back of my neck.

"I'm serious, Jack. Anyway, who is this man Slevin?"

"That's what I'm trying to find out."

"Well, you take very good care of yourself while you're doing it, Jack."

"Thanks, Phil."

"And I hope you find your girl."

"Morwenna...," I heard the phone pips then a click and a familiar 'hello.' "Yes, it's Jack."

"Everything alright, my lover, you sound a little, well, flustered."

"Oh, fine thanks, just in a bit of a mad dash. Look, is Sue Driver still staying with you?"

"Oh yes, booked in tonight and tomorrow."

"Can you give her a message for me?"

"Course. She likes you, that Sue."

"Good, but look, tell her this please. Have you a pen?"

"Hang on... alright."

"If she promises not to print anything about her Cornish coelacanth yet, I might be able to give her the scoop of the year."

"Have I got that right?" said Morwenna, reading the message back to me, with the two of us spelling out the word coelacanth twice.

"Perfect."

"Jack?" Her voice was for the second time that day, uncharacteristically sombre. "Are you alright?"

"I think so."

"Well take care, because I've had a bad feeling about things today, ever since I couldn't get those beer pumps to work. Come back safe and sound. I always need my boys back here safe and sound."

2:30PM

Wiping grease from The Lemon Sole Plaice's best fish and chips off my hands (I was disappointed to have been served by an old man, presumably not Rita), I looked at the newspaper wrapping. It was the Western Morning News, and I noticed the ubiquitous picture of Angel at the bottom of the front page with a small headline stating that the girl was still missing. Screwing this up and dropping it into a bin next to the bench by the quay, I walked across to Stocker's Body Shop, where my car stood ready outside the shed, the racing green and chrome bodywork shining from end to end.

"Washed her for you as well, Ted has," beamed Pete, clapping his hand on the boot. "Good as new. And he checked your points. Said you were misfiring a little. Timing all wrong."

"May I thank Ted myself?"

"Bookies." Pete jerked his head back in the direction Lemon Quay. "I'll tell him for you though."

"Looks good," I said, opening and closing the boot, which did indeed seem to work. "What's the cost?"

"Hmmm…," said Pete, pulling out a pair of spectacles and a long sheet of paper. "There'll be parts, new locking mechanism, handle, catch spring. Then there's labour, and Bob's lunch."

"Bob's lunch?"

"Well, more elevenses really."

"Really?"

"Yes, he had to stop on the way back from Plymouth."

"Doesn't he do that anyway?"

"Bob?" Pete called.

"Yes Pete," came the reply from under the same Transit van as I'd seen the day before.

"Do you do that anyway?"

"Do what?"

"Have your elevenses on the way back from Plymouth."

"Course, bacon sandwich and a cup of tea from Andy Dower's café on the A390, just after Liskeard. Never miss it." Pete just nodded at this.

"So?" I said to Pete, throwing my arms wide at this surreal duologue.

"I'll knock it off. That's just saved you half a crown, Mr Sangster."

"How much now?"

"Er, with eight percent purchase tax, sixty-seven pounds exactly." Pete held the paper close to his glasses. "Minus your fiver deposit, and that half-crown of course.

"Look, just make it a round sixty-seven, so here's the sixty-two I owe you," I said, counting out the notes. "And give me a receipt."

"Thanks, Mr Sangster." Pete signed his long paper, then scribbled 'paid with thanks' and handed it to me. "Now you watch out on the road, weather's on the turn." I looked up to see threatening storm clouds brewing all across the sky.

"I will," I answered, hearing Pete shout out as I drove away.

"Sangster's paid for your elevenses, Bob."

3:30PM

"Passing Place – No Parking' said the sign in the layby, but I parked anyway, and followed the track signposted to the Bethadew Well mine.

The main pump house lay about a hundred yards into the woods and, when I got there, I could see that the words 'Cornish Castle' had long since ceased to apply to this virtually extinct pile of stones. The roof was entirely collapsed, as were the upper parts of the walls, which were anyway largely obscured by ivy and surrounding brambles. The chimney had somehow managed to stay up though, and there was still an intact doorway that showed evidence of having held metal gates at some point by the remains of hinges either side, but other than that the Bethadew Well mine was little more than a ruin. I looked inside, to see more brambles, and occupying much of the floor, which was mostly earth (perhaps locals had 'liberated' building materials like flag stones from the building over the years), a large round indent filled with gravel.

Beside the doors was a sign from the National Trust, giving a little of the mine's history, warning against stones falling from the unstable walls, and explaining that the indent was the original mine shaft, long since filled in with concrete and gravel for safety. There was also a description of an entrance behind the mine, apparently listed as a national monument (the words 'There's a closed-up entrance to a fogou next to the building where we'd, you know, snuggle up,' then whispered in my ears). I walked around the building and found WPC Woon's erstwhile love nest, which was a rock-lined entrance. Another National Trust sign, naming the structure 'Bethadew Fogou, origin unknown', stood next to it, noting that the precise purpose of these 'fogous' (which the sign described as pre-Christian rock-lined shelters), was also unknown. This entrance, the sign said, also led to the remains of a shallow open cast mine (once again, origin unknown), predating the main Bethadew working by many centuries. I peered inside, to find the way blocked by an iron grille that had been permanently fixed into the rock, beyond which there was a short tunnel leading to a dead end.

I then saw a signpost to the Percuil River creek-side path next to a track leading away from the fogou, so continued on through the woods. And with the sky now thick with thunder clouds, I began to find the Plantation oppressive and almost threatening. Before today I would have said the place exuded tranquillity, but now, with the stench of the wild garlic that carpeted the woodland floor almost drug like, I imagined the very trees wanted something from me I couldn't give them.

'Garlic's really early.' I remembered Morwenna saying.

'Don't overdo it, Jack,' I then heard Sarah saying, as I walked on down the track, which wound steeply, loose soil and boulders constantly ready to catch my feet unawares, so that I stepped slowly and carefully. After a time, the going became easier, the terrain levelling out, although I could see from a glint of water ahead that I was still about fifty yards from the creek. Either side of me were what at first appeared to be odd shaped green bushes, but on closer inspection, proved to be overgrown stone walls. These looked to be ruins of what might once have been huts, and further on a moss-covered pavement of weathered granite blocks, that dropped squarely two or three feet at its far edge, formed what must surely have served as a jetty in the distant past. Ahead was a small pond, and beyond that an inlet, no more than a backwater of the main creek, and entirely surrounded by oak trees.

It was here that I'd seen Angel and Jonny disappear in the canoes from the ferry that day with Sarah, I felt sure, and here that the St Mawes Ferry crossing on Pengelly's medieval monks' map made its landing.

"You're near, Angel, I can feel you," I shouted, the echo of my voice fading as thunder rumbled in the distance, and for a moment thought I glimpsed someone by the water's edge.

"Hello," I called, but looking again I realised it was just shadows that I'd seen, from the sky's reflections on the surface of the creek, which was now beginning to ripple as the wind rose. I shivered, despite the warmth of the afternoon, and started back up the track, to the sound of more thunder, with raindrops beginning to tap on the trees as I passed the mine building. I ran to the car, and just as I sat down and the door slammed shut, the heavens opened, rain drumming mercilessly against the hood.

*

"Runtle, open up," I shouted, hammering at the postern door.

"Alright, Mr Sangster, come out of the rain a minute and I'll open the gates, then you can go back to your car."

I waited in the tiny postern room, watching Runtle at his space-age control panel, throwing the various switches needed to open the gates.

"Runtle, was there ever a village close by here, in the Plantation, near the mine perhaps?"

"No village, Mr Sangster, not that I know of."

"But there are the foundations of what look like buildings close by the creek. I just saw them."

"Ah yes, the old caretaker talked about those."

"And?"

"And what, Mr Sangster?"

"What did he say?"

"Never called it a village."

"Did he call it anything?"

"A settlement, he said. When the mine was working there were more folk around of course, and those buildings are by the old dried-up quay, where they'd ship the tin ore. Storehouses, lime kiln, oyster keep, small cottages for the men to sleep in. Been there a long time he said, ever so old."

"Did this place perhaps have a name?"

"Yes, now what was it again, that's it… Joseph's Pill he called it."

"Pill?"

"Old slang in these parts for a creek, I think."

"Thank you, Runtle."

I ran back to the car through the rain, hit the start button, and the engine immediately misfired, making a very similar sound to the Stocker's Land Rover when Mabel had tried to affect a quick getaway the night before.

'And he checked your points, said you were misfiring a little,' Pete Stocker had boasted about his brother Ted.

"Bloody Stockers," I yelled out loud as the engine finally sprang to life, and the car passed through the gates and up the drive.

4:30PM

"Velinda." I knocked on the study door to the sound of sobbing inside. "Velinda." The door remained shut so I turned the knob and entered to see 'Prinny' slumped at her desk in tears. "Velinda," I said again. "It's me, Jack. What on earth's—"

"It's Cyrus," she said, raising her head. "He's gone."

"Gone, what do you mean?"

"I mean left. Me, the academy, everything. Run away."

"I'm sorry," I said, sitting down, and immediately thinking Pengelly might have been wrong about Slevin, and that Flimwell was involved with Angel's disappearance after all. "Where… I mean how… can you tell me what happened?"

"Oh, I can. You remember the note you found in Angel's desk." I nodded." That was Cyrus's writing."

"Yes, I know that now."

"And he called her Iseult, Iseult I tell you."

"I believe that was what the 'I' stood for yes, and the 'T' for Tristan was Cyrus' name for himself."

"Iseult's what he called me, on our honeymoon. We were Tristan and Iseult."

"Oh."

"I kept the note after we spoke, I'm not sure you noticed, but I did, and—"

"I noticed."

"Well, I challenged Cyrus straight afterwards, and he admitted it all, said he couldn't help it, had become infatuated with Angel. We didn't really speak after that, then this afternoon he just upped and left. Took a suitcase, took the car, took a wad of cash from the safe as well."

"Do you know where he's gone?"

"He didn't say, but back up to London I suppose."

"We must tell the police. Find him, see if he knows what's happened to Angel."

Velinda sat back when I said this and looked hard at me.

"He doesn't have Angel."

"How do you know?"

"I'm sure, Jack. From everything he said, I'm sure, and apart from anything else, he was with other people during the time she went missing."

"She could have met him later or something, but okay," I said, Velinda's eyes, and everything else I knew, telling me Cyrus Flimwell probably wasn't the abductor. "I'll have to inform the police and the institute anyway I'm afraid, but if it makes you feel any better, we did run a check and your husband has no record of anything like this in the past."

"Yes," she almost spat, then lit a cigarette. "That's what makes it worse. If he'd had a roving eye, even for schoolgirls, it would have been better."

"It wouldn't, would it?"

"It would to me. You see Cy actually thought he was in love with Angel." She violently stubbed out her half-smoked cigarette (on the back of Cyrus Flimwell's hand, I imagined she imagined), then immediately lit another. "I gave up having kids to be with him, and then he does this, I…" She began to weep again, and I passed her my handkerchief.

"I'm sorry, Velinda, but I'm going to need you in good shape this afternoon I think."

She nodded, with a look of resignation.

"We've lost another eighteen pupils in the last two days by the way, Jack," she then said. "And the staff have all left for an evening out in Truro. Claimed it was just social, but I think they're going to discuss leaving en masse. There's only me, Runtle, matron and the girls' and boys' duty teachers here right now."

"Eighteen?"

"Yes, so are you any closer to finding Angel?"

"Maybe."

"The police haven't a clue by the way. They all left for the weekend, just after twelve."

"I think she's alive, Velinda, and I think she's nearby, somewhere in the Plantation. And if I'm right, before long we'll be calling the police back here to look for her."

"Oh, I hope they find her," she said, as rain beat against the office window. "But it'll be so hard to search in this deluge."

"Have you seen Canon Pengelly?"

"Why yes," she said wincing and looking up as another thunderclap sounded off, the storm now almost directly above us. "In the chapel I think, and oh, this is going to be a stormy night."

Yes, I thought to myself, this is going to be a stormy night.

*

I entered the academy study room, a large, high-ceilinged space which had been a dining room for the old hotel (a brand-new refectory had been built for the academy as part of the overall refurbishment).

"You still haven't finished the translation?" I asked Spider and Jonny, who were sitting in the corner, barricaded behind three tables which they had presumably pushed together.

"It's harder than we thought, Mr Sangster," Spider answered

without looking up, he and Jonny poring over a mass of papers and books. "Isn't it, Jonny?"

"Really hard, Mr Sangster. We have to translate the Aramaic into Koine Greek, then English. Wish Angel was here to help."

"That's the whole point, you dickhead," Spider said, slapping Jonny over the back of the head. "She isn't here. Keep going."

"So, when will you be done then, Spider?"

He muttered something as a thunderclap, powerful enough to pierce the thick stone walls and roof of the academy and blot out any other noise, crashed around us.

"Sorry?" I shouted.

"Six o'clock, yeah?"

"Sure?"

"I think so, Mr Sangster."

"I'll come back then."

*

The chapel at the academy 'sweated antiquity' as Sir John had once rather irreverently but very accurately said. It was small, with a central aisle, rows of oak pews either side, a stone pulpit with stairs leading up to it on the far right, and an ornate altar on a dais next to that, behind which was a disproportionately large pipe organ that was known to regularly deafen worshippers. Some walls were hung with tapestries depicting various biblical scenes, while others were covered by peeling frescoes which seemed to be (as far as my heathen eye was concerned), portraits of the disciples (at least I counted twelve of them). Above and behind the altar was a rather gruesome looking crucifix, made of brown wood except for eyes that had been painted a piercing blue, and high over that, on wooden beams where the pitched roof came to a point, hung a small bell.

"Probably makes a right racket, because it's never rung that bell," I remembered Runtle telling me when I'd first looked over the academy. "Clapper's been taken out, the old vicar and the one before him never fixed it, and the new chap's never got it fixed either".

I lowered my gaze to see a cassocked figure knelt on the stone steps leading up to the altar.

"Afternoon, Pengelly, Velinda Flimwell said I'd find you here."

"Sangster." He turned his head but stayed kneeling. "I am praying for Angel." He clutched a pewter communion chalice, its neck shaped like a crucifix, the body and outspread arms of Christ forming the stem that held the bowl.

"Have you been taking communion?"

"No. We don't actually serve wine from this chalice, bishop doesn't approve of it."

"Whyever not?"

"Thinks it, how shall I say… a little flamboyant, pehaps a bit papist. Chalice was here longer than anyone can remember but nevertheless, I have to use this one for services." He looked up at a more sober looking silver cup standing on the altar. "But this one," he went on, clutching the crucifix chalice even tighter. "Gives me succour as I pray."

"Can't do any harm I suppose, praying for Angel."

"Any news, Sangster?"

"Nothing more than when we talked at lunchtime."

He stood up and then beckoned me to the chapel's main door (I had entered by a separate passageway leading directly from the academy building), pointing to the stone archway above it (which most certainly did fit Sir John's epithet of sweating antiquity).

"You've never really been in here, have you, Sangster."

"I looked in a couple of times when we were organising the refurbishment, but it's listed, I suppose you knew?"

"Of course."

"We couldn't touch this place because of it being listed, so never really had the need to come here to oversee any building works."

"Well, I've been priest-in-charge for five years now, and I never cease to wonder at these symbols. It's difficult to tell at a distance but look hard and you'll see." I squinted, eventually making out various pictograms carved into the crumbling stone.

"This, Sangster, tells the story of Jesus coming to Cornwall."

"Is it really two thousand years old?"

"Oh no, not sure how old, but perhaps twelfth century at the most. Only thing that predates it is that bell up there." He pointed to the roof and the underside of the bronze-coloured bell. "That's been here since records began."

I looked hard again and failed to see anything that would help us in the stone symbols. There was no detail in the way of the etching on the dagger, or Angel's notebook, just vague pictures.

"I suppose you showed all this to Angel, Pengelly?"

"She looked at it once or twice, didn't seem to get too excited. In fact…"

"Yes?"

"She said something very odd." He looked around the church. "'Just an echo'. That's what she said."

"Alright." I looked at my watch. Five to six. "I'm going to check something out, then I'll be back. I'm pretty sure I'm going to need your help."

"I… I… cannot, I'm not able," he stuttered. "I must pray again."

*

I walked back through the connecting passage, and even there, surrounded by thick walls on all sides, could hear the thunder outside. After a minute I was standing next to Spider and Jonny.

"So, gentlemen, what have you got for me?"

"Grab a chair, Jonny," said Spider, "for Mr Sangster." Jonny obliged. "Now then," Spider continued. "Like I said on the phone, we can't believe what we've read. Basically, it says that Jesus' body was brought here—"

"Spider," I said, holding my hand up. "That's fantastic work you've done to find that out, but I know all about it, and the link with Joseph of Arimathea. Is there anything you translated that might tell us where Angel is?"

Spider looked a little crestfallen at this and pushed several sheets of translated notes to one side, before Jonny spoke up.

"Oh yes, she's—"

"Alright, Jonny, I'll tell Mr Sangster." Spider showed me one of the sheets. "We think the knife talks about a place here in Cornwall, close by, and, if you can believe it, a place in America."

"America?"

"Yes. I'm sorry, but we're pretty sure."

"But they wouldn't have had a word for America in Aramaic."

"They didn't. It talks about a great ocean, a river, and an inland sea, or maybe their word for a lake."

"That could mean anywhere."

"Yes, but look." He thrust more sheets of translated notes at me. "We found this note of Angel's…"

For the ocean that was at that time navigable; for in front of the mouth which you Greeks call 'the Pillars of Heracles' there lay an island which was larger than Libya and Asia together; and it was possible for travellers of that time to cross from it to the other islands and from the islands to the whole of the continent over against them which encompasses the veritable ocean…

"The Pillars of Hercules, which is…"

"I know, Spider, the Straits of Gibraltar, and before you tell me, I also know that's a famous quote from Plato about Atlantis." The lad looked even more crestfallen, in that way only the very young and very intelligent can when an adult displays even a little of some arcane piece of knowledge they believe to be their very own.

"Four hundred BC," Spider added hopefully, and I could tell he wasn't just trying to be clever and genuinely sought for appreciation of the work done, but I had no time for niceties.

"All that on a foot-long knife?"

"Not that bit, Angel had added to it in her notes. Took us ages to translate. She'd done them in the same Aramaic script, and the same Koine Greek."

"Didn't want anyone reading them then." Spider shook his head, as did Jonny.

"But you must see this. It's a place in America, I'm sure."

"Sure, of what?"

"Look," Spider said, showing me several sheets of notes, one of which showed a map of a lake, the outline of which was perhaps known to me. "State of Michigan, an island in Lake Superior. Isle Royale."

"Isle Royale, Spider?"

"Yeah. We're sure. I dunno why though."

I remembered the book with the fold-out map in WPC Woon's 'academic pile'.

"This was certainly important to Angel, but did you see anything that might help us find out where she is?"

"I'm not sure, but we found this." He held the notebook open at its centre pages, to show a sketch Angel had drawn, more a design really, of different sized cogwheels, looking like a watch with the back off. "We didn't try to copy it, just translated the words."

I saw a title, 'Star Sailor', and a note at the bottom, 'Antikythera type mechanism to navigate the Atlantic'.

"What does Antikythera mean?"

Spider and Jonny both shook their heads, but judging by the care taken with the drawing, this mechanism, whatever 'Antikythera' meant, was also clearly important to Angel. Nevertheless, it still didn't provide any clue to her whereabouts. I needed something more, something immediate.

"So, tell me what else she wrote, Spider, just the main points, because if this is what I think it is, we haven't much time."

"It's in these other sheets," said Spider, holding up more papers. "And everything points to a place near here, Bethadew Well mine. She's actually written 'Sepulchre of God' next to it, but we think she means Bethadew. You know, the old place up—"

"No stop," I said, holding up my hand in an effort to calm the almost hysterical Spider. "I know all that lad. Bethadew Well doesn't translate to 'Sepulchre of God'. Angel was wrong, and we have to look elsewhere."

"It does, it does, look." He held the notebook page up to my face and my blood ran cold as I read Angel's words...

'Found it, the Sepuchre of God!!! Original Cornish name Bedh Whel Duw anglicised = Bethawhealdew. Mining text book says English owners changed the name in 1790 to sound more English, moving the parts around to get Bethadew Well. Wonder if they really knew why they did it? Deep memory made them uncomfortable?'

...then remembered Morwenna's words ('It would have to be called Bethawhealdew to mean Sepulchre of God').

"Where at Bethadew?" I shouted. "Where?"

"Underneath."

That could only mean the fogou.

"Alright. Bring all of your notes, and Angel's notebook, and the etching drawing of the dagger, and meet me out front in ten minutes by the gatehouse with them. And tell Prinny to meet me by the front door." Lightning suddenly lit the room, then thunder banged through the windows, adding to the already deafening din of the rain. "Got all that?" Spider nodded. "Now go."

*

Coming back to the chapel, I saw the figure of Pengelly, now almost recumbent on the altar steps. His hands were held together in prayer, his arms still clutched the chalice, his head was elevated towards the macabre crucifix above the organ, and his voice rang out, almost shouting, though sometimes barely audible above the unabated storm.

"The Lord is my shepherd, I shall not want. He maketh me to lie down in green pastures, he leadeth me..."

"Pengelly."

The canon turned to me, and I started at the sight of his face, filled with fear and dread, eyes wild, and almost devoid of reason.

"I did this, Sangster. I let the weakness of my flesh lead Angel into the clutches of Satan."

228

"We need to find her, Pengelly, and most of the staff are gone, as are the police. Come on man."

"This is all in the Lord's hands now. We can do no more."

"I know where she is, now come on."

I placed my hand on his shoulder, but he merely knelt lower.

"Leave me," he cowered. "Leave me to face my sin alone. We cannot help her now."

I tried to drag him up to no avail, him slipping out of my grip and lurching forward to end up face down on the steps, before lifting his arms up and shouting at the crucifix.

"Take me now, Lord, a sinner, I will confess all—"

But he never got to make the confession. On the word 'all', every window of the church was illuminated, as lightning flashed all around. The chapel was silent again for a moment, and I waited for the thunder, but all at once there was another flash, this time accompanied by a sound that I could best recall afterwards as being like a zip fastener being done up very quickly.

"Oh," cried Pengelly, looking up to the ceiling, which was now making a cracking sound, the wooden roof beams creaking as they split one by one. Then the entire structure began to groan, and I saw it start to collapse, first plaster landing on the floor, then pieces of wood.

"Pengelly," I yelled. "Come back from there."

"Take me," the canon screamed, hands still held up towards the crucifix which itself then fell from the wall, along with the organ pipes which clanged as they landed against the stone altar.

I grabbed Pengelly's legs and pulled, as the thunder continued, rain now beginning to find its way in through the damaged roof. A clanging sound then made me look up, and I saw the bell moving, as the framework that held it gave way. I pulled Pengelly again, dragging him back down the aisle as the belfry collapsed and the bell hit the flagstones with a metallic thud. The granite floor then screeched as it shattered into star patterned cracks, and the bell rolled, still clanging, until it came to rest next to Pengelly's head.

"Am I taken?" he whispered as the chapel fell silent, the thunder now apparently in at least temporary respite.

"No, you're not taken, you're very much alive. Now get up, we have to find Angel."

"I cannot," he wailed, and stayed on the floor.

"Then stay here, man," I snapped, and ran back to the passageway, looking back to see Pengelly now cradling the bell, which was bigger than it had looked hung up in the top rafters. And as I watched this wretched tableau, I saw that the rim of the bell was marked with symbols that I'd seen before.

*

"What's happened, Jack?" shouted Velinda as I ran into the entrance hall. "I heard a crash from the chapel. Is anyone hurt? "

"No, but the bell fell down from the roof and Pengelly's in shock."

"Oh my goodness."

"You should get over there though. Canon needs someone with him."

"And you?"

"I think I know where Angel is, and I'm going there now."

"Do you want me to call the police?"

"Er, no." I tried to clear my mind and then think of the best thing to do. "Go straight to the chapel and help Pengelly. I'll call them from the gatehouse."

"Alright, Jack."

I climbed into the car and pressed the ignition. The engine, which normally started with a rich and deep sound, began with a stutter, then revved up as I pulled away and drove down towards the gatehouse, where I saw Spider sheltering by the postern, the sheaf of papers under his arm. Slowing down, I felt the car stall, and despite my pressing the ignition several times, it failed to restart. I jumped out and ran into the lodge, where Runtle stood holding a candle, shouting to Spider to put the papers in the car boot as I went.

"Storm's taken the electrics out, Mr Sangster," said Runtle.

"The phone, can I use the phone?"

"That's out as well. Phones in the main building should all work though."

"Spider," I shouted through the open door. "Run back and tell Prinny we couldn't drive up there and Runtle's phone's out. She needs to call the police, now."

Spider stood stock still, rain falling about him and frozen with, as he'd told me once before, 'information overload'.

"Runtle, what's the fastest way to walk to Bethadew. Up the road?"

"Oh no, if you're on foot you'll want the creekside path," the caretaker answered, sounding for all the world as if I were asking for directions on a sunny Sunday afternoon. "That's the best way, down to the ferry landing stage, then turn right about a mile and when you come to those old ruins you were talking about, turn right again and up through the woods."

"No quicker way?"

"Best way I know."

"Look," I said, taking him by the shoulders. "Go back and tell Mrs Flimwell to call the police and send them to Bethadew mine now. Okay?"

"No need to push me, Mr Sangster, I'm on my way."

"And take Spider here," I said, looking at the still catatonic youth.

Runtle put his arm through Spider's, turned the staring lad around then began to march him back up the drive. I watched them go, then walked out through the postern and looked down the road towards the landing stage. The tarmac was awash and seemed like a less than sure bet to walk down given what was at stake.

*

"Never mind that way," came a voice from behind. I turned to see, through the almost solid curtain of rain, the bedraggled form of the tramp standing behind me, wooden staff in one hand and an old-fashioned oil lantern in the other. I jumped, having heard no sound nor seen any sign of his coming. "You got to go, now, Mister, save the girl if you can."

"We should wait for the police."

"No time, Mister. Even as we speak, Angel's life hangs by a thread, now come." He pointed with his staff to a gap in the trees on the other side of the road. "There's a path here'll take us where we need to go, much quicker than the path by the water." With that he hobbled across and disappeared into the wood, calling me to come with him.

After an unsure backward look at the still-open postern door, I gave a shrug and followed the tramp, who, despite his limp and the downpour, moved quickly and easily through the trees, so that I struggled to keep up. He stopped and turned every now and then, beckoning me on, before continuing through the undergrowth. In my struggle to keep up I began to understand how this old man could apparently appear and disappear so easily when he wanted to.

The tramp's 'path', as I complained to myself while scrambling after him, was really no more than a vague (and by the undergrowth on it, little used), track. This made passing through the tangled scrub oaks and steep slopes of the Plantation, which would have been challenging enough in broad daylight, difficult to the point that I nearly turned back more than once, with only the calls of my guide and the dim glow of his lantern to persuade me otherwise. But I didn't turn back, and quite quickly found myself close by the ruined stone jetty, where the waters of the usually sheltered creek, with the tide now at full flood, could be seen through the trees, writhing in the wind and beating rain.

"This is it, Mister, this is the way he brought her," the tramp shouted as the sky thundered and the trees were momentarily lit like skeleton bones by an almost simultaneous lightning bolt.

"The police found no trace and there was no way out of the school, how could he bring Angel here?"

"Ah, he's a clever one, that priest," said the tramp, tapping the side of his nose. "And it's the clever ones that are easiest caught. Never think anyone else is as clever as they are."

I looked around at the lost walls of the buildings and the stone quayside, lit by the glow of the lantern. There was surely no place to hide.

"So, you say she's here?"

"No, Mister, she's not here. Got to go on, path that leads up to the castle." He levelled his staff towards the steep track leading inland from the disused jetty, the track that I'd descended only a few hours before. "She's in danger I tell you. I heard the bell toll just before."

"Oh, you mean the chapel bell. No, that was lightning, it struck the—"

"Bell only tolls when it wants to."

"But—"

"It's underneath the castle you'll find the girl."

"Angel's buried there you mean," I said, looking in the direction he was pointing, to see, as far as I could tell in the shadows and rain, and disoriented despite being here only a few hours before, the broken chimney of the Bethadew Well mine. "You mean buried alive?"

"I mean run. Save her if you can."

"Of course, but…" I looked around to see the lantern left balanced on the stone parapet of the jetty, and nothing else. I panicked at being alone. "Come back, it might need two of us, you brought me here," I shouted into the black woods.

Nothing but the sound of the wind and rain in the trees came back, and after several minutes of calling, I despaired, sensing by the lack of echo that the surrounding woods were immediately absorbing any sound I had hoped would carry. I picked up the lantern and started walking as the tramp had indicated, climbing up the track to Bethadew. As I walked, I counted myself lucky the track was at least narrow enough that the stunted scrub oaks either side could meet overhead and shelter me from the worst of the weather, and within a few minutes arrived, slightly breathless, at the base of the ruined pump house.

'Underneath', that was what the tramp had said, and that was what Spider's notes had said. 'Underneath'.

233

I looked around, the place seeming impenetrable in the fading light. Brambles guarded the walls, the interior of the derelict engine house was clear of any hidden rooms or entrances, and the single pit within just as full of gravel and concrete as it had been in the light of day before the storm.

I walked around the building, swinging the lantern in the vague hope of casting light on concealed steps, a trapdoor, a niche in the walls, or some other way that might lead underneath the mine, but to no avail.

Somehow, the way to Angel must be the fogou, I thought as I came finally to the entrance, with its iron grill and council sign looking as immovable as ever. I put down my lamp and placed my hands against the bars of the grill, shaking it in vain.

*

"Don't move, Sangster." I felt a blunt object press into my back and looked over my shoulder to see the face of Slevin, smiling at me from under a broad brimmed hat. "Now walk over there, no sharp moves, I think you know what this is in my hand. I'm not just pleased to see you."

"Where's Angel?" I shouted.

"Oh, you'll be pleased to see her shortly. Now stop and turn around." I did as instructed to see him standing in an almost floor-length leather coat, gun in one hand and canvas tote bag in the other, rain falling off his hat brim in torrents.

"You won't be able to cover this up you know, Slevin, whatever you do to me. The police know I'm here and they'll find you."

"Oh, I don't want to cover it up," he laughed. "Quite the opposite. Just want to get away."

"I thought you were from the Vatican, so—"

"Yes, I am," he laughed again. But that's not who I really work for. My real bosses have a vested interest in all this going public, now walk, Sangster." He jerked the gun towards the stone archway.

"But it's blocked by a metal grill."

"Not if you know how," he laughed again. "Now place your hands on the top of the two end bars on the left, that's right, at the very top." I felt the cold metal and waited for more instructions. "Just stay there and keep your fingers tight on those bars." He edged over to the other side, put his bag on the ground, then held the top of the righthand-most bar. "Now on the count of three, I want you to pull downwards. One, two, three…"

The grill fell away in my hand, surprisingly easily, both Slevin and I jumping back as it clanged to the ground. I fell against him, and he quickly turned, holding the gun level, and without noticing that a very large iron key was protruding from his coat pocket.

"Whoa," he said, looking upwards to steady his aim, so that I managed to grab the key and slip it in my pocket unseen. "Don't come close like that."

"Just an accident, Slevin, easy with that thing."

"For sure, Sangster, now Angel's inside."

"She's been there too long. We must get her out."

"That's not my problem," he grinned. "Tide's up and I've got a boat to catch."

'Boat' I noticed he said, not 'ship'. A submarine?

"You're in the pay of the Soviets?"

"Very clever. Been a lot of sea monster sightings in the last week, haven't there?"

"But what do they, I mean you… want from all this?"

"Oh, the Kremlin's very keen to see all this come out. The resurrection of Christ a sham, Western values a sham. I've got photos, documents, even a bone from that tomb in there." He laughed. "You get the picture, Sangster."

"You're a Catholic priest."

"I don't owe the church anything. Ruined my mother's life, sent her to a workhouse for having a child out of wedlock, and then sent me to be brought up by Jesuits. Give me the boy and I'll give you back the man, that's what they say."

"I heard that same thing the other day."

"Well in my case it was give me the boy and I'll do what I like to him."

For a moment after he said this, despite all the worry about Angel, and with Slevin pointing a gun at me, I was suddenly filled with a vision of this long-haired priest as a boy, alone and undefended against who knew what. This also made me think that any compassion or conscience had been taken from Slevin long ago, so that he probably wouldn't hesitate to kill me, Angel, or anyone else if it suited him.

"But I don't see it," I finally said, hoping he wouldn't sense my fear. "Despite that, you trained all your life for the priesthood, went to the Vatican."

"If you want to get even, first get close."

"But the betrayal of your country."

"Well, Ireland has no tolerance, and even so-called liberal England isn't exactly kind to a man of, well, my inclinations."

"It's getting better, you must see that."

"Well, this isn't my country anyway. British soldiers did things to my ancestors in Ireland a kid wouldn't do to the next-door neighbour's cat when nobody's looking."

"You used to torture cats, Slevin?"

"Look," he said, after pausing for a moment. "I'm not here to be, what do they say, 'psychoanalysed', and though it's always nice to chat, I really must be getting on. Now walk."

"But that passage is a blind end."

"Course not. My Russian mates supplied the gear and we dug it out easily enough, so that now a few carefully placed boulders behind the iron grill here look fine to anyone passing by."

He pointed to a pile of such boulders by the sides of the passage, and then poked the gun in my back again and we walked down the rock-lined tunnel, me in front with the lantern, eventually turning a bend to see a wooden framework with a block and tackle slung under it. Next to this were shovels, a pickaxe and a pile of rock and earth, dug I assumed, from a round hole in the floor beneath the block and tackle, about a yard deep and the same wide. Inside the hole was a circular stone slab embedded with a rusting iron ring.

"Grab the end of that boom and heave, Sangster." He pressed the gun barrel against my spine. "Go on, heave it."

I heaved as requested and, slowly but surely, the slab lifted, and like the iron grill, more easily than I expected, although the ring looked ready to give way at any time.

"Sure," said Slevin, as the slab was raised above head height to the ring's creaking. "I've been worrying about that ring holding up each time I've done this. Doesn't look too good, does it?"

"What now?"

"Just take your little tilly lamp and climb down," he said, tying up the beam. "Then you'll find a ladder."

I swung the lamp into the hole, then lowered myself down to the aperture, where sure enough, a metal ladder was leaned against the lip.

"Now down you go, and don't fall, it's a way to the bottom."

I turned and placed my foot on the first rung, hearing a moan from inside the blackness.

Angel!

"Why did you keep her alive for so long?" I whispered, my heart pounding at the realisation the girl I'd sought for so long was alive at all.

"I wanted more information, but she wasn't giving. And I'm not a murderer, Sangster."

"You will be if you leave us down here."

"Thought you said the police knew where you were. Now go on, we haven't got all night."

I stepped downwards, coming to the floor, perhaps twenty feet below, when the groan of stone against iron slowly began to pervade the atmosphere.

"Looks like that ring's finally given way," Slevin shouted to me as the slab crashed down into place, sealing Angel and me inside.

*

"Angel Blackwood, this is a friend. Is that you?"

"It is," came a whisper in the dark. I held the lantern high, and there she lay, on the floor next to an oblong stone structure that dominated the centre of the chamber. On the walls, which were smooth hewn rock, were numerous inscriptions, in the same style as the notes Angel had made, and the markings on the dagger and the bell. More disturbingly, there were also statues, standing silently by the walls and clearly of great antiquity, with the stone cracked and angles smoothed, by age rather than weathering. And they were life-sized figures; a weeping woman, a man kneeling with outstretched arms, another with an open book, and yet another with what might have been a fishing net over his arm. In one corner, a hook-nosed man in a full-length robe stood with his hands together, head bowed in prayer.

Angel herself had her head raised, but otherwise was barely moving. She lay, almost corpse like, in her torn skirt and blood-stained blouse, the rank smell of the clothes, along with urine and excrement stains, confirming if I needed such, the duration and confines of her incarceration. Only a metal flask next to her, and some scattered bread crusts on the nearby floor gave any clue that she might have been given sustenance or otherwise cared for during that time, so that I feared for Angel's survival.

Looking at her feet first, I saw one ankle was clearly sprained, swollen twice the thickness of the other (she was wearing what had once been white ankle socks, one of which was now stretched tight, cutting into the skin around the enlarged joint). Her upper body was cruelly bound with thick chains, attached to iron rings sunk into the flagstones, each secured with a massive padlock. Then I looked into Angel's face, and even in the half-light of the chamber, I knew this was someone different.

'Quite remarkable' as Pengelly had said.

The girl's features, while smeared with dirt and tears, were certainly as beautiful as they appeared in the police photo and when I'd briefly seen Angel around the school, but it was her almost saucer-like green eyes, and the sense of wisdom behind them, that took their hold on me. I tried (and failed in that moment), to avoid the feeling that Angel saw everything, missed nothing, felt intimate connections between the most insignificant and the most profound things, and with that had nothing less than access to an inspiration that was perhaps divine. In all my years as a convinced atheist, looking at Angel that night in the sepulchre was the nearest I had come to a religious experience. I shook myself, held up the key I'd snatched from the Monsignor and set to work on the locks.

Chains now discarded, I held Angel in my arms, body limp with fatigue and fear, hair and skin matted with who knew what? I laid her down as gently as I could, back against the side of the stone tomb, then offered water from the flask and, as she sipped it, looked again at the girl's darkly stained face and torn clothing.

"I'm—" I began, but she cut me off.

"I know who you are, Mr Sangster, and I can guess how you found me."

"Oh, you do, and you can, can you?"

"Yes."

"Well… er," I stuttered, never thinking to doubt her. "Did he… did he do anything to you, Angel?"

"No," she said immediately. "And I wanted him to, that's why I came here. I wanted him, not as a girl with a crush, but as a woman who wants a man. The priest though, well he didn't want me. Not like that."

'She's a true genius, Jack, but also a teenage girl with all the normal urges and uncertainties that go with it', I recalled Velinda Flimwell saying. And knowing what I did of the Monsignor, I could easily understand why he was able to manipulate an infatuated Angel whilst remaining entirely immune to her charms.

"So, once he'd found this place, why did Slevin keep you here?"

"He couldn't exactly let me go."

"No, I mean, you know… alive for all this time."

"He wanted more information. I didn't give it to him."

"There's more?"

"Oh yes, he hasn't guessed the half of it." She laughed a little, then winced in pain. "And he needed to wait until tonight to be picked up."

"In a submarine, he told me." She nodded.

"Does anyone know we're here, apart from Slevin that is?"

"I'm afraid not," I replied, knowing that even the best of white lies likely wouldn't work with Angel. "I came quickly. It was an old man."

"The tramp?"

"Yes, he said I should come quickly, showed me a short cut through the woods."

"He would do that," she said flatly. "He'd need someone else, someone he felt was right, like you, to enter the sepulchre. He'd think it wouldn't be right to enter himself."

"The school has called the police though." I tried to say this brightly. "So perhaps they'll find us."

"They weren't able to before, so they won't be able to now. Slevin will have covered his tracks and yours." She thought for a moment. "And even though the tramp probably guesses we're stuck here, he won't tell the police, or anyone else for that matter." She said this with a finality that made me despair. Would two more bodies, both starved to death, be added to the count of this sepulchre?

"Then we must wait and hope, Angel," I said flatly.

"Oh no, there'll be a way out. Anywhere you can get into, you can get out of."

'Try asking a lobster in a lobster pot' I almost said but thought better of it. Somehow, in this girl's presence, all of my thoughts seemed crass and childish, and I suddenly felt the truth behind Pengelly's comment.

'She's just quicker.'

"I've been watching since I was chained up. Each time Slevin puts the slab back in place when he leaves, there's a breeze, fresh air, can you feel it?"

I sniffed. Yes, there was a hint of a draught.

"Is there another way in, Angel, or out?"

"No, the air's coming through the edge of the stone covering." She pointed up at the roof. "The surround's been worn away over countless years, so the stone slab now rests on the thinnest of ledges."

"It's still got to weigh near on a ton though."

"Exactly, and that will work in our favour."

"How?"

"If we can scratch away at the stone on the right side of the ledge, just a little, that slab will come crashing in."

"Won't doing that just wedge it further down as it slips?"

"No, the edges of the opening have been worn so that only a few protruding bits of the ledge on the right are keeping the slab from falling. It will crash right through."

"But this is granite. I've a steel penknife, but that won't work and anyway it's too small. I'm sorry, there's nothing we can possibly use to scrape that will be big enough or hard enough?"

Silence followed, and I guessed Angel had resigned herself to the hopelessness of our situation.

"This is how we'll do it," she suddenly said. "There's a bag under those stones in the corner." The way she spoke, sure and deliberate even though her voice was weak, made me realise I had guessed wrong. Angel was merely calculating everything that needed to be done.

I lifted the lantern high, its light letting the statues cast grotesque shadows onto the walls behind them, then stepped carefully towards the corner where sure enough, behind the hooked-nosed saint, a loose pile of stones could be seen.

"Under here, Angel?"

"Yes, my backpack."

I set the lantern down and scrabbled to remove the stones, eventually feeling canvas.

"Got it."

"Bring it to me."

I sat down next to Angel and handed her the bag, which she unbuckled.

"I knew from the outset what the Monsignor was going to do once I'd shown him what he wanted, I just didn't want to admit it to myself," she said as she put her hand inside, pulling out a sackcloth bundle. "So,

I hid the bag when I first came here with him. Slevin was so caught up with the tomb and the inscriptions on the walls he didn't notice me put it under the pile of stones. Then, when he locked me up, I still didn't tell him about this..."

She unravelled the sackcloth and held up a metal blade about a foot long. I drew breath, knowing immediately this was the dagger, the bronze knife that Pengelly was so convinced held the key to the fate of the Christian church, and the modern chemical composition of which had so surprised Professor Polkinghorne. I watched the light from the lantern flame (which would fail soon I was sure), catch the dull metal, bringing out an almost greenish hue, especially on the raised edges of the numerous symbols etched onto the blade and handle.

"Why is this knife so important, Angel?"

"It is of a special metal, and the making is unknown to us today. Hard like a diamond when cold, soft as clay to fashion when hot."

"It's modern, Angel, a replica from America."

She smiled and nodded, stroking the blade thoughtfully. "No, it really is very old, and these symbols guard a great secret. That's why I couldn't let Slevin have it."

"And what is that great secret that—"

"No," she almost shouted, voice now very weak but still defiant. "Forget secrets. Right now, this knife is important because it will get us out of here. Now please, Mr Sangster, just climb the ladder, start chipping away at the weak part of the ledge, and the knife will do the rest." She passed me the dagger then slumped back against the tomb, eyes half closed.

I stood, lifted the metal ladder, and leaned it back against the wall at an angle that would let me reach up to the side of the slab. Then, taking the lantern and knife in one hand, I climbed, looking down and almost falling as the interior of the tomb came into view. The bottom was much lower than the surrounding stone sides (which were in truth just a parapet surrounding a deep pit) and strewn with the unmistakable shapes of bones. Many were scattered at random, but there were some, such as ribs and long bones like femurs, still arranged as they would have been in life, and a white rounded orb at one end was surely a human skull.

I steadied myself and, hooking the lantern on the end of the ladder, began to scrape at the granite with the dagger.

Angel was right, the blade did cut the stone, in a way I wouldn't have thought possible, grinding the solid granite to dust as I moved the knife back and forth. Spurred on by the sound of the slab groaning, I scraped harder, bringing down more dust and feeling the slab shift, once, twice, and then a third time. The ledge then cracked, and the slab fell away, knocking me backwards and crashing against the tomb, shattering the stone lid, the noise echoing around my head until I fell into darkness.

"Mr Sangster," I heard Angel say. "Mr Sangster, are you alright?"

I opened my eyes to see the girl, pale faced and wiping away blood from my brow with her sleeve.

"You fell when the slab came down. If you can walk, we can climb out."

I looked upwards, allowing my blurred vision to settle for a moment, to see the square entrance in the roof was now a gaping hole.

"Can you walk, Mr Sangster?"

I pushed myself up against the wall and took a step forward.

"Yes, just." I gave a slight laugh. "I'm supposed to be looking after you."

"We must leave this place; I don't like it here." She took the dagger, which was lying next to me, and wrapped it with the sackcloth before placing it back into her bag.

"You go first, Angel," I said, pointing to the ladder. She climbed slowly up, every rung clearly painful and almost beyond her strength, and I followed, still unsteady myself from the concussion. Despite this, within less than a minute we were safely in the rock passage.

"Come on, Angel," I said, as she paused and stared back down into the now darkened sepulchre which had been her dungeon for so many days. I thought at first she was perhaps trying to rid herself of the fear of the place, facing back at it now she was free. Then I wondered when, for the most fleeting of moments, I could have sworn a smile passed across Angel's lips, a knowing but enigmatic smile, perhaps triumphant.

"Mr Sangster, promise me something, please?"

"If I can."

"Don't tell them I have the dagger."

"Who do mean by 'them'?"

"Anyone. It will be for the best. Oh," she whispered. "And burn all my notes."

I wasn't quite sure why but felt that somehow what Angel wanted would be for the best, so just nodded my agreement. She nodded back, turned away from the sepulchre entrance, then held tight on my arm. Supporting each other like this, we walked slowly, the noise of raindrops growing louder as we came to the fogou entrance, where I saw that the pile of boulders had been replaced. Swinging the lantern and peering through gaps between the boulders, I also saw that the iron grille was back in situ.

Slevin could have made his escape and let the authorities know where we were but had chosen to leave Angel and me to our fate, concealed, and Slevin had done his work well. Anyone passing, including the police, wouldn't see us unless we could somehow shout out and be heard, which wouldn't be easy, given the ceaseless noise of the rain and the ongoing thunderstorm. I gulped, remembering Pentreath's comment about the dogs.

'Will still usually pick up a scent, unless it's raining heavily of course, then they can't.'

The only way out was to dig.

I grabbed the stones and pushed, but after several frantic minutes, it became clear that the way those boulders were arranged meant that they could only be removed from the outside.

"Don't leave me here," said Angel, now slumped against me. "I can't be alone. Don't leave me."

"I won't, and I can't get out anyway," I said. "We'll stay in here together, then try again when the storm dies down." I looked at her face, now ashen white, and wondered whether she would last that long, and with my own head cut and throbbing, and almost unusable bruised legs, whether I was anyway fit to raise the alarm if someone did happen by. "Or until someone comes," I added for comfort. "Whichever is first."

I gently removed Angel's arm from mine and went to help her sit down, but she stopped me.

"No, there's a way we can get help."

"How?"

"That jerrycan, by the block and tackle."

"What jerrycan?"

"The one Slevin carries, with the liquid that he uses to cover his tracks."

"Won't it—"

"Just get it," she said sharply. "While we still have a flame in the lantern."

"You'll be okay here?"

"Yes, now go."

I limped back, waving the lantern in front of me, seeing nothing at first, and then behind some sacking a glint, and there it was, a green can standing by the opening to the sepulchre. Angel was right.

I grabbed the handle, the can feeling surprisingly heavy in my already weakened hand, then stumbled slowly back to the rock covered entrance, where Angel now sat. Her face, if possible, was now even whiter than when I had left her a few minutes earlier.

"Was it heavy?" was all she said.

"Yes, how did you know it would be there?"

"Slevin's gone now, so he's no need to cover his tracks anymore. And if it's heavy all the better. That means the can's full, so all we need to do is make a fuse." I felt in my coat pocket and pulled out a handkerchief.

"This do?"

"No, it's cotton. Will burn in a flash, either blow us up or go out before the flame gets to the can." She looked downwards at herself. "Now then, I'm sorry, Mr Sangster, but I have to—"

"What are you doing?" I shouted, taking an involuntary step back when she began to unzip what was left of her skirt.

"Making a fuse," she answered, taking the torn garment, and rolling it into a tight sausage of material. "This skirt is acrylic. Will burn slowly if I soak it in the liquid, now roll it up and put it into the spout of

245

the jerrycan." I took the material sausage from her and unscrewed the top of the can, eyes stinging immediately as the liquid inside began to evaporate in my face. I plugged the spout.

"Now what?"

"We place the can behind the boulders," she said, pulling herself unsteadily to her feet. "Light the fuse, then go back down the rock passage until it goes off."

"Alright," I said, watching her in the lantern light, now only dressed in blouse, pants and shoes. "But for heaven's sake take my oilskin first, Angel, you'll catch your death, and anyway..." I pulled off the yellow smock and held it out, seeing the nine-tailed fish motif on Angel's ankle. "I can't have you sitting like that all night."

"I am sixteen you know."

"Never mind that."

She took the oilskin and silently pulled it over her shoulders, watching me intently as I set the jerrycan down, making sure it was as close to the front of the archway as possible while still out of the rain's reach. Then I took the lantern and undid the clasp, opening the guard and manoeuvring the precious flame towards the end of the makeshift fuse.

But just as I went to light the material, a lightning flash must have rent the sky as the spaces between the boulders were suddenly edged in blue, matched by deafening multiple thunderclaps. Whether from the surprise of the noise itself or an actual shock from the sodden, electrically charged air, I couldn't tell but, either way, I reeled backwards, knocking the lantern as I went, which tipped on its side, oil dripping out and catching alight. After a brief flare, the passageway darkened, lit only by the remaining oil glowing on the ground, which could never have been used to light the makeshift fuse. I felt my legs buckle and cursed myself that our last hope of raising an alarm was extinguished, then I saw Angel, standing over me and smiling.

"I think you'd better let me do it," she said, holding up a small object in her hand that I recognised as the matchbook from the Cassandra Arms. "You dropped this on the floor when you pulled out your hanky."

"Did I?"

"Yes, and I picked it up, now go back down the passage, quickly."

I got up on my knees and began to crawl, looking back to see the flare of a match, the skirt material fuse catch light, and Angel begin to stumble after me. Pulling myself upright I took her arm, and we rounded the corner together. Then, without any kind of a cue, we both turned away from the entrance and placed our hands over our ears.

I waited like that for what seemed an eternity, eyes shut as tightly as the palms of my hands were pressed over my ears. Then, through closed lids, I sensed the flash behind me, heard a crashing noise and felt almost intolerable force on my back from the blast, which threw me forward, as stones hit my legs repeatedly. Angel, too weak to stand against it, pressed hard into my chest as rock, wind, fire, and noise flew down the passage. Then, as quickly as it had come, the burning maelstrom subsided, leaving us clinging together in a bright glow coming from the direction of the stone archway.

"Angel," I mouthed, ears ringing so that I wasn't sure what I (or she) could and couldn't actually hear.

"That's done it," I heard her say, almost, it seemed, in slow motion.

"Done it?" I felt my senses returning as I spoke.

"Yes," she mouthed back, pulling away from me and pointing towards the glow. "Slevin's fluid's so volatile it will have split that iron grill into a thousand pieces and sent up a plume of flame through those rocks a hundred feet into the sky. Someone's bound to come now."

"Then let's go and wait by the archway." I offered my hand, before feeling my legs give way again, the pain from multiple rock hits now kicking in. She steadied my waist with her arm, leaned up, then kissed me on the cheek.

"Second time tonight," I said, trying not to groan with the growing aches I was feeling all over, especially in my ribs as she pressed against me. "What's that for?"

"It's another thank you, Mr Sangster. Not just for saving me tonight, but for everything."

SATURDAY,
MAY THE 30TH
12 NOON

"I'm not sure Mr Sangster can see anyone, I'll…"

"Don't worry, Matron," I heard an unfamiliar voice say. "We'll only be a moment. Police business and all that."

"Well, I don't know…"

"As I say, don't worry, Matron."

I opened my eyes to see the owner of the voice, a tall man of early middle age, rather oddly, or so I thought, wearing a dark suit despite it being a Saturday. His hair was also heavily slicked back with Brylcreem (rarely seen in this new decade, Sarah having banned my use of it the year before), which, along with a pair of black, heavy-rimmed glasses, gave off an air of decades past. Behind him stood three more familiar figures; DCS Pentreath, Sergeant Bolitho, and WPC Woon.

I looked around to see the whitewashed walls of the academy infirmary, and through the haze just about remembered being brought here the night before, then being woken up early in the morning by Mrs Davey sticking a thermometer in my mouth.

"Hello Sangster," said Pentreath, in what sounded to me, despite my still being half asleep, like a very uncomfortable voice compared with his usual measured and very deliberate tone. "Trust you're on the mend?" I nodded. "No broken bones then?"

"Just aching bones and a few cuts, Pentreath. I'll be up and about this afternoon."

"That's good to hear because you were certainly in a state when we found you. Must have taken the brunt of that blast."

"It's all a little hazy. Was I there long with Angel after the explosion?"

"About fifteen minutes. We found the two of you by that stone entrance to the fogou, both pretty well out of it."

"And Angel?"

"Dehydrated, saw her on a drip in Treliske hospital this morning."

"A drip?"

"Yes, but as far as I understand it, that was all, and she's pretty much recovered now. Parents were already there at her bedside when I went to visit."

"Did she, er, say anything to you?"

"Not much. Now may I introduce Mr, er... Smith." He looked at the stranger. "He's down from London. Would like a few words alone with you if that's alright?"

I looked at Mrs Davey and Velinda Flimwell for confirmation, both of whom shrugged.

"Good," Pentreath continued. "Now, we can all leave the room, and Mr Smith and Mr Sangster can have a chat."

"So," said the stranger when they'd gone. "May I sit?" He pulled up a chair and sat next to the bed without waiting for me to say yes. "You've had quite an ordeal I believe?"

"Smith's your name, is it?"

"That's right."

"And what do you do?"

"Oh, government matters, small cog, big machine, that sort of thing." He took a biscuit from my bedside table. "May I?"

Er... yes."

"Oh, thank you, I've such a weakness for bourbons."

"Mmmm…" I nodded, sensing a menace in his voice that made me try all the more to wake myself fully.

"So," he said, in between biscuit bites. "I'm here to make sure any loose ends are tied up. This Slevin character, what d'you know about him?"

This wasn't the first time I'd seen the likes of Smith (or whatever he was really called). His type had appeared now and again during my time with Naval Intelligence and, by coincidence, I'd encountered one of these invisible government people very recently during a case with the institute, so decided it would be futile to avoid any questions.

"Soviet agent, masquerading as a Vatican official."

"Well not masquerading," said Smith. "He was the real thing, Roman Catholic man and boy, but his loyalties didn't lie, er… with the church."

"Or the West in general I suppose," I added.

"Indeed. Now did you know there's been a Russian sub in these waters recently, Sangster?"

"The sea monster locals have been seeing?"

"Quite. Well, the sub dropped off the equipment Slevin needed, such as an inflatable dinghy, shortwave radio, and some kind of infernal chemical that Slevin could use to cover his tracks. Dog proof, makes it so there's no trace of his scent." Smith picked up another bourbon. "They even came ashore and helped him with the digging to expose the tomb. That lifting gear we found had Soviet markings on it, but," he laughed, "I suppose you already know all that?"

"I know about the chemical because we used it to cause the explosion. What was it by the way?"

"Soviet cleverness, Reds are good at that kind of thing. Not sure exactly what the stuff was made of though."

"No?"

"You rather selfishly blew it all up and didn't leave anything much for us to analyse."

"And did Slevin make his escape?"

"We think that sub picked him up at high tide. New class of boat, very manoeuvrable, came in close to a cove on the point. Carricknath, I believe they call the place."

"Yes, I've seen that boat, near the lighthouse."

"Oh," Smith said. "And how would you know it was that particular submarine?"

"Come on," I shouted, his urbane and obfuscating manner getting the better of my self-control. "How many Russian subs are lurking in these waters, and anyway, it's a class of one vessel." It was then my turn to laugh. "But I suppose you already know all that."

"Touché, Sangster." Smith smiled to himself. "Your calls to the redoubtable Admiral Anson and his subsequent, er… enquiries, are what prompted me to come here and visit in the first place. We'd somehow missed Slevin slipping out of London because he used the train, and we were only watching for him on the roads."

"Ha, so he was one step ahead of even you people." I laughed harder before groaning at the pain in my bruised ribs. "But what of the priest now?"

"Well, the police found Slevin's motorbike, with some equipment including a radio, abandoned in the car park by the lighthouse, and the empty dinghy washed up close by as well."

"There was a storm last night. Do you think he could have drowned?"

"That's a possibility, or the sub picked him up. Either way, I'm sure you'll agree this traitorous Monsignor is probably gone from our shores."

Smith was silent for a moment, glancing sideways in a way that told me he might be hiding something, before looking me directly in the eye.

"So, Sangster, you're ex-naval intelligence, commander in your own right and all that, so you've signed the official secrets act, know the importance of, er… keeping mum." I nodded. "Well, none of this comes out, understood?" I nodded again. "Now, is there anyone else who knows, other than that Blackwood girl." He frowned, slightly theatrically I thought. "I'm afraid she does worry me, Sangster, I—"

"You leave her alone, Smith," I shouted, sitting up. "She's young and fragile."

"Calm down, man," he said. "I've already spoken to her this morning, very gently I promise, and accompanied throughout by Pentreath's sweet little WPC Woon."

"Where?"

"Girl's in Truro hospital and seems remarkably well given her ordeal. Even her sprained ankle is almost healed, I was quite…"

"As I say, leave her alone, Smith. I mean it."

"Oh, I will. She doesn't know anything. Seemed to think it was hilarious, Slevin imagining he'd find the body of Christ buried in Cornwall."

"Did she?"

"Yes, told me the tomb is just an historical grave, of interest to people who dig that kind of thing up, but nothing more."

"How can you know she's right?"

"Well, for a start, the human remains in the tomb were of an old woman, not a thirty-something man. Police who went into the place established that straight off. And the idea of Christ coming to England, or his body being brought here, well, it's preposterous…" He snorted.

"Oh, I see."

"I'm glad you see," he said, licking biscuit crumbs off his fingertips. Now, there isn't anyone else who knows about these, er… extra details. Not that Canon Pengelly, or any of the other staff or pupils here?"

"Nobody."

"Not even your lovely wife?"

"You've crossed a line there, Smith, step back." I felt my voice gag, but nevertheless tried to speak with authority and conviction, which was difficult, lying in bed wearing a pair of borrowed pyjamas while Smith was suited and sitting in a chair. "And she knows nothing of all this."

"Then I know it's all safe, because any leak would have to come directly from you, and we both know that couldn't happen." He drew in a breath. "Got to be careful you understand, nothing personal."

"All safe," I said solemnly, feeling, for the first time I could remember the sensation that my veins (as I'd read in numerous books) had turned to ice. "Because Mr, er... Smith you said your name was?" He nodded. "Well I'll take your word for it, but remember, you found me so I can find you, and I'd take it entirely personally in the worst possible way for you if my wife was to, er... know anything of this."

"Um... of course," he said, his bland manner now ruffled. "I'll, er... take the opportunity to, er... bid you a speedy recovery and a good day, Mr Sangster." He quickly stood up. "Good day."

3 PM

I felt a hand on my cheek, its touch warm, soft, and familiar. Opening my eyes, saw Sarah standing over the bed.

"Jack, I've been so worried."

"Nothing to worry about now," I said, opening my arms and sitting up, only to feel my side shoot with a spasmic pain. "Oh," I groaned, lying down again. "Perhaps you'd better come to me, Sarah."

And she did, throwing herself around me, which also hurt my sprained neck ('sorry darling, is there any part of you that doesn't ache?'), clinging for several minutes before withdrawing her embrace and sitting down on the side of the bed.

"I got the call last night from the police but there was nothing I could do until this morning. Train took hours and hours. Stopped everywhere, almost no food, and changes in Birmingham, Bristol, Plymouth and—"

"Never mind, you're here now. Er... could you lift this pillow, help me sit up?"

"Of course, darling."

"Did you speak to the doctor?"

"I spoke to the school matron, what's her name?"

"Mrs Davey."

"Yes, Mrs Davey. Seems the doctor says your wounds are superficial."

"Superficial. Ha, he should see for himself what it feels like."

"What the doctor meant, darling," she said, kissing me again, "is that they're not lasting wounds, and he also thinks you could leave here today providing you're careful, don't wear a seat belt, and I do any driving."

"All the way home?"

"No, just back to the hotel for a quiet evening. And they'll all be keen to see you, Morwenna, Pasco and co."

"How d'you know?"

"I dropped my bag off on the way here. Ever so concerned they were."

"Alright," I said, envisaging anything but a quiet evening. "But let's move to a ground floor room, I don't fancy all those stairs."

4PM

"Now then, Mr Sangster, take it slowly, and rest the bottom of your crutch on each step as you go down." I felt Matron Davey's arm around one shoulder and Sarah's around the other as I slowly descended from the main entrance of the academy, to see my car gleaming on the gravel drive. "Now then, Mr Sangster, I—"

All at once there was an ear-splitting noise from the sky, followed by swirling wind as a green helicopter appeared from above the trees of the Plantation and lowered itself onto the front lawn, blowing patterns in the grass as it landed.

The door opened, and out stepped Sir John, ducking the downdraft as he walked towards us. He was followed by a man with striped epaulettes on the shoulders of his white shirt (the pilot I assumed), who then helped a man and a woman out of the door. I recognised them as Angel's parents.

"My goodness, Sangster, we are a mess, aren't we?"

"Thank you, Sir John."

"No, thank you, Sangster, sterling work, sterling." He looked down at Angel's mother, who had now caught up. "Don't you think so, Marjorie?"

"Oh yes, Mr Sangster, George and I cannot thank you enough, we really can't."

With this she threw herself against me in a bear hug, which would have knocked me on my back if it hadn't been for Sarah and Matron Davey's steadying hands.

"Be gentle with Mr Sangster," said the matron, gently pushing Mrs Blackwood back. "He's well enough but delicate."

"Oh, I'm sorry."

"Don't be," I said. "I'm just… you know, happy Angel's safe and sound."

"We all are, Sangster, and d'you know?"

"Sir John?"

"Marjorie and, er…" He looked at Mr Blackwood.

"George," said his wife.

"Yes, George of course." I smiled at Sir John's blundering attempt to ingratiate himself with Angel's parents, giving them a ride in his helicopter but unable to remember her (admittedly rather forgettable), father's name. "Well, they've agreed that a statement vindicating the academy can be made public. Angel's also made a statement endorsing the system as well. Sent the statements to all the parents and we're going to put them out in national newspapers and all that as well. This case has caused quite a stir in Fleet Street, I can tell you."

"Of course, nobody from the academy behaved inappropriately," I said, catching the eye of Velinda Flimwell. "So, the education department will let us keep our license, Sir John?"

"Almost a dead cert, Sangster. Now then, I'm billeted at the Grand Duchy Hotel in Truro tonight, and I've arranged a room there for the Blackwoods so they can be closer to Angel while she convalesces. Shall we see you and your wife there for dinner this evening?"

I looked at Sarah, who shrugged and looked at Mrs Davey.

"Doctor's told me I can discharge Mr Sangster," said the matron. "But I think he needs a quiet evening all the same."

"Course, Sangster, what was I thinking. Anyway, we'll be having a reception here tomorrow afternoon, so hopefully you'll be fit enough to come."

"I hope so."

"Until tomorrow then," called Sir John, striding back across the lawn, the pilot following with the now rather confused looking Blackwoods in tow. Sarah, Velinda, Mrs Davey and I said nothing as we, along with most of the academy pupils and staff (who I imagined had come down to the lawn when they first heard the noise of the rotors), watched the helicopter lift up then turn and swing back across the Plantation, disappearing from sight with its noise gone a few seconds afterwards, leaving the academy once again in tranquil silence.

*

"Alright, Mr Sangster?" said Mrs Davey as I eased my bruised legs slowly into the passenger seat of the E-Type, which seemed somehow to have become much lower and more awkward to get into than it ever had before. Sarah had put the hood down, which helped a little, but I still feared being able to get out again.

"Yes, thank you, Mrs Davey."

"And thanks again, Matron, for looking after my husband so well," Sarah added, while tying up a headscarf and then pressing the ignition button. "You and Velinda really have been marvellous."

Both women smiled, and we waved, before pulling away down the drive to the gatehouse, where Runtle stood poking a cylindrical metal garden incinerator that belched white smoke.

"Pull up."

Sarah slammed on the brakes, and I groaned.

"Now, there's a bag of papers in the boot. Take it and ask Runtle to put that bag into his incinerator."

"Sorry?"

"Ask Runtle to put the bag into his incinerator. The whole bag."

Sarah climbed out, more meekly than I expected, and took the bag to Runtle as requested. I watched as it was engulfed in flames, quickly reducing to ash. The last item to ignite was Angel's notebook, but even that, with its leather binding, burned hard, so that within less than a minute the last of Angel's evidence was gone (or so I thought, watching the flames).

Runtle then went inside the gatehouse, reappearing as the main gates swung open.

"Bye Runtle," shouted Sarah.

Runtle waved and we turned into the lane, where I instinctively looked into the woods of the Plantation, wondering if the tramp would be watching us. I saw nothing, and we carried on, past the layby with the Bethadew sign, the track to which was cordoned off with police tape, and where a van I recognised as belonging to Sue Driver and team was parked.

"Looks like a TV crew," said Sarah. "Must be doing a feature on the whole thing."

"I'm sure," I answered, as we sped past. "By the way, the car's running smoothly again, and I'd swear someone cleaned and polished it."

"Runtle, he fixed the car and cleaned it as well. Said to me someone must have, now how did he put it... 'Done a gashly job with the timing.'"

"Those bloody Stockers." I remembered Pete's words; 'You were misfiring a little. Timing all wrong.'

"Anyway, darling, I'm glad the doctor's given you the all-clear to come back to the hotel. We'll have a nice quiet evening and, as long as you're feeling up to it, go to Sir John's reception tomorrow afternoon. And you know," she said, pausing to look around as she drove, "I love the silence of these lanes, you can almost hear the—"

She was cut short by a bang behind us.

"What's that, Jack, I can't see a thing in the mirror?"

"Boot lid's just flown up."

SUNDAY,
MAY THE 31ST
12 NOON

"Still got the police cordon up," I said to Sarah as we drove past the turning to Bethadew mine, surrounded as it was by plastic tape. "I wonder why?"

"Suppose they'll hand it back over to the National Trust or the British Museum or whoever soon," she replied. "Can't be anything left to do with it as a crime scene now Angel's safe and that awful Slevin's gone."

"And now that I'm safe."

"Of course, darling," she laughed. "Now that you're safe. Oh…" Sarah swerved to one side as a white van careered past us. 'John Williams & Co.' said a sign on the side.

"He could have been a bit more careful overtaking, I… look, lying by the hedge, it's that old man we saw on the ferry, isn't it?"

I saw the familiar figure of the tramp flat out by the roadside, then heard our brakes screech, causing the old man to sit up as the car slammed to a halt. Sarah jumped out and ran to him.

"Are you hurt?" I shouted, winding my window down.

He shook his head.

"Can you move?" Sarah asked, placing her hand on his shoulder.

"Course I can move, young lady," he said, shaking off her touch.

"But you were hit, I saw—"

"Nonsense. I was just taking a rest here on the verge, minding my own business like you should."

Sarah gave a 'huh' sound and walked back around the car.

"Glad you're alright anyway," I called through the window as she sat down and slammed the door.

"And I'm glad Angel's alright," he answered, pulling himself up on his staff.

"We all are, and thanks for your help the other night."

"Least I could do."

"Excuse me," Sarah called across from the driving seat. "That Hamsa on your wrist, it's a real beauty. Do you mind telling where you got it?"

"You do pry, young lady."

"Please tell me," said Sarah quietly. "It reminds me of my childhood."

"Oh, well in that case," he said, staring at her with wide eyes. "Um... someone gave it to me a long time ago, as a thank you."

"A thank you for what?" Sarah asked.

"I was a shoemaker. Made a particularly fine pair of sandals for a lady in Aelia, and she gave me the Hamsa."

"Do you mean, er... Aelia Capitolina?"

"S'right."

"So, Jerusalem?"

"S'right," he said again, then leaned his head forward and looked even harder at us both. "You're bound for that academy I take it."

"Yes. All the drama's over, but we've still got to clear a few things up."

"Drama's all over, eh?" laughed the tramp.

"It is."

"Well, keep your wits about you. Never know who's hiding in these woods."

"Will we be seeing you around?"

261

"No, I'll be on my way now, work's done here. Maybe across the sea's where I'll go."

With that he turned and began to shuffle along the road, his staff tapping on the tarmac as he went. Suddenly the tapping ceased, and I looked around to catch a glimpse of his coat tails disappearing into the woods. I wound the window up and Sarah drove on.

"That was odd, darling."

"Him saying he's going across the sea?"

"No."

"Then what, the comment about never knowing who's hiding in the woods?"

"Well yes, but I could also have sworn that van struck the old man. You couldn't see it from the passenger seat, but I could. Looked like a hit and run."

"Can't have been. He was right as rain."

"And another thing. Him talking about Aelia."

"What of it?"

"Aelia's an old name for a new city the Romans built on the ruins of Jerusalem. Nobody's called the place Aelia for about two thousand years."

"Well obviously some people do still call it that. And after all, you knew the name."

"I suppose I did, Jack."

*

The gates were uncharacteristically wide open as we turned into the academy, with Runtle greeting us as we climbed out of the car by the main doors.

"Been like Piccadilly Circus here today, Mr Sangster. I've given up opening and closing me gates. Look." He pointed to a number of vehicles that were parked next to us, including several cars and, to my surprise, the Harlech TV van (I wondered what Sue Driver was up to now). "It's folks bringing their kids back, and that TV crew, and we just had Williams' builders from Grampound come to make the chapel safe." Runtle paused to take a breath. "And I'll tell you what," he then continued, in as animated a voice as I'd ever heard from the usually implacable caretaker. "If we get any more people coming, I'll have to put up—"

But Runtle never managed to tell us what it was he would have to 'put up', as all of a sudden, the noise of rotors above the trees blanked out every other sound and the shadow of Sir John's helicopter appeared on the lawn, its wind scattering pupils who had been seated on the grass as the aircraft set itself down.

Sir John then stepped out, ducking under the downdraft, followed by the white-shirted pilot and the Blackwoods, including Angel. Even from where I stood, the girl looked to be in much better shape than when I had last seen her, lying almost unconscious at the entrance to the Bethadew fogou.

"Sir John's just made his usual understated entrance," said Velinda Flimwell, appearing on the steps. "That contraption will break the windows one day," she laughed. "I swear it."

"Morning all," boomed Sir John as the noise from the helicopter subsided. "Or is it afternoon?"

"It's well past noon," said Velinda. "Anyway, everyone, please follow me."

She led us across the lawn to where several parents stood talking to members of staff (Runtle's 'folks bringing their kids back' I presumed), along with Sue Driver and team.

"Sir John," she said. "Shall we join you?"

"Got the woman doing a documentary on the academy, Sangster," Sir John said in the nearest he could manage to a whisper. "Marvellous publicity."

As Sue came forward, I was surprised to see Pengelly standing behind her. It then occurred to me that nobody, perhaps with the exception of Slevin and the shady Mr Smith, would know of the canon's true involvement, and I certainly had no intention of telling anyone. Pengelly looked at me with a pleading expression (to confirm my silence I assumed), then walked over to Angel and whispered something in her ear, and I watched her nod to him.

"We'll be having sandwiches and cake later, but for now may I offer you all tea," Velinda then asked, pointing to a long table set out on the lawn with cups, milk jugs, sugar bowls, saucers, teapots, and plates of biscuits.

And so, despite everything that had happened, there we stood, drinking tea, eating biscuits, and making small talk. All of us except Angel that was, who sat herself down on the grass, seemingly lost in thought.

"Marvellous news that we found Angel," interrupted Sir John, rubbing his hands. "Hope you're getting all this, Miss Driver."

"Oh yes, getting it all," said Sue, scribbling furiously in her notebook.

"And Angel's ever so grateful to Mr Sangster for everything he did," said Marjorie. "Ever so grateful, aren't you, Angel?"

"Pardon, Mum?" Angel asked, her voice, eyes, and general expression somehow very different to when I had last seen her.

"Grateful to Mr Sangster, aren't you?"

"Oh yes, I am." She stood up. "Actually, would anyone mind if I took Mr Sangster to the boathouse? I want to show him the boat we were fixing up before all this happened, maybe take him out on the water."

"Today?" said Marjorie.

"Yes please."

"I'm sure Mr Sangster doesn't want to—"

"Perhaps," I said, catching Sarah's eye and picking up the faintest of nods. "As long as we go slowly enough for an old cripple like me that is." Everyone laughed and then returned to small talk.

"Angel," I then said, rubbing my side with one hand and waving my stick with the other. "I really am a bit of a cripple right now though. And..." I added, pointing to a bandage round her right ankle, "you've got your foot strapped up. Perhaps another time."

"No, please," she said, in an almost desperate way that both surprised and flattered me (I supposed she was proud of the work on the boat and wanted to show it off to me). "Today, I'll bring you some seat cushions."

"Alright, as long as you manage everything, Angel. I think I can get in and out, but I won't be much good for anything else."

"After lunch then." Angel started to walk towards river.

"You going to the boathouse now?"

"Yes, I need to top up the outboard with petrol. Then I'm going to the chapel."

"The chapel?"

"Pengelly said he wanted to see me there."

"Did he say why?"

"No, but would you come and find me in there, Mr Sangster? I'm not sure why, but I'd be happier if you'd come and find me."

"Alright."

"See you in a bit then."

*

"Jack," Sarah called to me. "Velinda's been telling me everything. I had no idea about all the sleuthing you've done, makes me feel quite weak—"

"I know," I sighed with embarrassment. "Weak at the knees. Didn't want to bore you with the details."

"So, this really is a happy ending," said Velinda, rubbing her hands together after an awkward pause. "I wasn't sure at first, Jack, but Sir John's instinct was clearly right."

"Instinct?" I asked.

"Not to tell you Angel was missing until Tuesday evening. Leaving you to finish off the phase two plans in peace."

"What?"

"He said, now how did he put it, yes… wanted to keep his powder dry."

Of course, it made sense now, the delay in my being told that Angel was missing. I had been worried my finding out late would anger Sir John but now it seemed the whole thing was actually of his making. How did I not realise before?

"I'll give him powder." I turned to see Sir John holding court by the tea table, and was about to walk over and give him a piece of my mind when Sarah touched my shoulder.

"Leave it, darling."

I grunted, then took a deep breath and left it.

*

"Promised to go and find Angel in the chapel," I said to Sarah and Velinda. "Back in a few minutes."

I crossed the lawn towards the main building to see Spider coming the other way.

"Mr Sangster," he smiled. "That crutch, are you alright now?"

"Oh, I'll mend. It's more of a walking stick than a crutch anyway. And you?"

"I came round from my trance after a couple of hours. Can't remember much of what happened, but the others told me. Sounds like we saved Angel." I nodded and he nodded, both of us silently acknowledged his help.

"Anyway, I'm off to the chapel now to find her."

"Then you'll need to go outside. The builders blocked off the inside passage to the chapel this morning for the repairs."

"Thanks, I will. Oh and, Spider?"

"Yes, Mr Sangster?"

"All that translating and so on. Did you and Jonny keep any notes?"

"No, I gave you everything we had. All seems a bit of a blur now."

"Good. Forget you ever saw it."

*

Walking around the side of the main building, I came to the stone archway that stood over the entrance to the chapel, and noticed a wooden sign erected next to it.

'John Williams & Co, Grampound.
Roofer and General Builder'

I recognised the name from the van that had driven Sarah and me off the road earlier and determined to have words with the driver. At that moment, a middle-aged woman in a tweed suit and hat came striding out of the door, almost colliding with me.

"Terribly sorry," she said, looking down at my crutch. "Wasn't looking where I was going. Just had the most amazing experience."

"Is everything alright in there?"

"Oh yes, it's just that the bell, it's as sound as, well… a bell."

"Er… it would be I suppose."

"Sorry, let me introduce myself. Cynthia Blewett, campanologist. Brought in to tune the chapel bell before it's rehung."

"And did you?"

"Did I what?"

"Retune it."

"No."

"Was there a problem?"

"No, the point is, Mr er…"

"Sangster."

"Well, Mr Sangster, that bell is fully in tune, and it's a virgin."

"Sorry?"

"Bells generally need tuning every thirty years or so, and this one is hundreds of years old by all accounts but hasn't ever been tuned as far as I can tell. It's what we call a virgin bell, and I can't explain it."

"Mmmm…"

"And do you know what, Mr Sangster?"

"No."

"The bell cracked the granite paving stones on the church floor when it fell but wasn't damaged itself. Not at all. God knows what it's made of but, anyway, I got the strangest feeling that..." She stopped herself, visibly shivering.

"Feeling that..." I encouraged.

"Well, the girl was in there, the one from the newspaper picture, but she seemed scared."

"And Canon Pengelly?"

"Yes, and he seemed scared as well, and there was another man I didn't like the look of, long hair, one of the builders I suppose." She shivered again. "I can tell you, there was an atmosphere in that chapel, and I couldn't wait to get out. Now good day."

With that she hurried off down the path, and I stepped inside the chapel, to see the 'virgin' bell that had so nearly killed Pengelly and so completely amazed Mrs Blewett the campanologist, set upright on a temporary wooden trestle table. The fallen organ pipes were still lying on the ground, but now sitting neatly in rows, so that the whole place looked tidy and ready for repair, giving me a reassuring sensation that turned out to be very short lived.

*

"Alright, Sangster, that's far enough," came a bark from behind the altar.

I jolted, then stood stock still.

"Slevin, is that you?"

"Right again, Mister Special Investigator man. Back from the dead."

"But you..." I stammered. "You were drowned, or picked up, or..."

"And I've got a friend of yours wants to say hello."

I heard the gagging sound of someone trying to cry out.

"Go on, love, say hello."

"Mr Sangster..." It was Angel's voice and, as she spoke, I saw her and Slevin come out into the light. He had one hand round Angel's waist, while the other held a wicked looking flick-knife that he opened with a sickening click against her throat.

"Now I don't want to do anything rash." Slevin pushed the knife hard against the girl's neck.

"Then what do you want?"

"Just the dagger. This girl wouldn't tell me where it was for five long days in the tomb, so perhaps you can tell me now."

"I don't know." He pushed his knife up to Angel's throat, making her gag louder. "Alright, Slevin, alright." I felt my heart pound. "Now Angel, just tell us where you've hidden it, please."

She said nothing, shaking her head despite the knife now scratching her skin. I realised Slevin held all the cards and was about to shout again at Angel to tell him when I saw movement, and recognised Pengelly, fingers held to his lips, tiptoeing out from behind the stone pulpit. The canon held the crucifix communion chalice by the neck, which he brandished while nodding towards Slevin.

"Slevin, just see reason," I said slowly, trying to bring a sense of calm (although I felt anything but calm), while giving Pengelly, who took silent, deliberate steps past the altar, time to come close to the priest. "Take the knife away from her throat."

"Nothing doing, Sangster. Now I mean it." He pushed the knife harder, Angel whimpering as blood droplets ran down her neck.

"Angel, please, tell him, you can't—"

I saw Pengelly raise the chalice, then take one last silent step, but the look on my face must have given him away, Slevin jumped to one side, still clutching Angel. Pengelly's blow then fell harmlessly past him, the weight of the chalice pulling the canon forward as it did so.

"Think I was born yesterday?" shouted the priest, kicking sideways at Pengelly's knee as he spoke, so that the canon collapsed with a groan. Slevin followed this with another, even more vicious kick, this time to the head, rendering Pengelly motionless in front of the altar, the chalice rolling back and forth beside him with a grating noise until it halted next to his face.

"Slevin," I said, holding my hands up. "I know where the dagger is. Let the girl go and I'll tell you."

"No, Sangster, tell me first, then we'll see."

269

Did he know I was bluffing? And even if I had been able to tell him, he could easily keep Angel as a hostage. The only chance was to get as close to Slevin as I could before he realised the bluff. Then get the knife off him, somehow.

"We'll make an exchange, Slevin. I'll come up there, you give me Angel and I'll tell you. Now, I'm coming up." I walked slowly up the steps to the altar dais, exaggerating my limp and use of the crutch as I went. I approached Slevin and Angel.

"Alright, Sangster, close enough. Now tell me."

"Let her go."

Slevin pushed Angel away but kept brandishing the knife. Angel let out a gasp as he released his grip, then caught my eye. She seemed to know what I was going to do.

"Now, Sangster, last chance."

I stepped forward, exaggerating my limp even more, then pretended to trip with the crutch, before lurching forwards and smashing my stick down on the hand holding the knife.

"Run, Angel," I shouted, as the blade clattered to the floor. She jumped from the dais, I grabbed the knife, then followed her, a spasm of excruciating pain shooting through my leg as I landed on the floor (although I just managed to remain on my feet). Angel stood behind me and we both began to back away.

"It's over, Slevin," I said to the priest, who was cradling his bruised hand. "You can't carry on now." Angel and I were now close by the stone archway, and I turned to grasp the door handle, only to hear a familiar click that made my heart miss a beat.

"Like I said before, Sangster, that's far enough." Slevin stood on the dais smiling, pistol in hand. "Now you can see I've nothing to lose, so please, save us all a lot of fuss. Where is that bloody dagger?"

Angel shook her head.

"Alright, girly," said Slevin with a sigh. "I can see Sangster doesn't know, so this is what I'm going to do." Here he clicked the pistol. "Mr Sangster will tell you that was me switching off the safety catch by the way," he laughed. "Now, I'm going to count to three, then if you haven't told me, I'll shoot Mr Sangster." He levelled the pistol at me, and Angel let out a cry. "Not kill him straight away, just a shot to the stomach and you can watch him bleed out. Then I'll count to three again, take another shot, and so on until you do tell me. Get the picture?"

Angel nodded frantically, apparently lost for words.

"So, one…"

I felt my heart pound.

"Two…"

I felt my head spin.

"Three—"

My senses were suddenly confused, as Slevin dropped his gun and fell down to the floor, his body lying straight so that he didn't even collapse in the normal way but keeled over, rigid. I heard a loud sigh from behind him, then saw a shocking vision of Pengelly, his face a dark purple on one side from bruising, standing with the crucifix communion chalice in his hand.

"Knew this chalice would come in useful one day," he said, as Angel grabbed me around the waist with both arms, burying her head against my chest. Pengelly, meanwhile, looked up at the chapel roof and crossed himself, muttering what sounded like a prayer of forgiveness, before collapsing unconscious next to Slevin.

*

"So, this is our abductor," said DCS Pentreath as he stood over Slevin, who was now sitting on a pew in the chapel, head recently bandaged by Matron Davey. "And we all thought you'd drowned."

"I don't drown that easily, ah…" said Slevin, with what he had clearly intended to be a laugh but turned into a low whimper as he held his hand to his head. "So, what happens now, Mister Policeman?"

"Oh, we'll keep you at the holding cells in Truro, for tonight at least. Now, Bolitho, could you escort Mr Slevin to the car while I take some statements here."

"That'd be Monsignor Slevin," said Slevin, still holding his head and wincing.

"Plain Mister where you're going," laughed Pentreath. "Now then…"

Sergeant Bolitho and another officer I didn't recognise stepped forward and took Slevin by either arm.

"Come along, sir, this way."

Slevin stood up and seemed about to say something else when he stared behind me, mouth open wide. I looked around to see a familiar figure appear through the chapel doors.

"Thank you, officers, but we'll take it from here." It was Smith, dark-suited as usual, and followed by two similarly dressed men. "This prisoner is ours."

"Now hold on," said Pentreath, stepping in front of Slevin. "We've got Devon and Cornwall police jurisdiction here, and the correct procedures will be followed.

"I think you'll find this gives me jurisdiction, Chief Superintendent," said Smith, holding a leather wallet (with what looked like an identity document inside), close-up against Pentreath's face.

"Well, er…" stammered Pentreath, stepping aside. "In that case the prisoner is yours."

"Thank you again, Chief Superintendent. Gentlemen, if you would." He gestured to his two companions, who walked forwards and took Slevin's arms from the two uniformed officers, then marched the clearly disoriented priest (who was now muttering what mostly sounded like gibberish to himself, although the occasional lucid word told me he was terrified of Smith's men), out of the chapel.

"Oh, Matron?" said Smith.

"Yes, Sir?"

"We'll be driving Slevin to London. Is he fit to make the trip?"

"This man needs to see a doctor. Possible concussion, perhaps even internal bleeding."

"We have doctors where we're taking him, so I ask again, Matron, is he fit to make the trip?"

Matron Davey looked at Pentreath, who nodded back to her.

"I suppose so," she said. "I checked vital signs, dilation of his pupils and the like, and given he's taken a nasty blow to the skull he seems well enough for now. You should watch for any concussion symptoms though, dizziness, vomiting and so on. If that happens go straight to the nearest hospital."

"Thank you, Matron," said Smith, waving Slevin's two escorts away. "Now then, I'll say my goodbyes." He turned towards the door. "Oh, and Sangster, would you be kind enough to walk with me to my car. Just a couple of questions if I may."

I followed him out of the chapel and round to the front drive, where his two suited friends were already pushing Slevin, who was now shouting out insults and sounding somewhat delirious, into the back of a large black Rover with dark tinted windows.

"I thought you were up in London, Smith."

"Oh no, London was a ruse, been staying quite close by. We were pretty sure Slevin had faked his own drowning and was in hiding. Wouldn't have dared go to Moscow without a result."

"So how did you know to come here now?"

"Oh, we left instructions for someone here to call us when Slevin turned up."

"Someone here?"

"Yes, never mind who."

"But I do mind."

"Looks like you're still struggling to walk, Sangster." Smith patted my stick. "So, I won't keep you standing long. As I say, just a couple more questions and a request."

"Request?" I said, heart sinking at the word.

"That journalist."

"Sue Driver?"

"Yes, and I gather she rather likes you."

"I don't know what you want, but she—"

"I want, Sangster," he interrupted, "no, I insist, that you put her off the scent with the Soviet sub and the, er... alleged true nature of the tomb. You could, er... do that couldn't you?"

"I suppose," I said slowly, remembering the phone call with Sam Youd. "I could tell her the monster sightings were a long-tailed whale."

"She'd believe that?" Smith asked, his usually serene voice filled with incredulity.

"I'll try to be convincing."

"And you'll make sure she doesn't get any ideas about the tomb?" I nodded. "Talk of the devil." Smith looked across the drive, where Sue Driver and her team, cameras and microphones in hand, were running towards us.

"Is it true, Jack?" she shouted breathlessly, looking around at the parked police cars.

"Is what true?"

"That there's been an incident in the chapel. We were filming inside and heard police sirens, then someone said that the priest Slevin had been holding Angel."

"Er... I'm not sure—"

"Miss Driver, isn't it?" interrupted Smith.

"Yes, do you know me?"

"Oh no, we've never met, but I've seen you on television. Anyway, if you and your team go to the chapel now, you'll find the police there. I'm sure there's a story in it."

"Well thanks," she said, before skipping across the gravel as fast as her high heels permitted and calling to the others as she went. "Clip, Nora, Jimmy, quick, to the chapel."

"Ah, nothing like a journalist with the scent of a story in her nose," Smith laughed, as Sue and the others disappeared around the side of the building. "But I'm afraid she'll find her priest-bird's flown." He looked at the car where Slevin was now sitting securely inside, still ranting as far as I could tell. "Now then, Sangster, just one more question before I go."

"Go ahead, Smith," I sighed.

"You're sure there's no evidence that proves any profound, shall we say, religious significance to that tomb."

"If by that you mean any physical evidence giving a connexion to Jesus, then no. You said yourself it was nonsense."

"Of course it's nonsense, but the public are impressionable. Wouldn't do for anything to get out and give people the wrong idea. Say, er... someone found..." He audibly drew breath and looked from side to side. "A ceremonial dagger, Sangster?" I shrugged. "I heard Slevin shouting something about a dagger just now."

"He's concussed, Smith." I shrugged again. "Shouldn't take too much notice of anything he says if I were you."

"I'm sure you're right, and anyway, time I got on the road." He walked over to the car and was about to get in when he turned back to me. "Really, Sangster, it wouldn't do for something like that dagger to be found. Put the cat among the pigeons and no mistake." His expression, previously smiling so that any threat had at least been hidden behind a veneer of pleasantry, now visibly darkened. "We couldn't let that happen," he said in a tone as cold as death. "You do understand?"

I nodded, remembering Admiral Phil Anson's words.

'People playing at that level sometimes disappear'.

Smith seemed to see my thoughtfulness and nodded back, then without another word, climbed into the car before pulling the door shut. The clunking sound as he did so said finality, and I watched with a sense of growing wellbeing, almost liberation, as Smith's black Rover (taking away not only the man but somehow the whole menace that walked with him), disappeared down the drive.

3:30PM

"Now then, if I may interrupt, everyone," shouted Velinda, pointing to the long table on the front lawn, which was now set out with sandwiches and cakes. "I know it's been an odd day, and there has been an, er... incident in the chapel as you all know." A murmur rose up from the crowd on the lawn. "But for those of you who haven't already spoken to them, I can assure you," here she looked at Pentreath, standing close by, "that the police confirm everything is now under control." The murmur grew louder. "But," Velinda continued, with somewhat forced enthusiasm, "the good news is that cook and her team here," she looked at three women in white aprons standing smiling by the table, "have rustled us up a wonderful lunch, and we've tea, coffee, orange juice or water if you'd prefer."

She began to clap, and soon everyone else joined in. I looked around to see the Blackwoods amongst parents bringing back their children, pupils, support staff and teachers. I also saw Runtle (who had picked up an adder with a forked stick and was showing the wriggling serpent to whomsoever might be interested), as well as the TV crew and the remaining police officers, so that all in all, perhaps a hundred people stood clapping on the lawn that sunny afternoon.

Sir John, taller than those around him and ever the centre of attention, clapped loudly above his head and yelled at the top of his voice.

"Bravo for those cooks, bravo, bravo."

"So please," said the principal, once Sir John's bellowing had subsided, "dig in."

At that, the crowd, especially the pupils, descended on the table, Sarah and I taking a step back to let them pass, while Sue Driver and team circled around, filming from every angle.

As I watched, I remembered Smith saying someone at the academy had told him about Slevin. Who could it be? Certainly not Sir John, and not Runtle, nor Mrs Davey, and most of the staff didn't know any details. Pengelly was also an unlikely candidate. I then looked over at the table where Velinda was directing people towards the drinks and sandwiches. She looked up and caught my eye and, just for a second, I thought there was a spark of recognition and guilt. Was Velinda Smith's contact, his spy amongst us? The idea seemed outlandish, but I knew after that one fleeting glance I would never see her in the same light again. The thought took me back to Smith's comment about Sue Driver.

'Put her off the scent with the Soviet sub and the, er... alleged true nature of the tomb.'

I excused myself to Sarah, who was anyway talking with the Blackwoods, gulped, then walked over to the journalist.

"Got your story?"

"Jack," said Sue, looking me, and my crutch, up and down. "How are you?"

"Oh, on the mend."

"A lot's happened since I interviewed you outside the Watersmeet."

"You could say that."

"And it's only been what, three days?" I nodded. "And I still haven't got my big story."

"Apart from, let me see..." I shook my head. "The fire at the pub, the incidents in the old tomb Friday night and in the chapel today, as well as Sir John asking you to make a documentary on the academy."

"Ah, that was just regular news, my day job." She took a notebook and pen from her handbag. "I'm talking about Morgawr, and those sightings. All the witnesses describe something like a plesiosaurus."

"A dinosaur?"

"Yes," she said, her womanly composure now melting in the excitement of the subject. "Or perhaps a Zeuglodon."

"A what?"

"A primeval toothed whale, extinct for millions of years." Sue looked at me with wide eyes. "Or maybe not extinct, Jack?"

"So, you think you've stumbled on a Lazarus taxon?" I felt guilty at using my friend Sam's words in vain, but not too guilty, remembering the veiled threats of Mr Smith. I needed to give Sue a good story after all.

"Jack," Sue gasped, making me feel even more guilty. "You never cease to amaze me."

"Well…" I feigned modesty.

"But when you said Morgawr's not what I thought it might be, what did you really mean?"

"I don't want to spoil it for you. Just print what you like on the monster and let's talk about the tomb. That's a far better story."

"No," said Sue, grabbing my arm so that I wobbled on my crutch. "What did you mean?"

"Alright, odds on it's a whale. A fin whale to be precise. Very rare inshore in Cornwall, but one's been reported in Falmouth Bay, and I have it on good authority that this whale could easily be mistaken for some long-necked animal."

"A whale, a big fat whale?"

"Quite slim I believe, and the tail fluke, Sue, it looks like a neck and a head apparently." I felt my ears burning as I said this, not so much out of guilt over the monster but for the lies I would now tell her about the tomb.

"Oh," said Sue quietly, looking down at her feet with a sigh. "You're sure?"

"I was told by an expert."

"Why were you talking to someone about fin whales, I mean—"

"Never mind that, Sue. Now look, you've only had the basic police statement on the business with the tomb, correct?" She nodded. "Then get your notebook back out and let me tell you the full story. Exclusive, that's the word, isn't it?"

"As long as you haven't told anyone else what you're about to tell me?"

"I most certainly haven't, Sue. Now then, it all started, from my point of view at least, when I got a call from the academy last Tuesday evening. I'd just finished eating and…"

I resolved to try and speak the truth as far as I could (just not all of it), telling Sue the story of Slevin's ambition to find historical links between Cornwall and the Holy Land. I explained how he had taken advantage of Angel's genius, luring the impressionable girl from the academy, and incarcerating her in the very place he had previously been searching in vain. I added that Slevin became infatuated with Angel along the way.

"So," she said, when I paused for breath, "Slevin lured Angel to this tomb, and then what?"

"Er…" I stumbled, trying to think what to say next.

"Well," she said slowly. "We know he didn't kill her but, I have to ask, did he, you know…"

"Violate her?"

"Mmmm…"

"No, thank goodness. Just kept her chained up there, then when I came upon the place, left us both shut up inside, to rot away for all he seemed to care."

I described how Slevin had sealed us in, how he had made his escape by boat, and the way Angel had worked out how we could escape (but didn't mention the dagger).

"And how did you find this place, this hidden tomb, when so many police had failed?"

"Well, I was mandated by Sir John to use any means at my disposal to find Angel, I had full access to police material, and perhaps got a bit lucky."

"A bit lucky, eh?" I nodded. "You got help from some of the kids, didn't you?" I nodded again. "Spider and Jonny. We spoke to them."

"Did you now, Sue?"

"Yes. And those kids seemed frightened to talk to us."

"Both a bit highly strung."

"Oh, and by the way, we tried to get inside the tomb yesterday, but the police only let us film the outside."

"Yes, I saw your van parked. Let me help you with what I know."

I went on to tell her the details I could remember of the interior of the tomb, and its apparent historical significance, holding, amongst other things, the remains of a woman of some importance, and how the whole place would be opened to the public at some point.

"Hmmm…" She shook her head. "And this priest, this Slevin, seems he was in cahoots with Pengelly. I saw the canon being led away from the chapel by the police, head all bandaged and walking with a crutch. He looked in a real state."

"Yes, but Pengelly had a change of mind at the last minute."

"I'm sure," she said, in a manner that said she was anything but sure. "And I hear you were also quite the hero."

"Oh," I said, looking away. "Just lucky to be in the right place at the right time."

"The second right place at the second right time in so many days?"

"Well…"

"And Slevin had already made good his escape, but risked his neck coming back, plotted with Pengelly, went to all that trouble hijacking the builders' van to enter the academy."

"Is that how he got in undetected, Sue?"

"Yes, the police found the driver bound and gagged a few miles back up the road apparently. Seems Slevin had pretended to hitch a lift. The van was his escape plan as well."

"Makes sense," I said, remembering the van speeding past our car and seeming to hit the tramp.

"And all this because you say Slevin became infatuated with the girl?"

"She's quite a beauty."

"Yes, most of the country's seen her picture." Sue stared hard, journalistic instincts clearly aroused. "Mind you, Jack, from asking around, and the fact he had the girl at his mercy for best part of a week but didn't lay finger on her, I wonder if Slevin's idea of beauty didn't lie, er… elsewhere." I shrugged again. "And if so, what was his real motive in kidnapping Angel?"

"Who knows what maniacs are thinking?"

"And why escape by boat when he could far more easily have ridden off on his motorbike?"

"Knew the police would be looking for the bike I guess." I shrugged yet again. "Like I say, Sue, who knows what maniacs are thinking?"

"Who knows what anyone's thinking, Jack?" Sue stared even harder at me, then placed the pen and notebook back in her handbag.

*

"Hungry?" I felt a tug on my arm and looked round to see Sarah.

"Not so much, you?"

"No, I'm fine. Let's walk if you're up to it."

"Hardly a cripple just yet," I said, taking her arm. "If you'll excuse us, Sue?"

Sue Driver nodded and turned back to the crowd.

"Funny, all this," said Sarah, looking over her shoulder at the gathering on the lawn as we walked to the water's edge.

"Funny how?"

"Well, one minute we have drama, with the priest taking the girl in the chapel, next minute everyone's behaving like it's school sports day or tea outside the cricket pavilion."

"I suppose that's one way of bringing back normality. After all, the police just spent about two hours taking statements. By the way, Pentreath just cleared up a little mystery for you and me."

"What do mean, Jack?"

"The creature we saw on the moor last week. It was a dog."

"What," Sarah snorted. "At that size?"

"Yes, Great Dane apparently. Slipped its owner's leash and ran away."

"And ripped that sheep apart?"

"No proof of that but, anyway, mystery solved."

"Shame," said Sarah, shaking her head. "I rather liked the idea of Pasco's spectral Dandy Hound."

"Great Dane's not quite so romantic, is it?"

"Pentreath say what will happen to Pengelly?"

"He'll be charged as an accessory."

"Accessory?"

"To kidnap, I think that's what Pentreath said. After all, Pengelly lured Angel to the chapel when he knew Slevin was waiting there."

"Deserves whatever he gets then."

"Yes, but I can't help feeling sorry for the man. Shows what lengths someone will go to for love, even if it is unrequited."

"Very magnanimous and poetic of you, darling," laughed Sarah. "And maybe Pengelly braining Slevin with that chalice will sway the judge a bit."

"Maybe, and thank goodness he did brain Slevin, but nothing to worry about now." I hadn't yet told Sarah that Slevin was about to shoot me, so merely took a breath and smiled. "That's all out of our hands, and on a brighter note, Sir John did say the academy's avoided closure. If we can manage a staged intake for phase two, and finish the new science block in time for start of term in September I'll be—"

"Shut up, Jack, and enjoy the view."

I shut up and looked across the river, its water once again calm, reflecting my emotions.

"Sarah?" I asked after a few minutes.

"Yes darling?"

"Angel, she's desperate for me to go out in her boat this afternoon. It's an old racing gig that some of the kids did up."

"Yes, I heard her say earlier, but can you, though?" She looked at my crutch and shook her head. "With that leg, your ribs and so on."

"Yes, I think so. I was more wondering why Angel was so insistent."

"Oh Jack," laughed Sarah, punching me on the shoulder. "You're such a dimwit."

"Am I?"

"Well look, she's clearly proud of the boat. Wants to show you what she's done."

"But she's a genius. Why show me?"

"She's a teenage girl as well." I nodded. "And, Jack, in case you've forgotten, you rescued her twice from what… certain death?"

"Well maybe not certain death."

"What's her father like?"

"Adopted father."

"Okay, but what's he like?"

"Oh, very ordinary. Foreman in a factory that makes insulating bricks. Both parents seem permanently in awe of Angel."

"So," said Sarah. "Let's think about that. Girl's supremely gifted but languishes in a very normal environment, then comes to the academy, meets Slevin, gets into who-knows-what trouble, and is rescued by this silver haired knight in shining armour."

"Who?"

"Don't be silly, Jack, you know what I'm saying. Now you become father figure, hero, everything she expects a man to be. From now on she'll measure the men in her life against you."

"What?"

"And so, getting back to the point, of course Angel wants you to see that boat."

"But she's special, different, a genius, wouldn't behave like other girls, wouldn't latch on to someone like me as any kind of figure, father or otherwise."

"We're all the same, darling," Sarah said, stroking my cheek. "Women, under the skin."

"I'm not sure, I—"

"We're all the same." She continued her cheek stroking.

"Sarah," I said with rising anxiety. "You're saying Angel now has some sort of what, Oedipus complex about me?"

"It's called an Electra complex with girls, but no, at least I hope not. I just meant that you've likely occupied a niche with her. It's no bad thing, as long as you're not some unattainable role model."

"Well," I said, trying to affect a superior look. "I am a hard act to live up to for any would-be lover, I mean—" Sarah pushed me and wagged her finger.

"I seem to remember a night not so long ago at all at an inn in Wales," she laughed. "When you promised me the most romantic evening of my life, then drank so much whisky with the landlord that you were, well… not exactly sexual performer of the year."

"I don't remember any of that." I laughed back. "And it was very good whisky. Eighteen-year-old Macallan as I recall."

"You remembered that bit."

"Touché, but anyway, surely I'm not a father figure to Angel?"

"Maybe not in the way I described," said Sarah, looking out across the river. "But is she a daughter figure to you?"

"Well, you couldn't ask for more in a daughter, I suppose," I answered, remembering Pengelly's words.

'Were I to have a child, Sangster, and if that child possessed even one tenth the mind of Angel, I would be the very proudest of fathers.'

"But no, Sarah," I then said, after considering the thought. "I've worked on so many cases since I joined the institute. Some of the kids were vulnerable but not remarkable, some of them remarkable but not vulnerable, and some just plain odd but, all round, lots who needed saving in less obvious ways than Angel. So, you see, Angel's special, but she's still just another one of those kids at the end of the day."

"I love you, Jack," said Sarah, taking my hand and kissing it. "Now let's walk back, have a sandwich if there are any left, and then you go out with Angel in that boat of hers."

"Thanks, Sarah."

"And mind those ribs of yours."

5 PM

"Let me get in and start the engine first," said Angel, climbing into the boat. "Can you grab that backpack, then cast the painter off?"

"A bit difficult with this," I said, holding up my crutch and wondering once again why Angel was so keen to take me boating.

"Sorry, Mr Sangster. Just throw it in then do the rope."

I duly threw the pack, thinking by the weight she'd brought enough Coca-Cola for a long trip, with the cans inside clanking as it landed on a seat, then undid the mooring line from a hook on the jetty, threw in the crutch and slid myself into the boat after it. Angel, meanwhile, began pumping at a plastic bulb on the fuel line then pulled the engine cord, which caught after three attempts, the outboard springing to life with an ear-splitting buzz.

"Better when we get outside," Angel shouted, turning the tiller hard so that the gig pointed towards the double boathouse doors.

"Have you enough fuel?" I shouted back.

"Filled it up this afternoon, remember?"

"Shouldn't we take oars or paddles, just in case?"

"They get in the way, we'll be fine."

"You sure?"

She nodded, and without giving me a chance to argue further, opened up the engine throttle and took us out into the main channel where the water was green and calm, and the sun shone safe and bright against a cloudless sky as the gig, now riding the swell at some speed, cut its way towards the harbour mouth.

"Coke?" she asked, reaching into the backpack and passing me a can and an opener.

"Thanks."

"Can you do one for me?" She passed me another can, and I punched two triangular holes in the top ('one for me to drink from, one for the displaced air' as Angel observed), then passed it back. Doing the same with my own can, I then raised it to make a toast.

"To a newly recovered lady. Good as new, in fact even better."

"Do you mean—"

"I mean the *Igraine*, Angel."

"She's what Runtle called a 'real treffy.'" Angel stroked the side of the boat.

"Not sure what a treffy is, but she really is a lady."

"Lady, how ?"

"Ah," I laughed. "Something you don't know." Angel shrugged. "A lady's what sailors call a boat when everything's just right." I remembered seeing the gig laid up on the roof rafters, Spider standing underneath. "You say you did this boat up yourself?"

"Jonny, Spider and I mended the *Igraine*, but with quite a lot of help from Runtle."

"And that?" I asked, pointing to a stylised fish symbol painted on the bow planking.

"Ichthys, the fish. Two arcs, crossing to make a tail, with a single dot for the eye."

"What's that got to do with Igraine. Surely she was—"

"Yes, yes, King Arthur's mother. The fish has nothing to do with her, I just..." Angel suddenly seemed distracted, uncharacteristically lost for words. "I needed to paint that on the boat, I don't really know why." She looked at the fish symbol for a few seconds, then laughed, and we both drank. The *Igraine*, which must have been listening, suddenly sped up, passing the headland and coming close in by the lighthouse, which stood white and tall above us, its glass top looking down with what felt at that moment like a benevolent gaze.

"It's lovely and calm," said Angel, squinting out to sea. "Let's go towards the Helford River, okay?"

"Alright," I said, looking at my watch. "But not too far, it's getting on."

Angel turned the *Igraine* west and headed out to sea.

*

"Engine doesn't normally sound like that, Angel."

The boat jolted a few times before the outboard shuddered to a complete halt, and I cursed myself for not having personally checked the fuel before we left. A quick check in the petrol tank confirmed my worst fears.

"It's alright, Mr Sangster, you haven't lost your nautical touch."

"How do you mean?"

"I made sure there was just enough petrol to get us here, and I left the oars back in the boathouse on purpose as well. Now we won't be bothered for a while."

"That could get us into real trouble," I shouted, almost standing up before remembering the narrow gig might tip over. "We've no way of getting to the shore."

"There'll be a boat along soon." I looked around to see sails in the distance, in front of us and behind us. She was almost certainly right, I thought, we would be picked up before too long.

"Bothered by who?" I then asked. "And about what, Angel?"

"I want to tell you some things."

"Better have another coke then." I opened her a new can from the sack.

"None of them really understood, Pengelly, Slevin and so on.

Didn't matter what they were shown, staring them in the face. People like that scrabble around, but they've no vision."

"You don't suffer fools gladly, do you?" Angel shrugged. "I mean, they had their own weaknesses, but both were well-educated men of the church."

"Perhaps, but they couldn't see. Things are simple, you just have to look." I smiled at Angel's complete confidence, that confidence only the very young and very old possess.

"Prinny doesn't understand how you do what you do."

"Do you?"

"I think so. You soak it all up then put it all together. But then again…"
She looked at me, wide eyed. "Yes?"

"You can do things others can't, or you wouldn't be who you are, wouldn't be at the academy, would you?" She didn't answer, gazing away from me across the water. "I know you don't think much of Pengelly, Angel, but he put it well."

"How?" she said distantly.

"Said you're just quicker."

"Maybe I am." Her gaze was still distant as she spoke, but then she suddenly turned to me. "The dagger's genuine."

"But Polkinghorne thought it was modern, I—"

"I know, they all did."

"Look," I said, "We're not going anywhere, so just tell me about what you think happened, from the beginning."

"That's why I brought you out here," she grinned.

"And there was me thinking you wanted to show off the boat. Anyway, tell me everything but in words my little mind can understand. Okay?"

"I did want to show you the boat, Mr Sangster," she said, kissing me on the cheek. "And your mind is anything but little, but yes, I will try and tell you everything."

And so began a most remarkable hour.

*

288

"I found the lessons at the academy tedious," Angel began by saying. "So, one of the first things I did was to look around for something else to do. I was brought up on sailing in Essex, and that's why I volunteered for boathouse duty. Mending the holes in the canoes, painting them up, things like that. Jonny and Spider joined in as well, and we worked on my canoe first, then Jonny's."

"Why didn't Spider have a canoe?"

"Can't swim," she laughed. "I named my canoe for Morgawr, after reading about the Falmouth Bay monster in an old newspaper."

"Monster's suddenly in the news again."

"Soviet submarine, K222 class?"

"How on earth did you know that?"

"Doesn't matter."

"Well, it does matter, so don't tell anyone." I remembered Smith's warnings. "Anyone at all, understand?"

"I do," she nodded. "Anyway, I began exploring the creeks of the Fal estuary in *Morgawr*, starting with the Percuil River. It really dries out at low tide though, and the first evening I went up there I got stuck, high and dry. Then this old man came from nowhere, waded out knee deep into the mud and pushed me back into the channel."

"The tramp?"

"Yes and, as he pushed me, I saw something glinting in the mud, and lifted out the dagger. I guessed how old it was straight away."

"How?"

"Oh, I saw Aramaic script once."

"Just once?"

"Yes, so I cleaned the dagger, looked it all up and made the translation. Aramaic follows rules, just like anything else."

"Then?"

"It made sense that there was a link with Jesus, the Holy Land and so on."

"Again, how?"

"Just putting together things I'd read, and the writing on the knife. Aramaic was a street language, not just for priests."

289

"Was it?"

"Yes, so that told me the dagger wasn't just some religious thing but had a practical message for anyone who could read it. It was after the talk on Jesus in Cornwall by Pengelly that the penny dropped."

"So what did you do?"

"I learned everything I could from him, got access to the cathedral library."

"You found that old monks' map of ferry crossings there?"

"You know about that?" she laughed. "Well yes, and it told me where the tomb would be, the name Joseph's Pill and the angle of the crossing from St Mawes."

"And you told Pengelly?" She nodded. "And then he introduced you to Slevin?"

"Yes," she said, looking downwards, and at that moment I thought perhaps there was a slight tear in her eye. "I didn't want boys, I wanted a man who could, oh, I don't know... keep up. More than keep up, do you know what I mean?"

"You're a woman, Angel, a young one but a woman, nevertheless."

"And I fell for him from the start, even though our meeting wasn't too romantic. I was looking at some books on the old trading links between Palestine and Cornwall when he spoke to me, and, well... that was that. Slevin bought me a coffee that day in London while Pengelly was busy and I just opened up to him, told him about my family, being at school in Essex, the academy, and even the dagger. He seemed to understand. I now know Pengelly set it all up."

"Then what?"

"I kept in touch with Slevin, via telegrams from the post office."

"Yes, I've seen them."

"Course you have. WPC Woon's mum took them down." It was impossible to surprise Angel. "Pengelly was always badgering me after our trip to London, but I kept my distance. Anyway, in a few weeks I'd figured out what I needed to know."

"Which was?"

"Jesus came to Cornwall as a boy with his uncle, Joseph of

Arimathea. Then, immediately after the crucifixion, that same uncle removed Jesus' body from the tomb in Jerusalem, taking it far away, to Cornwall, safe from the Romans, or so he thought."

"Why wouldn't the body be safe from the Romans here?"

"Because the Romans invaded about ten years later."

"I thought it was Julius Caesar, before Christ, veni vidi vici and all that."

"No, proper invasion was much later. Plus, Joseph had a good reason to come back here, and that's the big thing neither Slevin, Pengelly or any of the others have understood."

The boat rocked a little as she said this, the surface of the sea totally calm, but with a slight Atlantic swell. Looking at Angel in front of me, blonde hair and green eyes shining, I felt that everything made sense.

"This chat wouldn't work if we were ashore, would it, Mr Sangster?"

"Stop reading my mind."

"Alright," she laughed. "Anyway, Joseph's reason for coming back here, it's all about the metal in the dagger. Bronze, but harder than we can make now."

"You said that same thing in the tomb."

"Did I? Anyway, the key lay in the copper, bronze is mainly made with tin and copper."

"That fallen bell in the chapel's made of the same stuff?"

"Yes," she nodded. "And you'll know that Polkinghorne found the copper in the knife to be American, highest grade in the world. That's what I expected."

"But he said to me—"

"I know, I know," she interrupted. "And that meant the dagger should have been modern, but it wasn't. That blade was made two thousand years ago, using European smelting methods and American copper. You see, Joseph of Arimathea and his forebears sailed to America long before Christopher Columbus."

"How on earth can you know that?"

"The symbols on the dagger. They tell you where Joseph went, and how to get there. A place in Lake Superior."

"And how on earth can you know that?"

"You say 'how on earth' quite a lot, don't you," she laughed. "But look, those ancients were better sailors than we give them credit for. Dead reckoning, stars, trade winds, ocean currents, lode stones for compasses, you should know about all that, being in the navy."

"That might not be enough to cross the Atlantic."

"Ah, but they had a secret device, something they called by a weird name. Nearest I could think of in English was a 'Star Sailor.'"

"That thing you sketched in your notebook?" I said, remembering the carefully drawn diagram of interlinking cogwheels. "Looked like modern clockwork to me."

"No, it's very old."

"Can you be sure?"

"One was found in a Greek shipwreck from before the time of Christ. Predicted movement of the moon, stars, even tides."

"Okay, say these people did cross the ocean, how would they manage the overland trip, I mean, Lake Superior's hundreds of miles from the sea?"

"They sailed up the Mississippi, like the copper traders that went before them."

"How on earth…" I stopped to laugh. "Sorry, I mean, how can you be sure of that?"

"Maps from an Ottoman Admiral."

"Piri Reis?"

"You know of Piri Reis?"

"You had a book on him in your room."

"I did, didn't I," she laughed. "Well, his maps of the New World were based on much older ones I'm sure, and they show the river that led the European copper traders all the way to the Great Lakes and let them carry their heavy-metal cargo all the way home by boat."

"So, you're saying people from Palestine already knew all about America?"

"The ones who sailed with the Phoenicians did, and when the time came, Joseph took the body of Christ to this far off land, to lie in peace, safe from the Romans or anyone else, for all eternity."

"And will it be, safe I mean?"

"If I read the dagger right, the body was hidden deep in an abandoned mine under a lake on an island in another lake."

"Isle Royale?"

"Well done. Did you get that from the book on Indian copper in my room?"

"Yes. And what of the old woman's body in the tomb?"

"Do you read the Bible?"

"No."

"Jesus wasn't the only one who disappeared from a tomb in Jerusalem and was assumed to have ascended to Heaven."

"Wasn't he?"

"His mother."

"Mary?"

"Joseph brought her to Cornwall when her time came," said Angel, in a dreamy voice while gazing out to sea. "Laid her in the tomb that her son had occupied."

"You know this?"

She nodded.

"And I think that somehow, others knew as well. You can't ever really keep a secret, so perhaps this one echoed down the centuries. Those carvings on the arch in the chapel at the academy, they're eleventh century or older."

"Very old then."

"Old yes, but how did they know about Jesus a thousand years after he was brought to St Anthony? And what about the cathedral?"

"Truro?"

"Yes, the cathedral name for a start."

"Lots of churches are dedicated to the Virgin Mary."

"Not so many Anglican ones, and if you take the halfway angle between the transept and the chancel, you get a bearing that points directly to the tomb."

"Do you?"

"Yes. What compelled someone to go to all the trouble of building Truro Cathedral as cruciform, and at that angle, if not a memory of where its patron saint lay buried?"

I said nothing and she said nothing for a time, both of us looking out over the water.

"Nobody else knows all this, Mr Sangster."

"Are you sure?" I tried to think who else might know.

"Slevin is caught, Pengelly hasn't a clue, the Russians don't have any evidence, and the establishment, including the government, the Church of England and the Vatican, are all probably breathing a sigh of relief, so I think…"

"Yes?"

"We're safe."

"What about Smith?"

"I put him off the scent I think."

I wasn't so sure.

"Smith has Slevin in custody now," I said slowly. "And he's no fool."

"Maybe, but I'm pretty sure Smith'll just think it was all a dreadful mistake by Slevin and, anyway, with all those notes burned, the dagger's the only real proof now."

"Not the writing around the rim of the chapel bell?"

"No, that script's Aramaic alright, but it doesn't tell you anything."

I still felt a niggling doubt, suddenly remembering the police Polaroid photo of the dagger etching, and WPC Woon's comment.

'Oh, all these papers will get stored somewhere and forgotten about, but we never throw anything away.'

"Then let's leave it at that, Angel," I eventually said. "There's no evidence and nobody else knows."

"Except the tramp of course."

"What does he know?"

"You said you didn't read the Bible, Mr Sangster."

"That's right."

"Then you won't know that it tells of a man who mocked Jesus as he carried the cross to Golgotha, the hill of the crucifixion, and for that was cursed to wander the Earth for eternity, and to limp as he went. Perhaps it was this man you call the tramp, and he was then sent to protect the last resting place of Christ, and of his mother."

"Is that what you think, really?" I struggled to square such ideas with Angel's excessive faculty for logic.

"I don't just think, I know. He's the…" She lowered her voice, almost to a whisper. "Wandering Jew, the Fisher King, the—"

"Whoa, Angel, what are all these names?"

"Just that," she snapped back. "Names, but whatever we call him, perhaps the tramp chose me, put me in the way of finding the dagger that evening in the mud of the dried-out creek. And…" She looked at me with wide green eyes and that same piercing gaze I'd seen when I first shone the lamp on her face in the tomb. "Perhaps he chose you as well, Mr Sangster."

"This is crazy."

"Is there nothing about the tramp that tells you I might be right?"

I remembered the grainy photograph in the saloon bar at the Cassandra Arms, one hundred and twenty years old, and the tramp being so often inexplicably there when I needed him. I also remembered his comment…

'Here, and in America. Wherever I'm needed to protect the righteous.'

…and as I remembered I wondered, just for a moment, if she might be right.

"Do you believe in the supernatural then, Angel?"

"No."

"Not even when it's dressed up as religion?"

"No."

"Then how can you explain all this stuff about the tramp?"

"It's just a part of things, Mr Sangster. I can't say it better than that."

We lapsed into silence again, and I wondered again about Angel's theories (which is surely all that they were, the ideas of a supremely gifted but also young and naïve girl).

"What do we do now?" I finally asked her.

"Drift and wait to be picked up, Mr Sangster. Drift and wait."

7 PM

"We're almost at the mouth of the Helford River, Angel."
A half hour had passed with neither of us speaking again and, although several boats passed close by, we'd made no attempt to signal to them. Looking at the nearing shore, then back across the bay towards St Anthony, I saw we were much further west than we had been, the lighthouse reduced to a white dot amongst the rocks of the headland. In front of us, above the green line of the Lizard peninsula, the sun, now a weakened and engorged orange ball, hung low in the western sky.

"We've drifted a long way," I said, and, despite the stillness of the air, shivered with that slightly heat-stroked tingle you only get after a long time out in the open. "And there's deep water here, look at the green colour."

"As good a place as any then, Mr Sangster." Angel opened her backpack and pulled out a sackcloth parcel.

"As good a place for what, Angel?"

"This."

She unwrapped the cloth, and held up the dagger, no longer looking dull as it had in the sepulchre, but sparkling, the blade reflecting sunlight from the sea, catching not just the myriad Aramaic markings on the blade, but also something I hadn't noticed before. Etched on the hilt were the intersecting twin curves of Ichthys.

"Do you think it'll make as many ripples in the sea as it did on land?"

I didn't answer, glancing down at Angel's unbandaged ankle, tattooed with her glum looking fish, its nine tails oddly twitching when the girl's calf muscle tensed as she threw the dagger from the boat. I raised my eyes, and we both watched the knife arc through the air, flashing as it went, hitting the water with the blade tip facing directly downwards, making only the tiniest of splashes before disappearing completely.

There were no ripples that I could see.

ALSO BY THE AUTHOR
THE FACE STONE

Do ancient rocks and woodlands really harbour a secret that could bring about worldwide catastrophe? And can saving the health, life, and even mortal soul of one missing boy avert that catastrophe?

The year is 1969, and Jack Sangster, newly taken on by the Granville Institute as a special investigator, is sent to an elite school, where the son of wealthy local family has disappeared.

Sangster, despite his talent for dealing with people and problems, only comes upon more mysteries as the case unfolds, struggling to reconcile his natural pragmatism with disturbing questions.

Follow as he navigates clues and red herrings, learning at every turn that if his eyes and ears are to be believed, the stakes linked to this case are rising at an alarming rate. Sangster tries to do the right thing even as his uncertainty rises; all the while a seemingly well-ordered and rational world is slowly revealed to perhaps be older, darker, and more chaotic than he ever imagined…

JEHOVAH'S WIND

Unwillingly thrown into the search for a missing teenager, Sangster must try to thwart an obsessive man from exploiting captured Nazi technology and even his own son to achieve a twisted ambition…

It is summer 1970, and Jack Sangster has been sent to investigate the disappearance of a local boy at a remote Dartmoor hotel.

Already suspicious that the government is taking a far greater interest than the case merits, Sangster senses that not everything is what it seems in this wild and illusory part of England, a feeling compounded when he comes under intense scrutiny from his boss as well as the highest authorities.

And as the case unfolds, despite emotional distractions and frequent wrong turns, Sangster eventually comes to believe that shocking events, which at first seem potentially epoch-shifting, may just as likely ensue from the tragic imaginings of a man driven to madness by grief and disease.

Nevertheless, with more than one life at stake, and a connection to his own wartime past making Sangster wonder if the unbelievable really is taking place before his very eyes, it becomes a desperate race against time to do the right thing in the face of a discovery that could literally 'change everything.'